"You are a great temptation, Maggie Landers, a very great temptation,"

Jared murmured fiercely. "With the face of an angel and a body that would tax the resolve of Saint Jude himself."

"Mr. Michaels!"

He bent his head and captured her lips with his. Being a well-brought-up young lady, Maggie was perfectly aware that at some point, she ought to lodge a protest: cry out; struggle to free herself; run from the room. Something. Instead, when Michaels pulled her toward him—"crushing her to his bosom" was how she would always think of it—bent and kissed her, though not as savagely as she might have hoped—that is, expected—she leaned into the embrace willingly and raised her lips eagerly for the kiss.

Dear Reader,

Hot off the presses, the February titles at Harlequin Historicals are full of adventure and romance.

Highland Heart by Ruth Langan, another title in her popular Highland Series, is the story of Jamie MacDonald, a continuing character in the author's tales of sixteenth-century Scotland. And from Donna Anders comes *Paradise Moon.* Hawaii during the turbulent days following the end of the monarchy is the setting for this fast-paced romance between star-crossed lovers.

For those of you who enjoyed Sally Cheney's first historical, *Game of Hearts,* don't miss her second. *Thief in the Night* is a humorous tale of a British detective and a pretty young housemaid who may or may not be a thief. The author's quick wit and delightful secondary characters make her a wonderful storyteller. And readers of Westerns should be sure to pick up a copy of Jackie Merritt's *Wyoming Territory.* This well-known writer's first historical is a sensual romance between two headstrong neighboring ranchers.

From your cherished favorites to our newest arrivals, take a look at what our writers have to offer you this month. We appreciate your support, and happy reading.

Sincerely,

The Editors

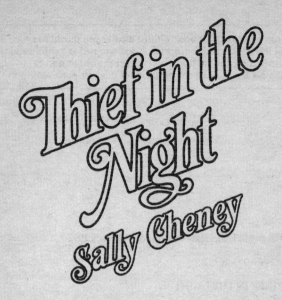

Thief in the Night
Sally Cheney

Harlequin Books

TORONTO • NEW YORK • LONDON
AMSTERDAM • PARIS • SYDNEY • HAMBURG
STOCKHOLM • ATHENS • TOKYO • MILAN
MADRID • WARSAW • BUDAPEST • AUCKLAND

Harlequin Historicals first edition February 1992

ISBN 0-373-28712-7

THIEF IN THE NIGHT

Books by Sally Cheney

Harlequin Historicals

Game of Hearts #36
Thief in the Night #112

SALLY CHENEY

was a bookstore owner before coming to her first love—writing. She has traveled extensively in the United States, but is happiest with the peaceful rural life in her home state of Idaho. When she is not writing, she is active in community affairs and enjoys cooking and gardening.

To Dr. Paul Dearing,
the very stuff of Harlequin romances.

Prologue

London, 1820

Two men sat huddled over a greasy table in one corner of the smoke-filled room. Each held a mug, half-full of the watery house beer—which was as much as Mr. Hazard allowed his customers for a ha'penny. Both men, however, seemed more interested in their conversation than in the libation before them.

" 'Er name's Greta Briggs. She's somethin' of a legend down 'ere, Mick. Not even any of the pros can tell me how she runs it," the smaller, weasellike man was saying to the other.

Above the door of the narrow, four-story building wherein the men sat was a sign that said Hotel, Gentlemen. But there was also a picture of a bear identifying the establishment and giving the lie to the first sign.

The Brown Bear was what was known as a "flash house." Mr. Hazard boasted a large and varied clientele: pickpockets, jewel thieves, counterfeiters, sneaks, knuckles, those adept at Milling a Kin or Touching the Rattler. Kidds, Caps and Pickups. None of whom, regardless of how adept he was in his chosen line of expertise, could be called a gentleman.

Snitches also frequented the Brown Bear. Usually they were men who had tried their hand at the demanding profession of illegally appropriating someone else's wealth and now found it much simpler merely to sell out kith and kin for the price of a mindless binge.

"I thought you knew everything, Danny." The other, larger man was talking now. Among frequenters of the Brown Bear were one or two "pretty boys," well-favored men who employed their faces, physiques and wholesome appearances in relieving gullible women of their liquid assets, utilizing their natural talents the same way the safecrackers utilized their unusually fine senses of touch and hearing in their gainful pursuits. Therefore, one was careful never to make a quick, favorable evaluation of anyone in the Bear. Reporting only observable fact, the young gentleman talking now was extremely good-looking, with dark brown hair, straight nose and firm jaw. He was broad shouldered, tanned and vibrant, and his dark eyes were disturbingly keen and direct.

"I thought nothing happened out there that you couldn't and wouldn't sell," he continued. "As I understand it, that is the reason you are paid so handsomely."

The first man, Danny, snorted loudly and then took a sip of the dishwater beer—a guaranteed cure for light spirits—to quell his amusement.

"If I was paid so 'andsome I'd be sittin' in the Theatre Royal, up in one of them fancy boxes, with a 'alf-naked woman on each arm. Instead I'm sittin' across the table from a snag-toothed runner who won't cough up the price of a decent gin." Danny gulped down the rest of his beer and *plunked* down the mug on the table defiantly.

The other man smiled ever so slightly and held up his finger. In a moment the barman was at the table, refilling the mug.

"Ah, you're a right one, Mick," Danny said, grasping the handle as if it were a lifeline, though willing to talk for another minute or two before drinking the liquid in his endless pursuit of forgetfulness.

"Has she got a partner?"

"Dunno."

"She works alone, then?"

"Could be. I've heard it both ways."

"Have you seen her? Is she in town? Has she been selling anything?"

After each question the smaller man shook his narrow head, his dark, close-set eyes darting around the room, ferreting out salable information even in the midst of present negotiations.

At his failure to get an answer to his last question, the other man sat back in his chair and grimaced with impatience. Danny shrugged and took a drink of his beer.

"I can't 'elp it, Mick. 'Ave I seen 'er? 'Ell, I might've seen 'er every day. Word is you never know 'oo she's goin' to be, the grand lady of the 'ouse or the charwoman sweepin' ashes out front."

"What does she look like? Blond? Brunette? Fat? Skinny? Short? Tall?"

"That's right."

The runner shook his head and took another drink of the beer, though he didn't finish his. Instead, after a sip, he put down the mug and pushed it away with something like relief.

"So I wasted my shilling and the price of three beers. I suspect your services have been highly overrated, Danny."

"Make it four beers and you won't leave with nothin'."
The little man leaned across the table and grinned a gray
grin with several gaps in it. The other man narrowed his
eyes distrustfully but held up his finger again.

"Top it, Bill," Danny said as the beer leveled off at the
standard half-full volume. The bartender looked questioningly at the other man, who nodded slightly, and the
glass was topped.

"What have you got?" the man asked, once more
leaning forward with his arms on the table. Danny
shushed him and took a swallow of beer before he answered.

"She's workin' in the country."

"Where?"

"The word is she's hooked up with a couple called
Benson or Dennison. Somethin'. 'E's a banker. Lots of
money, lots of loose goods lyin' round the 'ouse."

"How did she get in with them?"

"Oh, she's very smart, this one. Keeps 'er ear to the
ground, she does. Knows 'oo's goin' where and when,
and 'oo's goin' with them, and maybe what kind of 'elp
they'll be lookin' for or what kind of folks they're apt to
meet up with. The lady of the 'ouse thinks she 'as a right
new maid, but all of a sudden what she really 'as is a
whole lot of missin' jewels and silver. They're gone, the
maid is gone, and nobody knows where or how."

"Doesn't make my job any easier, does it?"

"You'll 'ave to work for this one all right, Mick,"
Danny agreed.

"You say the new mark is a banker?" Danny nodded.
"Benson or Dennison."

"Somethin' like that. Didn't 'ear the name so clear."

"Right. Well," the other man said briskly, pushing
back from the table and standing, "it's a place to start."

"You won't be bad-mouthin' me down at the Street, now will you?"

"Your reputation remains intact." The tall man looked down at the emaciated figure on the other side of the table and began to fish around in his pockets. At last he withdrew a silver coin and laid it on the table. "Get yourself something to eat, man, before your bones break through the skin."

He was lost in the crowd at the door before Danny had the coin in his eager, sweaty palm.

"Right, Mick," he mumbled, even as his thin legs carried him to the bar to purchase the coveted bottle of gin.

Chapter One

Maggie Landers was not aware that she owed much of the initial good impression she made on people to the two deep and darling dimples in either of her rosy cheeks. Those dimples gave her the appearance of playfulness and unfailing good humor. The appearance was not always reliable.

"DeRay, give me that bowl!" she scolded her younger brother.

Raised in a strong tradition of teasing, with four other boys and poor little Maggie thrust in the middle of them all, DeRay held the coveted bowl just out of his sister's reach. Even in her frustration and exasperation the indentions in her cheeks manifested themselves occasionally, and the boy, younger, though hardly Maggie's "little" brother, refused to take her scolding seriously.

"DeRay, if you want any supper at all tonight, give Maggie the bowl and go see to your chores," his mother ordered gently.

Dutifully, if a bit reluctantly, the boy relinquished the bowl and trudged heavily out the door, muttering something about "Randy and Arnold cleaning up the barn tonight." But only very softly. He wasn't frightened of the tired-looking woman with the mousy gray hair, but he loved her dearly, as did all her boys, and made an effort to do her bidding. Some days it was more of an effort than other days.

Maggie, now in sole possession of the wooden bowl, seemed less delighted by that fact than she should have been, considering the hotly contested battle. The potatoes were on the fire and now, instead of the promised Yorkshire pudding, she laid the bowl aside and took one of the heavy iron pans off its hook.

"Lumpy dick," she offered as an explanation over her shoulder. Her mother nodded, and for a few minutes the only sounds in the kitchen were those of sizzling grease and the pouring of milk into the pan and the spoon against the metal.

Finally, watching the gravy begin to thicken around the globules of flour, Maggie cleared her throat.

"I think I'll do it, Mama."

Mrs. Landers was mending the armhole of one of her husband's work shirts. The material had been washed thin and gray and Mrs. Landers was well aware the thread she was using would last considerably longer than the rest of the garment. But George would as soon consider throwing the new guernsey calf he'd just bought out onto the garbage heap as this shirt. She sighed and pulled the thread between her teeth. She wasn't sighing over the thread, the shirt or the guernsey calf.

"Your mind is made up, then?"

"I think so."

"London is a long way away, Maggie. Your father nor I could do a thing for you if anything happened."

"Nothing is going to happen, Mama."

Mrs. Landers's frown deepened, but she didn't bother to refute her daughter's dogged optimism.

"What does your father say?" she asked instead.

"I haven't told him yet."

"Don't you think you had better?"

"I was hoping . . ." Maggie turned to her mother with raised, encouraging eyebrows, but Mrs. Landers shook her head.

"You're the one who is going. You have to tell your father yourself."

Maggie turned back to the stove and pulled the pan away from the flame. Her trim little figure and pert little nose, along with her dimples, belied the fact she was a young woman of twenty, eager to try her wings and see the world. Her father and five brothers, she knew, were all expecting her to marry one of the neighborhood boys and settle down a half mile away, giving birth to new babies regularly and visiting her childhood home daily. When she left her childhood home. Someday. When she grew up. At a date in the distant future.

Now it was Maggie who sighed as she went to the door to call her father and the boys to supper.

"What have they got in London town that you can't find here?" Mr. Landers asked.

This was after Maggie's hesitant announcement, a number of incredulous gasps around the table, a guffaw from Arnold, and her father looking first at Maggie and then at her mother and then back to Maggie for confirmation of the startling proposal.

"I don't know," Maggie said helplessly. "But *something.*"

Maggie didn't say it all. She didn't tell her family that she felt a restless urge to break out of the neat little niche where she had been placed by everyone who had ever known Maggie Landers. She wanted to travel farther than the ten miles to St. Ives her mother had traveled in her married life; she wanted to see more than cows and corn and meet someone besides Marlin Tucker. Cows and corn were all very pleasant, and Marlin Tucker was perfectly unobjectionable. But surely there was something better in the world than "unobjectionable."

"And what will you do in London? Gather the gold nuggets in the street? What have you boys been filling your sister's head with?" Mr. Landers looked sternly around the table. Rob shrugged his shoulders, LeRoy shook his head, Randy opened his eyes wide in an attempt to look innocent, which, surprisingly, he was this time. DeRay sniggered uncertainly and Arnold shoveled another spoonful of the potatoes and lumpy milk gravy into his mouth.

"They haven't been filling my head with anything, Papa. I know there is no gold to be found in the streets, nor a storybook prince to whisk me away."

Mr. Landers humphed ominously. There had better not be any "whisking" taking place as far as his little girl was concerned.

"I am going to work," Maggie finished.

More incredulous gasps and upturned lips.

She had heard of the Greenleaf Employers Agency in London from a girlfriend who had left their rural community the year before to seek her fame and fortune. Sadie Cullingham was a remarkably homely girl, ignored by the boys-fast-becoming-men she knew, and she decided London offered a broader field that just might include men of less discriminating taste. She wouldn't find anybody as good as Marlin Tucker, she knew, but there might be some well-to-do old codger in London with failing eyesight who needed a serving girl. One could always hope.

Maggie was not as desperate and might have been placed by a better agency, but she didn't know that and only had the address Sadie had given her.

"Greenleaf Agency? Old Bennet Cullingham wouldn't let his girl go unless he knew something about the place, I don't suppose." Mr. Landers picked up the tin cup and and took a swig of the country ale his wife had poured for him tonight with wise foresight. "Why don't you write to them? There's no harm in that."

Maggie drew in a breath and held it for a calming moment. The first hurdle had been met and crossed. Her father had given his permission to a letter of inquiry.

The letter was not allowed to call her away from household tasks, however. She washed and swept and mopped and finally, with her brothers and father all dozing in front of the fire, she brought the paper and ink to the table, where her mother sat struggling to see the faded words of a favorite book by the light of a sputtering candle.

Her mother, having ceded the inevitability of her daughter's venture, put aside the book, and together the two of them composed the letter, Maggie listing every qualification she could think of. It was a very short list.

Arnold was not yet in his teen years and was frankly disbelieving of his sister's plan, so blithely he took the letter up to Forkston for her the next day, and Maggie waited. And waited.

In time she began to despair of her glorious dream. No one had said anything about her going since that night over the potatoes and lumpy dick, and when Mrs. Landers laid the envelope in front of her one morning three weeks later, Maggie didn't grasp its significance for a moment. But only for a moment.

In the next instant the envelope lay torn in her lap, her eyes running over the few lines on the page.

The Greenleaf Employers Agency secures employment in respectable homes for young women willing to work. If your health is tolerable and you have no outstanding debts nor attached embarrassments—

Maggie wondered briefly over the ominous sound of the vague phrase.

—you may present yourself at my office in a fortnight from your receipt of this letter.

Maggie raised her eager eyes over the top of the sheet and met her mother's troubled gaze.

"So, they want you?"

"He says I may present myself at his office in two weeks."

In dazed bewilderment the men in the Landers family heard the news and silently counted the money Maggie triumphantly produced, which she had been carefully saving from the butter she made and sold to the neighbors.

"I think it's enough to get me to London, don't you?"

"Should be," Mr. Landers said numbly.

Ignoring the wounded looks, Maggie set about packing her little satchel, which held all of her earthly belongings, then, carrying it and the tin of homely edibles her mother sent along with her, she went off to discover the world.

"She'll be back," George Landers said. His voice was unusually gruff and he wiped impatiently at his eyes.

"I don't know," his wife said softly.

Neither did he.

Chapter Two

At the top of Wellington Street in London, close to the busy Strand and the great theaters of Drury Lane and Covent Garden, is a street that arches like a bent longbow. It is therefore called, quite appropriately, Bow Street.

Before the Pinkerton agency in the American colonies, before Scotland Yard in London, there were the Bow Street police.

Henry Fielding, author of the scandalous *Tom Jones,* was also a magistrate judge. In the middle of the eighteenth-century, appalled by the wholesale crime that teemed around him at his very doorstep, he organized a body of men to police the city and headquartered them in his Bow Street court.

By the turn of the nineteenth century, the police department boasted a foot patrol that would constitute the nucleus of Scotland Yard when it was formed in 1829. There was also a horse patrol to apprehend the swifter, more far-ranging criminal element. In 1836 the horse patrol of Bow Street was reorganized into the famed mounted branch of London's police.

And then there were the runners.

The Bow Street runners averaged fifteen men; fifteen brave, stalwart, clever men who were the detectives of their time and place. Names and deeds became legendary, so that by the early 1800s the introduction of a runner meant instant recognition, instant respect and often, if there were members of the fair and impressionable sex present, palpitating hearts and occasional vapors.

The force grew over the years and the magistrate office was held by many judges, most of whom were eventually knighted in recognition of their service to crown and kingdom. But in 1806 James Read, a comfortably situated and remarkably conscientious citizen, was made magistrate of Bow Street and refused to be knighted for what he considered his plain duty.

"Come in," Mr. James Read called in answer to the tap at his door. It was early in the morning of a day early in the week. He had just sent down for his morning coffee at Kelsey's in the street below, but the man who entered at his summons carried nothing in his hands but a hat.

"Oh, Michaels," the magistrate greeted him. The other man inclined his head but kept his clear, direct gaze on his superior. Unlike many other men, Mr. Read did not find the gaze disconcerting. "Have a seat, Michaels," he said.

The gentleman sat.

"Cigarette?" Read offered. The officer refused. Mr. Read had known he would and approved. He took one of the expensive French cigarettes himself, though, and lighted it with a Lucifer match, a whole box of which he kept on his desk for just such occasions. "The name you wanted is Denton. Franklin Denton. With the Fidelity National Banking Concern. Well enough off, though not spectacularly wealthy. Just the sort this Briggs woman goes after." The magistrate leaned back in his chair and studied the other man through narrowed lids and a fog of smoke.

"Then Danny was right," Michaels said.

"That is what you have to find out."

"The question is easily solved—approach the Dentons, inform them of the situation and apprehend any recent addition to their household, say a serving girl they just took into service."

Mr. Read nodded slowly but took another puff on the cigarette before he replied.

"*If* the Franklin Dentons are the intended prey. If there is any new employee in their household. If there is only one new employee in the house."

"If the thief has not already struck and fled," Michaels offered. Mr. Read nodded.

"If the disguise she has assumed is that of a servant. According to your report, she has assumed a variety of identities. You see the complications. The success of this Briggs, or whatever name she is using now, has caused unease in a number of the city's most influential minds. We can be grateful that, so far, she has stayed away from the peerage or our position would have been made even more uncomfortable. As it is—" He leaned forward again and tapped the ash from the end of the cigarette.

"As it is, you would like a runner in the Denton home."

"If you can arrange it." Mr. Read reached across the desk for the *Morning Chronicle*. He opened the page and shook it out before he seemed to remember the other man. "That will be everything. 'Luck, Michaels."

Officer Michaels stood and left the cramped room Magistrate Read used as an office. The judge was not due on the bench until ten o'clock and these few moments of ease and solitude were jealously guarded.

On the other side of the door Jared Michaels presented the very picture of grim determination. The Bow Street runners were also determined men.

He would first see the Denton fellow to explain the situation and make certain arrangements. And then he would stop this notorious thief.

Chapter Three

Maggie's ride from the Huntingdon stage stop to the grand city of London was long, damp and chilled. It was raining when her family solemnly bade her farewell, it rained the entire trip down, and it was raining when the coach arrived in the busy, friendless city. The droplets pelted against the roof and sides of the heavy coach, accenting the *clop* of the horses' hooves in the muddy lane.

Being a friendly soul, Maggie had hoped for a riding companion to share the trip and his or her life story. But the girl was alone in the dark cavern of the carriage, alone and cold and beginning to question if indeed there was anything in London town to make this trip worthwhile.

Her doubts were not laid to rest when she descended the rickety steps set outside the carriage door to stand in the misty drizzle. In the time it took for the driver to hand down her bag, the water was streaming off the narrow brim of her black bonnet. A drop of water splashed into her eyes and she blinked hastily to reduce the distorted figure of the man who was approaching her.

"Miss Landers? Maggie Landers?"

His figure, as it turned out, was not as grossly distorted as she assumed it must be. He was a large man, frankly a fat man, whose several chins undulated under his jaw and whose belly shifted and quivered when he moved, like gelatin that was not quite set.

"Yes, sir," she answered.

"I'm come from the agency. Is this all you brought, then?" His voice was high and nasal and Maggie shrank back when he took her arm to pull her after him. "Come along," he said impatiently. "My wagon's over this way. I was expecting more luggage. If you'd told me this was all you would have we could have walked it back to Greenleaf's. As it is, I had to hitch Jugs up and drive that heavy old wagon down these streets. Got stuck twice."

Maggie, who was by now unenthusiastically allowing herself to be dragged along, was not surprised to learn that the wagon this man had been sitting in had gotten stuck in the muddy streets; not as she watched the wide expanse of derriere in front of her sway from side to side like some ponderous pendulum.

The man stopped and Maggie could only assume that the manure-splattered wooden box set atop the iron wheels was the wagon he had brought for her conveyance. He took her satchel, which he had never offered to carry for her, and flung it carelessly into the box. Next he released her arm and began the elaborate procedure of hoisting himself onto the driver's seat.

Grasping the edge of the box with one hand and the wooden pole that ran from it to the horse's strap with the other, he pulled himself forward once, off the ground on the second try, finally finding footing on the board that braced the bottom of the box on the third lunge.

Heaving himself onto the driver's seat was another three-try effort, and then settling himself, finding the reins, soothing the horse and steadying the box took another several minutes.

With each of his heavy-handed attempts the wagon swayed dangerously, and with his final heave onto the seat, even the big horse was rocked off its feet and stumbled back.

Maggie watched the whole procedure, eyes wide with horror. She was certain that she was poised on the brink of disaster, that at any moment the man would fall and pull the wooden box, and possibly the horse, down onto his bulky form. Now, though, he sat securely in the driver's seat and gave her a look of profound scorn, as if *he* had been waiting for her for ten minutes.

"Well, get up here, girl. Unless you want to walk back to the agency anyway."

Maggie scrambled up and into the box, landing next to her satchel, since there was no room for her on the seat. Indeed, the man's flesh drooped loosely over the edge of the seat for two inches on either side.

Maggie had an unsettling moment of vertigo when she knew she had come to a rest in the box yet felt herself still moving. The man had jounced the reins and the horse, Jugs, had started wearily down the street. The raindrops fell into the box, making puddles here and there on the uneven wood, puddles that insisted on flowing under her skirts and person with every sway of the contraption. And there were many sways.

She began to think back fondly to her ride from Huntingdon to London and wonder what on earth she'd had to complain about, when the wheels dropped into two ruts filled with water and the horse made no attempt to pull them out.

"Here we are, then. Take your things and go right in. I hope the fire didn't go out. If it did, build it up again and put on the kettle for some tea. Tea's what we need now, some good, hot tea."

While the man spoke, Maggie had been wrestling her way out of the box again, this time handicapped by the bag she was trying to bring with her. Oblivious to her struggles, the fellow continued to extol the virtues of good, hot tea. And scones. And crumpets. And cakes. Finally he said something about getting Jugs out of the rain—never mind about getting Maggie out of the rain—and absently jogged the straps he held in his meaty hands. Fortunately, Maggie, at that precise moment, jumped free of the wagon and clear of the heavy wheel, even managing, as she did so, to keep a grip on the handle of her bag.

The horse and wagon sloshed away to whatever haven protected the livestock from inclement weather, and Maggie turned to inspect the establishment into which she had chosen to entrust her destiny. The prospect was not encouraging. The Greenleaf Employers Agency was a small, shabby building in a narrow, grimy street. As she picked her way to the raised boardwalk in front of the various stores and offices, Maggie began to despair as much for her destiny as she did the sumptuous tea her driver had fantasized.

The fire had gone out and Maggie was not able to breathe life into another one before the door was pushed open and the big man filled the room.

"Where's the kettle?" was the first thing he asked. And then, "Why haven't you got that started yet?"

Maggie was unable to answer either question. She had not taken time to inspect the two rooms that comprised the Greenleaf Employers Agency and so did not know where the teakettle was kept. She also did not know why her fire hadn't started. It was not for want of great puffs of breath, she could have told him, if she had saved enough breath herself to answer him.

He slammed her aside, though perhaps he only meant to nudge her, and Maggie stumbled back and away to find the teakettle.

The front room was dim and bare. There was a counter and a desk, and the stove, of course. There were several chairs against the wall opposite the stove, but Maggie really could not imagine that any more than one chair at a time was ever occupied in here. There was not, however, any teakettle. Not even under the counter, where there was a flat money sack and a loosely folded news sheet.

Maggie, hurrying by now because the man had taken advantage of her exhausting effort and had promptly started the fire, went through the door behind the counter into the inner office. This room was the very antithesis of the other, filled with the chaos of a lumpy divan, a little table, chairs, shelves with plates, eating utensils, three rolls threatening to turn moldy in the humid air, and even, if she was not mistaken, a nightcap. On the table, logically next to a tin of tea, was the kettle. Maggie grabbed it, was relieved to feel the weight of water in it, and took it out to the main office and the man and the merry little blaze in the stove.

"Well, well, well," he said, putting the kettle on the heating plate and then turning to her with a moist smile. The prospect of his much admired "good, hot tea" had cheered him. "So you are Maggie Landers, come to London to find fame and fortune."

Maggie was flushed with the heat from the stove and the uncomfortable feeling the man's tone gave her.

"I don't know about that, sir."

"Of course you do, my girl. They all come to London looking for excitement. It might be here, all right, but a little hard to find on a maid's wages, eh?" He stepped back uncomfortably from the fire; he was seldom ever cool, carrying with him his own considerable layer of insulation. "But you will find out all about being a maid, girl. We will get you placed soon enough, don't worry." He ran his eyes, like a heavy hand, over her slim figure, and Maggie, for her part, shivered slightly and took a step nearer the stove.

The kettle began to whistle and the man instructed Maggie to carry it back into "his place." He was settling down into a squeaky chair at the table when she joined him and set the kettle down. He brewed the tea while he directed Maggie's setting of the table.

"The big cup's mine. That's the one. You can use any of those others." The "big cup" would hold a pint and a half of liquid; the "others" were a miscellaneous collection of cracked and chipped teacups and saucers of the formally recognized thimbleful capacity. "Sugar, there. Cream in the pitcher. It should still be all right—hasn't been very warm in here, I don't suppose."

Maggie shivered again and agreed with him.

"The rolls, don't forget the rolls. See any jam up there? No? I must have used it all. Just have to sprinkle sugar today, I suppose." The man picked up the sugar bowl and dumped a great mound of sugar into the damp middle of the roll he held in his hand.

Maggie sipped at the tea, which *was* good and hot, but refused his offer of a roll. The man did not seem offended as he took another and tore it in half.

"Now, you understand, girl, that I will put you up in a respectable boardinghouse, across the way there." He motioned vaguely toward the door with his sweetened roll, filling the air with fine crystals of sugar that settled and dissolved on, among other things, Maggie's damp skin. "You must reimburse me that cost, of course."

Maggie nodded. The terms had all been spelled out in the letter she had received from this agency. Or rather, she realized, the letter she had received from this man, since this man evidently *was* the Greenleaf Employers Agency.

"The less time you are at the boardinghouse the less you have to pay me. And I shouldn't think you would be long there." Again his heavy glance traveled over her body. "I arrange for your employ in a house of good character, and you pay my fee from your wages, either one lump sum or several installments, however you want it."

Maggie nodded again. The fee had seemed exorbitant to her, but in the man's letter he had also quoted the wage she could expect to be earning. Maggie saw then that all things must be viewed relatively.

"Then there's just one final bit of business," the man said, draining the liquid from his cup—liquid thick with cream—and reaching for the tea. His hand brushed the knuckles of her clenched fingers that held her own cup. Maggie could hardly compress herself into a more compact mass.

What had she gotten herself into? she couldn't help wondering as another drop of water fell from the brim of her bonnet into the cup.

Maggie couldn't help wonder the same thing when the matron of the Miller Boardinghouse showed her into her room. The room was bare and cold, but not as bare as the agency's outer office, and nothing had ever chilled her as much as the inner office.

Maggie didn't bother to unpack her little satchel, since there was no place to put the unpacked articles. The furnishings of the room consisted of a cot, two blankets, a small stand with a pitcher and bowl atop, and a wee chip of mirror, which lay next to the bowl. This boarding-house was regularly used by clients of the Greenleaf Employers Agency with the understanding that these girls were looking for work and would want to present their best image at any interview. But Mrs. Miller doubtless had the business sense to see that the longer her guests stayed here, the more money she would receive, so it could not be said she exhausted herself in accommodating the girls in their job hunting.

Maggie's stay was one long, dreary week. It rained most of the week, being the spring rainy season, and Maggie was trapped like a little canary behind the dingy walls of her cage.

Mrs. Miller's food was quite good but never wastefully abundant, and the mealtime gatherings, which might have been gay at another season of the year, were, like everything else in this city, dampened.

Then, just when Maggie was beginning to despair and seriously wonder where she could get the money to return to Huntingdon, a note was delivered to her from the agency.

"There is an opening in the staff of a banker and his wife—a Mr. and Mrs. Franklin Denton," the heavy-set man from the agency informed her when she arrived at his office.

"Really?" Maggie breathed.

The man peered at her blankly through his puffy eyes. He didn't answer but picked up two sheets of paper in front of him instead.

"Take these papers with you. You will be interviewed by—" he glanced down at another paper on the desk "—a Mrs. Bern. The housekeeper. Now this is the address." He handed her the first paper. "And this is a sheet of your credentials compiled by the agency."

Maggie looked at the paper and quailed at the sparsity of lines of print. The man was watching her and reached out to pat her hand comfortingly. Maggie did not feel comforted.

"Don't worry," he said, then stopped to wheeze fitfully for a moment, which he did occasionally. "I have appended my personal recommendation at the bottom."

Maggie glanced at the bottom of the sheet and the two brief lines there.

"Girl is clean. Believe she is a good worker."

Maggie also did not feel particularly recommended.

Nevertheless, with a determined smile on her lips and dimples in her cheeks, she took the letter and address from the agency and came to beard the frightful Denton housekeeper-dragon in her den.

The "den" was a fair-sized town house near the banking district of London. It was not huge or flashy, but the brass door knocker was polished and gleaming. The steps that led to the front door had been swept and washed and looked almost as if they had been polished, too. Maggie could tell that the requirement that she be willing to work would not be taken lightly.

With address and letter of recommendation in hand, she climbed the steps to the front door. She was aware that inquiring help probably should present itself at the servants' entrance, but Maggie didn't know where the servants' entrance was, and besides, she really wanted to feel the weight of that brass knocker in her hand.

When she let the heavy metal fall against the door, a dull *boom* reverberated through the house and the girl was sorry that she had insisted upon using it. Nevertheless, it produced the desired effect almost immediately.

The door opened.

The woman who looked out at her did not look like a dragon. She had gray hair and crinkles around her eyes, but no other glaring evidence of age. Her cheeks were remarkably smooth and her eyes were keen, and at the present moment inquiring.

"Yes?"

"Maggie Landers, ma'am, from Greenleaf Employers."

"Ah, yes," the woman said. "Won't you come in?"

Maggie stepped into the cool dimness of a receiving hall and looked about her. The appointments were quiet and tasteful, light fixtures, wall hangings, rugs and furniture purchased with an eye for harmony and comfort rather than ostentation.

The lady who admitted her had excused herself and Maggie stood nervously twisting the papers she held in her hand. But in just a moment, the older woman returned and the girl turned to her with a smile of relief.

Mrs. Bern, the housekeeper, was, like a myriad of people before her, favorably impressed by the dimples in the girl's cheeks and the pleasant nature they seemed to promise. She was also impressed by the silky hair, the tidy dress and the sensible shoes the girl wore.

She motioned to Maggie, who followed the woman's lead uncertainly. Dimples and a good nature were not helping her measurably in this moment of crisis. In fact, as the heavy oak door swung inward with only a faint breath of sound, no more than a quiet exhalation, what the young woman was most aware of was the tremor in her knees and the trickle of perspiration crawling down her back.

"This way," Mrs. Bern said. "Mrs. Denton will see you now. Don't smile too much or chatter. We don't want Mrs. Denton to think you are a silly featherhead, now do we? And stand up straight.

"Mrs. Denton, this is Maggie Landers, sent over by the Greenleaf Agency. Give Mrs. Denton the letter, girl."

Maggie offered the lady of the house the two sheets of paper and Mrs. Denton took them and smoothed them out against the dark wood of her desk.

"Mmm," the lady murmured, glancing at the papers and then raising her eyes. But she didn't raise them to Maggie; she looked instead at the other woman with an expression of inquiry.

Mrs. Bern was a matronly woman of medium height, with a comfortable girth that was witness to the comfortable position she held in the Denton home. She had a pleasant, double-chinned face surrounded by a fluff of gray white hair, topped with a crisp white cap, which Maggie was to find never lost its gleam or its stiffness.

She kept house for the Franklin Dentons both here in town and in their summer cottage near Dover. Other servants came and went, but Mrs. Bern was a permanent member of the Denton household.

"I couldn't do a thing without her," Mrs. Denton regularly claimed. She said it with a smile that suggested she was, of course, exaggerating. It was no exaggeration.

Mrs. Bern had come to work for the Dentons right after her husband died and had been with them ever since. She came as Leticia Bern, although her husband had called her Letty. However, it was uncertain if Mrs. Denton even remembered her housekeeper's first name, she had been "Mrs. Bern" for so many years.

Mrs. Bern and her husband had been together only four years and they had had no children. But over the years Mrs. Bern had seen countless young people grow into responsible adults under her watchful eye.

"She is one in a million," Franklin Denton said more than once, though not as often as his wife said she couldn't do without their housekeeper. Mr. Denton didn't smile when he made his claim because he knew he wasn't exaggerating.

Now Mrs. Bern nodded her head almost imperceptibly. Mrs. Denton looked down at the letter again, and when next she looked up, she fixed the girl with a look that was neither as cold nor as imperial as it seemed to Maggie.

"It says here that you are just arrived in town from a farm near Huntingdon. You are aware, are you not, that we are engaging the staff that will accompany us to Dover for the summer?" Maggie nodded but didn't have a chance to reply before Mrs. Denton continued. "So if you've come to London to see some of the city life, perhaps you are not prepared to leave it again quite so soon?"

"Oh, no, ma'am. I am very willing to leave," Maggie said eagerly. The girl had seen London for herself now and was ready to see more of the country, especially a part that would include a view of the fabled ocean and some fresh air once again.

Mrs. Denton smiled coolly at Maggie's response and returned her attention to the paper.

As often happened when the Dentons made their annual summer pilgrimage to Dover, the hiring of new servants had become necessary. But that didn't mean Caroline Denton enjoyed the hiring process. She was often tempted to leave the positions unfilled and do for herself, until she considered that if she left the positions unfilled she would have to do for herself.

The announcement to the staff that they would be leaving the first of June was met with a loud lamentation from Tam MacPhillip, their cook of short duration, and an announcement of her own from Sally Darwin, their maid.

"Mr. Studge has asked me to marry him," Sally said proudly, glancing at Mrs. Bern to see if she should smile. The housekeeper wore a tolerant expression so Sally dared a wide grin.

Mrs. Bern did not entirely approve of David Studge. He was bold and loud and chewed tobacco, than which Mrs. Bern could think of no filthier habit. But he had a good job, was fond of Sally and didn't become a bully when he drank, so the two of them had Mrs. Bern's qualified blessings.

Mrs. Denton was surprised, not even having been aware that Sally had a young man—Mrs. Bern was very strict about the staff keeping their private lives private— but she accepted the announcement with good grace and slipped in an extra five-pound note with the girl's final pay.

For his part, when his wife told him that Tam Mac-Phillip refused to go to Dover with them, Franklin Denton displayed a marked relief that went considerably beyond "good grace."

Tam MacPhillip, who had been the Denton cook for six months, had fed them all of the cock-a-leekie Mr. Denton ever hoped to see. She packed up and left the very day Mrs. Denton told of the summer plans and by evening had been replaced by Ethel Cranney.

Once the Dentons had employed a French chef, Anton Latreque, who fought with all the servants, includ-

ing Mrs. Bern, and was as temperamental as a hothouse
orchid. But he prepared *rognons de veau au champagne*
that would bring tears to the eyes of even an irreligious
man. Since his employ, which had been all too brief for
Franklin, it had been hard to find a cook who satisfied
Mr. Denton. Certainly he wasn't satisfied by the bland,
heavy English dishes that Ethel Cranney served, but his
wife had an undemanding palate and seemed pleased
with their hasty replacement. Mr. Denton consoled himself with the reminder that at least the cook wasn't Ger-
man.

Sally Darwin's place had not been as quickly filled.
Mrs. Denton made excuses and put off the interviews
until Mrs. Bern dropped some rather heavy hints that she
could not do all of the packing herself and if Mr. and
Mrs. Denton planned on leaving for Dover before next
fall she would have to have some help.

So Mrs. Denton had sent inquiries to the employment
agencies and they had begun to send the procession of
brassy, uncouth young women who invaded the Denton
home once or twice a year.

The first girl she had seen that morning was an excellent example. She had arrived at a quarter to seven that
morning, which did not impress Mrs. Bern as much as it
might have when it became clear to the housekeeper that
the girl was an early bird more interested in the worm
than in any position she might secure.

"I know I'm early. I'll just wait in the kitchen till the
lady is ready to see me," she had offered, turning, without direction, like a compass needle to the North Pole,
toward the kitchen.

Mrs. Bern, being a charitable soul, had instructed
Ethel to give the girl a cup of coffee and a sweet roll, but
when she showed the young woman in to Mrs. Denton

she silently noted the splotch on her blouse where she had sloshed some of the coffee, nor did she offer any of the advice she now gave to Maggie.

This second girl, though, this Miss Margaret Landers, suited Mrs. Bern much better. She was a quiet, pleasant little thing, wearing a fresh dress, with hair combed smooth and pulled back, and even with clean fingernails. The whispered admonitions Mrs. Bern had given were kindly meant and, by the stiffening of the girl's spine, evidently taken to heart.

Now they stood together in front of Mrs. Denton's desk, Mrs. Bern with hands folded quietly across her stomach and poor little Maggie trembling like an aspen leaf, awaiting the verdict the lady of the house would soon deliver.

"It is unfortunate that you have held no former positions," Mrs. Denton said, raising her eyes once more over the top of the paper she held now in front of her face. "I always like to see some references."

Maggie mumbled something about being sorry and felt her hopes sinking, but Mrs. Bern next to her cleared her throat softly and the mistress of the house glanced at the housekeeper.

"What is your appraisal of—" she referred to the paper "—Margaret, Mrs. Bern?"

"I believe the young woman would do nicely, Mrs. Denton." The two women spoke over the head of the girl as if she weren't in the room. Rather than being insulted by their dismissal of her, Maggie was relieved to be out of the line of fire for the time being. "She seems willing to learn and knows how to care for her own person, which, it has been my experience, are the leading requirements for giving satisfactory service."

"Well, Margaret, you seem to have found favor in Mrs. Bern's eye, which, I admit, bears more sway with me than the highest recommendations from someone I neither know nor about whom I care. I suppose we will have to speak to one or two more girls before making a decision, however?" Again Mrs. Denton raised her eyes to her housekeeper's.

"Do you think?" Mrs. Bern asked.

"Or perhaps not," Mrs. Denton amended. Having girded her loins for this undertaking she felt almost disappointed to have the position filled so quickly and easily. She looked over the paper the girl had given her once again, but its few lines of print could hardly give her a great deal of insight into Miss Landers's character. She glanced once more at Mrs. Bern's calm face and then at the slight figure directly in front of her.

"I suppose we will consider your services engaged, then. You may collect your things and report to Mrs. Bern, who will give you your instructions. Welcome to the Denton home, Margaret."

"Maggie, ma'am."

"Maggie?"

"Everybody calls me Maggie. They have since the day I was born. I don't know why they bothered to tack on those extra letters since no one's ever used them. Why, if you were to ask for Margaret Landers anywhere around Huntingdon, I don't think—" Mrs. Bern cleared her throat ever so gently and Maggie realized she was chattering. Abruptly she stopped.

"You don't think?" Mrs. Denton prompted.

Maggie Landers was a cheery sprite who would have gladly told anyone else that she had always considered Margaret to be a bit of pretension on her mother's part. With any other audience Maggie would have laughed and told tales of the rude country life she had come from and the five tormenting brothers who had never let her take herself or the name her mother had given her too seriously. Why, from morning to night it was "Maggie this" and "Maggie that," she would have said, with the Landers boys chasing after their sister with worms and spiders and fresh killed rabbits dripping blood on the kitchen floor.

But under Mrs. Bern's ponderous gaze, instead of her merry tales, she dropped her own eyes in confusion.

"Nothing, ma'am," she murmured. "Only folks call me Maggie."

"Certainly, if that is what you prefer. Mrs. Bern, will you get Maggie settled in and then perhaps this afternoon you two can work on the packing."

Mrs. Bern said, "Certainly, madam," and led the girl from the room.

Mrs. Denton heaved a sigh of relief to think that that was taken care of, and hadn't she done a clever thing to have hired another girl so quickly? Franklin would certainly congratulate her on a job well done.

Mrs. Bern, for her part, recognized that getting the missus to hire this girl was just the first step, merely the overture, to the job of teaching the girl to serve in this house.

And Maggie was happy to have any job at all.

Chapter Four

Knock, knock, knock.

"Mr. Denton, I am sorry to disturb you, sir..."

"What is it, Jeremy?"

"There is a gentleman here to see you."

"You know I am trying to get ready to leave, Jeremy. I told you no visitors today."

"Yes, sir, but he is from the Bow Street police."

Franklin Denton looked up from the piled papers on his desk with a surprised frown. The Fidelity National Banking Concern was hardly in the habit of entertaining representatives of the celebrated police force, but after their success in apprehending certain thieves and counterfeiters in recent years, the Bow Street police had earned themselves a prominent position of respect in the London banking world.

"The Bow Street police?" Denton repeated. His secretary "yes, sir-ed," and Denton waved impatiently. "Do not keep the gentleman waiting, Jeremy," he said. The young man closed the door, but in a moment the soft tap was repeated.

"Come in, come in," Denton said, this time in his most jovial banker's manner, rising from behind his desk and pulling at his vest, which had slipped above the bulge of his ample stomach.

The gentleman who entered the office, though taller than Mr. Denton by half a foot at least, was considerably leaner. However, his broad shoulders and vibrant air were almost too large for the close office. He stepped forward and received Denton's hand in a firm grip, fixing him with dark, direct eyes, and the office, which had seemed close before, suddenly gathered itself directly about the banker's shoulders.

"What can I do for you, my good man?" Denton asked with loud and determined goodwill, reminding himself that he was neither guilty nor accused of any wrongdoing, and certainly glad of that fact.

"My name is Jared Michaels, Mr. Denton. I am a runner for the Bow Street police."

"Indeed?" Denton said. "Won't you sit down, Officer Michaels?" Denton indicated the chair and returned to the safety of his own chair behind the desk, relieved to be once again barricaded behind its massive bulk. "To what do I owe the signal honor of a visit from a member of the redoubtable Bow Street police force?"

"For some time now we have been on the trail, if you will, of a certain female criminal. She is a clever woman who has stolen at will from some of the finest homes in London. Apparently she accomplishes this by establishing herself as some sort of intimate in a wealthy household—trusted, unsuspected, ingenuous and as elusive as a will-o'-the-wisp. Our services have been called upon half a dozen times in the past two years, but always after the fact, after she has absconded with the booty."

"I commiserate with you on your frustrating investigation, Officer Michaels, but I am afraid I do not see how the bank..."

"As I said, always before we have been approached after the crime has been committed, when there is no hope of apprehending the woman. However, we believe we know who the woman has marked as her next victim."

"And who might that be, sir?"

"You, sir."

"Me, sir?" Mr. Denton's mobile face recorded his various reactions to the young man's claim as Michaels merely nodded stonily. At first Denton was shocked, then unbelieving, then outraged. Under that last there was a hint of fear. "Who is it? What can I do? Surely we have discovered nothing missing," Denton sputtered at last.

"No, Mr. Denton, we do not believe she has struck yet. We understand it is her practice, her modus operandi, to first infiltrate the household, to inveigle her way into the very working heart of a home, from which safe vantage she is able to steal at leisure."

Mr. Denton sat behind his desk, eyes wide and protruding, the muscles of his jaw opening and closing his mouth, though he did not say anything. Officer Jared Michaels couldn't remember ever having seen a finer impression of a fish. That thought was responsible for the first crack in the officer's impassive armor. With a kindlier note in his voice and a relaxation of the muscles at the corner of his mouth, he attempted to reassure the foundering gentleman before him.

"Tell me, Mr. Denton, have you filled any recent vacancies in your serving staff?"

"Our cook and one of the serving girls quit not long ago. It always happens." Michaels raised his eyebrows questioningly. "We leave for our summer vacation in a few days. My aunt left me a cottage near Dover. Comfortable little place, though necessarily a bit old-fashioned for our modern tastes.'' Mr. Denton pulled again at his vest, his feet once more on solid ground as he spoke of his secure possessions, things no thief, as clever as she might be, could steal from him. ''Some one of our servants refuses to leave town every year. This replacement business is a regular ordeal in the Denton home.''

Michaels nodded.

''And the vacancies have been filled by whom?'' he asked. For the first time in the interview the police detective took his eyes off Denton and the banker experienced a giddy relaxation, like a marionette whose strings had been cut. Michaels was searching through his pockets and in a moment he withdrew a bent pad of paper and the stub of a pencil. Another crack in his armor appeared and Mr. Denton allowed himself to be hopeful that he was talking to a flesh-and-blood mortal.

''My wife immediately hired Ethel Cranney to cook for us. Of course, we would have starved without her, but one cannot help wishing sometimes that Mrs. Denton would be a trifle more selective . . . Ah, well, that is neither here nor there.''

''The woman is not a skillful cook, then?'' Michaels asked, looking up from his notes.

''Oh, no, nothing like that. She can roast and boil well enough, I suppose—one must not always expect imagination.'' Mr. Denton sighed heavily, remembering Anton's *oignons farcis*.

''And the maid?'' Michaels prompted. Mr. Denton recalled himself.

''Mrs. Denton is in the process of filling that position this very day.''

''Ah,'' Michaels said, writing something on his pad.

''Ah, what? Is that significant?'' Denton asked eagerly.

"Just 'ah,' Mr. Denton."

"No. You said 'ah' as if hiring a maid today meant something. What have you heard?"

"It's nothing, Mr. Denton. Really. Please go on."

"There is nothing to go on to," Denton protested. "As soon as the two vacancies are filled we are leaving for Dover for the summer months. At least—" He looked at Officer Michaels, eyes brimming with hopeful disappointment; his wife loved to "get away" for the summer, but Mr. Denton had long since found this annual upheaval a royal, if His Majesty would forgive him, pain in the… "—we always have, though maybe we shouldn't leave town this year?"

Michaels jerked his eyes away from his pad to lock Denton's in a viselike grip.

"Indeed you should, Mr. Denton. By all means. Your trip to Dover is imperative. I have only one suggestion…."

"Caroline, my dear." Mr. Denton entered his wife's sitting room and bent to kiss the cheek she offered. "I've been wondering all day if you got the new maid hired?"

Mrs. Denton looked up at her husband with a glimmer of surprise.

"When did our serving staff become a matter of prime interest in your banking world, Franklin? Or perhaps you don't trust my judgment?"

"Certainly, certainly. You know I have never had any quarrel with your choice of servants." Mr. Denton smiled a bit widely, but not so wide as to cause his wife to suspect his sincerity.

"I am relieved to hear that."

"I only ask because I am anxious to leave for the Channel and I know the positions have to be filled before that happy event takes place." He smiled again but saw from the look in his wife's eye that he had overstepped the bounds of credibility with his hyperbole. His impatience with the rigmarole of relocation had been too loudly expressed in years past for his wife to believe in his eagerness now.

"Oh?" she asked, but Franklin did not rise to her challenge. Finally Mrs. Denton relented and smiled faintly. "Well, to relieve your fevered uncertainty, yes, we are fully staffed once again and Mrs. Bern and the new girl should have the packing finished by tomorrow morning."

"Capital!" Mr. Denton exploded, and now Mrs. Denton would not be put off.

"What is the matter with you, Franklin?" she demanded. "You act as if this trip would fulfill your heart's fondest dream, which, in view of this morning's frosty response to my announcement that we would be leaving as soon as possible, I fail to understand."

"It is only that—"

There was a knock at the front door. The Dentons hastily looked at each other, like culprits caught in some nefarious act.

"I imagine that is..." Mrs. Denton began, rising to her feet, grabbing at a sheet of paper that began to slip from her lap as she stood.

"Perhaps this will explain..." Mr. Denton said, turning to face the door.

They saw Mrs. Bern hurry past the sitting room door in answer to the summons.

"Darling..." Mrs. Denton said.

"My dear," Mr. Denton interrupted her, hoping to explain hastily before Mrs. Bern showed in the visitor. Before he could say anything further, however, that worthy lady's healthy bulk filled the doorway.

"Miss Christian, madam," she said.

"Who?" Mr. Denton asked.

Mrs. Bern's figure was replaced in the doorway by a tall, slender form swathed in trailing silks and rustling satins, with a river of glossy black hair flowing out from under an elegant bonnet.

"Elizabeth!" Mrs. Denton gushed, stepping toward the figure. "Franklin, I would like you to meet Miss Elizabeth Christian. An old friend of Hubert and Melinda Randolph." She turned back to her husband and held up the paper in her hand, evidently believing it answered all of her husband's questions. "I only received their letter this morning, my dear," she said to the lovely creature in the doorway.

"Oh, I thought..." the girl stammered in pretty confusion. "If I had had any idea...I am sure I did not mean to..."

Mrs. Denton put her hand reassuringly on the girl's arm and drew her into the room.

"You mustn't think a thing about it, must she, Franklin?" Mrs. Denton smiled.

"Certainly not," Mr. Denton said, returning her smile and stepping forward genially, though in all actuality he would have welcomed further explanations from someone.

"Did the Randolphs get away, then?" Mrs. Denton asked the girl.

"Just. The coachman brought me here from the dock."

"Hubert and Melinda are finally getting to the Continent, Franklin."

"Are they? How nice for them," Mr. Denton said.

"And though they invited Miss Christian to join them, she only recently returned from France herself...."

"Just," the girl said, smiling a dazzling smile.

"And so they thought it would be ever so much more pleasant for the young lady to visit Dover."

"I see," Mr. Denton said.

"I am so delighted," the girl breathed.

"With us," Mrs. Denton said.

"I see," Mr. Denton said again, and then he finally did see and replaced his hesitant smile with a sincere smile, though to the naked eye there was no difference between the two. "In that case, how very nice for *us.*" Mr. Denton pressed the girl's thin, delicate hand, but not too firmly. He didn't want to break anything.

"I believe we know your mother, Miss Christian," Mrs. Denton was saying. "Ruth Christian?"

Miss Christian shook her head. "That would be Aunt Ruth," she said. "Though, to be precise, I believe she is a great-aunt, or a cousin of my father's."

"Near enough to be family, anyway," Mr. Denton said brightly.

"And how did you find France this time of year, Miss Christian?" Mrs. Denton asked.

"It was..." Miss Christian began, but her report on the current condition of the Land of the Gauls was interrupted by another loud knock at the front door.

Once again the Dentons searched each other's faces.

"My dear?" Mrs. Denton asked.

"Darling..." Mr. Denton began.

"Well, my word!" Mrs. Bern's exasperated voice filtered in to them through two open doors and the short
hallway that separated the sitting room from the room
where the housekeeper and the new maid were working.
"Maggie, why don't you answer that this time?" they
heard her say, and then there was a timid little sound and
a murmur of what must have been instructions, and soon
the watchers in the sitting room, who might have been
spectators at a stage play, saw a small, blond-haired figure hurry past the door. The figure was unfamiliar to Mr.
Denton, though he assumed it was the new maid, and in
view of the conversation of this morning, his eyes narrowed suspiciously.

Aware that by now any forewarning to his wife was too
late, Mr. Denton waited patiently for the girl and the
caller to appear. Which they did in a moment.

"Mrs. Denton?" the girl said. She was a pretty little
thing, with wide blue eyes in which there did not appear
to be the slightest flicker of guile. Just as Michaels had
described, Denton thought. There were two bright spots
on her cheeks, suggesting physical or emotional exer-
tion. Maggie's form did not fill the doorway, and as the
intense dark eyes swept the room over the top of her head
and silently acknowledged the banker, Franklin Denton
could understand the girl's fluster and hoped there were
not two bright spots on his own cheeks.

"Mr. Michaels, welcome. Do come in. Caroline, this
is Jared Michaels. Perhaps you have heard me speak of
Mr. Michaels before—son of old man Michaels at the
bank, bright young student?" Denton watched his wife

carefully to see how much of this horse crappy she would believe. So far she appeared to accept his word as gospel. "Well, my dear, Mr. Michaels has recently graduated from the university and finds himself at loose ends for the summer until a position at the bank opens up. I suggested he accompany us to Dover. This comes as something of a surprise, I know, but he came into the bank today and we got to talking and I realized this could very well be the last summer vacation he is able to take until he gets to be as old and plump as myself. I am a welcome figure at the whist table, Miss Christian, but mine has long since ceased to be an admired figure on the boardwalk."

Miss Christian laughed, but only very softly and only with polite appreciation of Mr. Denton's witticism, while at the same time flatteringly dismissing his self-deprecation.

His wife put her hand on his arm and offered a comforting "Nonsense, dear," before she turned her smile on the handsome gentleman who stepped into the room.

The man was surely the best-looking thing she had seen in London this season; in fact, in more of London's social seasons than Mrs. Denton liked to admit she had been alive. Her husband's carefully prepared and rehearsed introduction and explanation of the young man's inclusion in their house party was entirely unnecessary. Franklin would only have had to present the gentleman and he would have been welcomed to come, to stay, to make himself a permanent member of their family if he would.

"Mrs. Denton," Michaels said, bending over her hand. "Your husband suggests this is an unexpected intrusion on your summer plans. Please . . ."

"Hardly an intrusion, Mr. Michaels. We had thought to be leaving for a very dull and uneventful summer. Instead we have two young and energetic people who will join us and add life to our party. I, for one, am very pleased by the prospect." She was forced to raise her head considerably to smile into his eyes. He returned her smile—at least she presumed that was a smile his lips were approaching—and then turned his attention to Miss Christian, whom he greeted with the warmth she seemed to evoke from any male she deigned to acknowledge.

"Miss ... Christian?"

"And Mr. Michaels," she said, offering her hand, which Michaels did not immediately relinquish.

"Mrs. Denton only echoes my pleasure at finding a contemporary member of this house party. And a very lovely contemporary." He smiled his quiet smile again and Miss Christian returned her own before withdrawing her hand from between his fingers.

Called back to matters at hand, Michaels glanced once more at Mr. Denton, who raised his chin toward the door. Jared half turned and noted the little serving girl who had admitted him, still standing by the door, evidently awestruck by the brilliant gathering.

He raised his eyebrows at Denton, who nodded slightly before his attention was reclaimed by his wife.

Michaels once more turned his unsettling gaze on the slight figure against the wall. She was standing in a ray of sunlight that entered through the west windows. The light created dazzling highlights in her golden hair and surrounded her form and the coarse material of her housemaid's clothing with an almost religious nimbus.

Maggie, for her part, was frozen by the gaze, only distantly aware of the tingling in her stomach that was wit-

ness to the fact that there had been *no one* like this back
in Huntingdon.

Miss Christian spoke to Mr. Michaels, who turned in
her direction, and like a stiff noodle suddenly immersed
in boiling water, Maggie melted limply around the door
and returned to Mrs. Bern.

"What have they got there in London town that you
can't find here, Maggie?" her father had asked.

"That!" she could have told him.

Chapter Five

"Who *is* that?"

Mrs. Bern looked up from her folding operations. These downstairs rooms were nearly finished, the furniture shrouded in dust covers, what was going packed, what was staying put away. Mrs. Denton had instructed them that the dark, heavy drapes would be drawn across the windows, but she wanted the lighter curtains that backed them taken down and put away when they left the house. The curtains were long, hanging from the top of the windows and falling to the floor. It had taken two of them to get them off the rods, and Maggie had naturally assumed that the folding would take two of them, as well. Yet in her absence, Mrs. Bern had folded and neatly stacked three of the curtains and had the fourth reduced to a manageable rectangle.

"Who is whom?" Mrs. Bern asked.

"The gentleman who just arrived?" When Maggie said "gentleman," she put a breathy emphasis on the word.

Mrs. Bern, though not totally devoid of romance, certainly did not encourage it in her girls. One never has to encourage romance in girls anyway. Now she recognized the threatening spark in Maggie's voice and spoke with an extinguishing flatness in her own.

"I did not see whom you admitted," she said, shaking the material in her hands vigorously and folding it one more time. "But if it is a gentleman he is doubtless a friend of Mr. and Mrs. Denton's." She didn't speak the words but the message rang clear: And he is *not* a friend of yours.

Maggie blushed faintly at Mrs. Bern's words, spoken and unspoken, and hurriedly gathered up the pile of white material on the table at the housekeeper's side.

"What do you want done with these?" she asked.

"You can put them with the tablecloths in the pantry," Mrs. Bern said, her voice, now that the reprimand had been delivered and received, resuming its natural warm tones.

Arms laden with the compact material, the girl left the room, blindly trusting that her feet would encounter no obstacle on her way to the pantry, since she could not see them at all and could see her way down the hall only imperfectly.

The Dentons and their guests were no longer in the parlor. Maggie assumed they had moved into the main sitting room and was disappointed that she didn't even have the hope of peeking into the room and catching another glimpse of the gentleman.

Even in her private thoughts "gentleman" had a certain breathiness.

The pantry was a little room on the other side of the kitchen, close to the back entrance. Maggie managed to traverse the length of the kitchen, though the way was strewn with obstacles and she came very close to dropping her whole armful a time or two.

The kitchen was a large, bright room, with copper kettles gleaming against the wall, the light dancing across them. The pantry doorway was like the dark mouth of a cave, gaping at the end of the room. Maggie was concentrating her full attention on keeping the bundle in her arms for seven . . . six more steps, when suddenly Ethel Cranney loomed up in front of her and scared a year's growth out of the girl, which little Maggie Landers could ill afford.

"Oh!" she cried, starting back and dropping most of her armful of drapes. Then, "Ethel! What on earth are you doing lurking in the dark like that?"

Ethel Cranney was a large, pasty-faced woman with dark hair streaked with gray and gathered informally into a bun either low on her head or high on her neck. Rising out of the dark pantry she did, very decidedly, give the impression of lurking.

"Just checking things," she explained vaguely.

"Well, you nearly scared me to death," Maggie complained as she stooped to gather the drapes that Mrs. Bern had so neatly folded. Ethel squeezed past her to get back to the kitchen.

"Where should I put these?" Maggie called out to her. Ethel was clattering pots and pans on the stove and didn't hear her, so Maggie found a box with fabric of some kind in it, which she assumed was tablecloths, and dumped her armload of drapes on top.

"Bring me some potatoes," Ethel called over her shoulder as Maggie emerged from the storeroom.

"Where are they?"

"Down in the cellar," the cook said, handing the girl a bent pan.

"I am supposed to be helping Mrs. Bern, you know," Maggie said as Ethel opened the back door for her and pointed to the cellar. "She will wonder what has become of me."

"Then you'd better hurry," was Ethel's unsympathetic reply as she shut the kitchen door behind the girl.

Maggie wasn't a mutterer but the protesting thoughts that "this is not my job" and "Mrs. Bern only sent me to bring the drapes" and "it certainly is dark down here" marched around her head as she descended the cellar steps and filled her bucket with the small, soft, year-end potatoes.

In a few minutes, bucket full, she emerged from the hole in the ground and dropped the cellar door shut.

Inside the kitchen Ethel stood at the sink cutting the remainder of yesterday's leg of lamb into a pot. Maggie put the pan of potatoes on the counter, and then, with the vegetables gathered and delivered, Mrs. Bern and her anxiety over the maid's whereabouts suddenly became much less important.

"There's a young gentleman and lady here, visiting," she said, leaning her elbow on the counter and her chin in the cup of her hand. "I think they are coming to Dover with us."

Ethel nodded.

"I know," Ethel said.

"Who are they?"

"You said it yourself—visitors." The cook shook her head, putting aside the plate, which now had nothing on it but grease and bones, and pulling the pan of potatoes over next to her. "And they are going to be two more mouths to feed," she said sourly.

"Oh, don't be such a grumpy goose, Ethel. You have to cook the food anyway, but just think who is going to be eating it now."

Ethel Cranney looked at the girl and finally she smiled. She was a plain woman whose appearance was not markedly improved by a smile, but it was a friendly signal from someone who did not telegraph many friendly signals.

"I suppose you're right. I guess she's a real lady and probably pretty, too."

"I really don't know," Maggie said. "I didn't get a very good look at her."

"No?"

"But *he* is beautiful," the girl sighed, collapsing down onto her hand again. "He works at the bank, or, that is, he will soon. He's taking the summer off and spending it with the Dentons. How thrilling."

"It's thrilling that he will be spending the summer with Mr. and Mrs. Denton or that he has nothing to do but sit around for three months?"

"Oh, Ethel, you don't understand," Maggie said with a hopeless little sigh. "He is so very elegant and sophisticated. A person shouldn't have to work if he is *very* elegant and sophisticated."

Ethel snorted derisively as she heaved the full pan over onto the stove.

"We all have to work for what we get, Maggie. Even your lovely gentleman."

"Well, I am glad he doesn't have to work this summer," Maggie said, moving aside for Ethel as the cook reached for the flour and began bread-making operations. "Will there be parties and dances and summer fetes, do you think?"

"I should hope not," Ethel groaned.

"I bet there will be. And bathing in the ocean. Just imagine it, Ethel, you and I are going to be part of it all!"

"You and me are going to be working our fingers to the bone, feeding and picking up after these people. Don't get to thinking that *you* are going to be on vacation, girl," Ethel warned seriously.

"Oh, Ethel," Maggie chided, remembering Mrs. Bern at last, because Ethel's warning had sounded so much like her, and starting for the door. "We can share some of the fun just by being there with them."

The cook, busy stirring the warm milk and yeast mixture, didn't turn to look at her but spoke loud enough to be heard—Maggie feared all over the house.

"I suppose you'll imagine you're some sort of poor waif and he's a handsome prince come to rescue you, or some such thing. Anyway, you'll have plenty of chances to get under his feet and into his hair."

Mrs. Bern had gone from the front receiving hall, where she and Maggie had been taking down the curtains, to the small office where Mrs. Denton wrote her letters, made out the menus, compiled shopping lists and kept all the household accounts. Since that room was mostly for Mrs. Denton's personal papers, Mrs. Bern made only a cursory inspection and, in Maggie's long absence, moved into Mr. Denton's much larger office, where he did much less work.

"That took you a while," she said when Maggie finally found her again.

"Ethel wanted to talk."

"Mmm," Mrs. Bern said. It wasn't a very convincing lie and Mrs. Bern had no trouble deducing who it really was who wanted to talk and who did most of the talking. But it would have surprised her to learn how much talking the reticent Ethel Cranney had done.

"Well, help me finish packing these books Mr. Denton wants to take with him, then you had better run along and clean yourself up. Mrs. Denton wants you to serve supper tonight so we will need to go over a few things."

Serve supper? To the Dentons and their guests? Maggie was stunned and suddenly all aquiver. This was turning out to be even more exciting and romantic than any dream she had ever had.

Maggie Landers was a girl of modest dreams.

Ethel's supper of lamb stew and fresh bread appeared, on the surface, plain enough. Why, Maggie had loaded the family table at home with the same supper a hundred, a *thousand* times. Nor were the Landers savages who ate with their fingers and growled at one another between bites. They expected silverware and cups besides bowls and serving dishes on their table. They waited until grace was said to reach for the bread and almost always remembered to allow their mother the first bowlful of stew.

Maggie was stunned to find out how uncouth her family was and how complicated the proportioning of stew and bread could be made. Mrs. Bern had been hoping to have several days to drill the new girl before her specialized services were called upon, but that was not to be.

"Now, Maggie, there will only be Mr. and Mrs. Denton and the young lady and gentleman. This will be relatively simple."

Maggie didn't believe that. Neither did Mrs. Bern. They were in the dining room, setting four places at the table. At each place was a plate and silverware, plus a wine goblet, a water goblet, a bread and butter plate, a salt cellar and a napkin, which Mrs. Bern was showing Maggie how to roll into its respective napkin ring.

"The tureen will be the centerpiece. You must place it close to Mr. Denton when you bring it in and he will fill the bowls."

Maggie listened carefully as she tried to make her hands do what Mrs. Bern's clever fingers were doing.

"As each bowl is filled you will take it from Mr. Denton. Serve the young lady first, Mrs. Denton next and the gentlemen last."

"Which side?" Maggie asked.

"Left. Always left. Once the stew is served you may bring in the hot bread and place it in the middle of the table, nearer to Mrs. Denton this time. Understand?"

Maggie nodded solemnly.

The lesson proceeded as rapidly as Mrs. Bern dared, and she was pleased by Maggie's quick comprehension of the intricacies of informal dining.

The table setting was barely completed when the two women heard the sound of the approaching party.

"Hurry to your room and brush your hair and straighten your apron. A maid's primary goal is to be unnoticed, but if, heaven forbid, you *are* noticed—" Mrs. Bern paused for a moment as she and Maggie both breathed a silent prayer against any such unfortunate occurrence "—we want you to present a pleasing aspect, don't we?"

Maggie nodded as she left for her room, escaping the dining room as the doors opened behind her.

"Mrs. Bern?" Maggie heard Mrs. Denton say.

Then, less distinctly, she heard Mrs. Bern answer, "Dinner is ready, madam. Your guests may be seated."

Hair and apron both smooth and straight, Maggie rushed back to the kitchen, where Ethel had the filled and steaming tureen ready for her.

"Now?" she asked Mrs. Bern, who stood by the door.

"Catch your breath first. Mr. Denton is telling a story."

Maggie took several deep breaths, willed her knees to stop shaking, which they did, and her heart to slow down, which it did not. There was a soft murmur of amusement behind the door, Mrs. Bern nodded, Maggie took one more deep breath and pushed open the door.

Mrs. Bern had instructed her to put the tureen on the table near Mr. Denton. To do so it was necessary for her to approach the table between the two gentlemen. Carefully, softly, hardly daring to breathe, she set the heavy bowl down. Keeping in mind Mrs. Bern's ideal of being unnoticed, she was pleased when Mrs. Denton continued talking when she entered and the beautiful young woman next to her answered in a soft, slow voice.

"Ours is a modest little country cottage, not far from Dover Castle and the cliffs. We cannot actually see the Channel, but we have a lovely view of the surrounding countryside, although you mustn't go expecting too awfully much of the house itself."

Miss Christian laughed quietly, a rich laugh that reminded one of the purr of a contented Persian kitten.

"I am sure your Dover property is lovely," she said. Mrs. Denton smiled modestly, suggesting with the curve of her lips that the Denton "summer cottage" was enough to impress this or any other young lady.

Maggie, though she was endeavoring to be invisible, was neither deaf nor blind herself, and she knew that *she* would be impressed, but she wasn't as confident as Mrs. Denton that Miss Christian would be.

Maggie was paying only fragmented attention to the brief snippet of conversation she heard, though. As she inserted herself in the gap between Mr. Denton and Mr. Michaels, what she was most aware of was the muscular shoulder nearly touching her hip, the individual dark strands of hair that she saw out of the corner of her eye.

He reached for his goblet at the same time she leaned forward to put the tureen down and she hoped the beating of her heart would not disturb Mrs. Denton's further description of Dover. Then, for the barest fraction of an instant, Mr. Michaels turned his dark eyes on her. She felt them as she pulled back from the table.

"What is the matter?" Mrs. Bern asked worriedly when the girl returned to the kitchen for the bread basket. Maggie looked at her with a self-consciousness she was trying to disguise as surprise.

"Nothing. Why?"

"Your cheeks are so pink. I was afraid you had sloshed the soup or nudged someone's arm," Mrs. Bern said, closely watching the girl's reaction.

"It went fine," Maggie said, this time with genuine innocence.

"I suppose it was the heat from the heavy tureen," Mrs. Bern said.

Maggie mumbled something about "it must have been" and returned to the dining room with the bread.

When the meal finally ended she was justifiably proud of her serving. True, her duties had been kept to the minimum this first time, but the girl nevertheless found her introduction to the grand world of society thrilling.

She really did nothing more than brought in the dishes for Mr. or Mrs. Denton to serve, removed them at the right time—from the right, always the right—crumbed the table, poured some water and served the cobbler dessert in the tiny glass bowls with the gleaming silver spoons and the tiny *and* gleaming silver cream pitcher.

She was not particularly quick in her service, but Mrs. Bern assured her that slow was better than sloppy, and besides, it gave her a chance to be in the dining room longer, breathing the air *he* breathed, though she never

did hear him say anything. Once in a while she was so
bold as to look right at him, the last time being when she
offered him the cream. He raised his hand to the pitcher
and his eyes met hers. He studied her for a long three
seconds and then relaxed the line of his lips into the closest approach to a friendly smile to which he had come
that evening. Anyway, Maggie viewed it as a warm and
friendly smile, and without conscious effort, her own lips
curved and two deep and darling dimples hollowed in her
cheeks.

Mrs. Bern told her to return to the kitchen after the tea
was served and not to disturb the diners again.

"Remember, Maggie—tea is a very agreeable diges-
tive. The pleasant interlude must not be hurried by a busy
little maid clearing dishes and clattering silverware."

Therefore, having delivered the heavy tea tray, the girl
removed her spotless white apron and replaced it with her
soiled work apron and assumed her station at the sink to
wash up the dishes.

Maggie was frankly amazed, looking around, by how
many dishes had been dirtied to prepare and serve stew
and bread to four people. At home, for all eight Landers, there would have been the stew pot, the mixing bowl,
the bread pans, one knife, eight spoons, eight mugs and
eight bowls to clean. And at least one emptied milk
pitcher.

If the cooking utensils dirtied were any indication of
the quality of a cook, Ethel was a very fine cook indeed.
Maggie shook her head as she looked around the kitchen
at the counters and tabletops piled high with pots and
pans and silverware and knives and ladles and serving
platters and at least thirty bowls of every size and description.

Mrs. Bern occasionally looked in on her, but Maggie gathered she couldn't help because Mrs. Denton was keeping the housekeeper busy with last-minute arrangements and a debate of some importance.

The house party would be moving to Dover by the end of the week, and someone needed to go ahead to open the house for the Dentons and their guests. Ethel couldn't go, of course. The party would starve, never mind the fact that the larder was stuffed to overflowing with meats, vegetables, flour and sugar. And Mrs. Denton, it will be remembered, really could not do a thing without Mrs. Bern. That left Maggie, and though Maggie was the logical one to send on ahead, how was she to get there?

Even allowing that the girl was intelligent enough to direct a hired coach to the house, how was she to transport the cartload of household goods that would have to go with her?

The dishes were completed at last, replaced on the shelves and covered with the cloths that would ward off a fraction of the dust while they were gone. Counters had been wiped, soiled linens had been taken to the laundry, the kitchen had been returned to a neat orderliness that would have been unbelievable an hour earlier. And Maggie was exhausted.

This morning she had been a rude country girl, boarding in a room the size of a matchbox, hoping to find work in a London town that staggered one's senses. In the sixteen hours since then she had been hired by a wealthy couple, introduced to the workings of this grand house, met the people that were to be her new family and had been smiled at by the most compelling, gorgeous man in the United Kingdom.

She was almost to the point of collapse, kept on her feet and awake by excitement. She had her hand cupped over the lantern to extinguish it when Mrs. Bern bustled into the kitchen, wiping her hands on her own apron and nodding smartly as she came.

"Well, it's all settled then. I will send you into town tomorrow to purchase a few things we will need in Dover while I finish packing. Of course—" she cupped her hand around the lantern that hung by the door where she stood and blew out the flame "—I may not get everything done, so you may have to help me even when you finish. But I will try to see that you have time to pack."

"Pack?"

"For Dover."

"Dover?"

"I suppose I will need to go over a few things with you before you leave, but Mrs. Denton and I agree that you are fully capable of opening the house on your own. Now you mustn't let me forget to give you the key before you leave." Mrs. Bern took a final swipe at the counter to make sure the grease had been cleaned off and turned toward the door. "We wondered for a time how you were to get there, but Mr. Michaels has been kind enough to volunteer his services. Hurry now. Finish in here and then meet me in your room. Let's see, I wonder if Mrs. Denton wanted to send her fur wraps ahead with you?"

Chapter Six

Maggie gloried in her feeling of imperial importance. Mrs. Denton had ordered a coach that was to deliver her to several prominent London shops, where Maggie was to procure a long list of "absolute necessaries!" and instruct the various proprietors to "put it on the Denton account."

The informal meal she had served paled into a modest glow when compared to the glories of her Errands.

She sat up tall and straight as the coach bounced along the cobblestones or skimmed across the luxuriance of smooth pavement. She was wearing a simple black dress, one of Mrs. Bern's crisp white caps and a darling lace shawl the housekeeper had handed her as she slipped out the side door.

"Now, you have the list of what you are to get?" Mrs. Bern cautioned. Maggie nodded and patted the right front pocket of her dress. "And your letter of credentials from Mrs. Denton? Shopkeepers will not charge the Denton account with everything any stranger takes from their stores." Maggie patted her left front pocket. Mrs. Bern nodded and stood at the door watching as Maggie climbed into the coach, just like an anxious mother duck witnessing her duckling's first plunge into the pond.

The first stop was at the milliner's, where Maggie was to pick up a new summer bonnet Mrs. Denton had ordered.

The effete young gentleman behind the counter was quite friendly when Maggie produced her letter and explained her mission. As he boxed the loose collection of straw, lace netting, silken ribbons and cloth posies he seemed inclined to gossip. But Maggie could have none of that today. She had many important Errands to run.

Next was the haberdasher's, and trousers and riding coat for Mr. Denton. They were both of a coarse tweed material and the shopkeeper commented, "Off to the coast again this year? The Dentons do seem to enjoy Dover, don't they?"

Maggie confirmed his guess and agreed with his estimation. The man's familiarity with her employers, their yearly migration and the fact that Mr. Denton would not be caught dead in the city in so bold a tweed made Maggie feel even more important. If that was possible.

The driver of the coach delivered her to the next block of shops, but since she had a number of things to buy along this street, Maggie told him he might wait for her at the corner. The girl was perfectly aware that there was a tavern on that corner and not so naive as to believe she would find the driver sitting atop his carriage when she arrived, but she felt indulgent and wanted that worthy gentleman to enjoy his day as much as she was enjoying hers.

The hat and men's clothing were left in the coach, and now Maggie carried a shopping bag over her arm, which soon began to bulge here and there and drag on her arm as she entered and exited the various businesses.

"And a box of those butterscotch candies. Mr. Denton is very fond of butterscotch candies, though he has complained that Mrs. Denton does not keep them on hand the way he wishes she would.'' Maggie spoke with a familiar superiority that was meant to convey the fact that she was on the most intimate of terms with Mr. and Mrs. Denton; that the discussion of family matters with the maid was the usual order at the Denton house.

The man behind the counter smiled and bobbed his head as he weighed out a pound and a half—or perhaps a trifle less than that, though the girl or her mistress would never know the difference—of the hard candies she pointed out. He had weighed butterscotch candies for Mr. Denton enough times over the years that his fingertips on the scale had saved him twenty-five pounds of candy by now.

Maggie emerged from the candy shop, near the center of the closely packed block of stores, and stopped to review the list Mrs. Bern had been so careful about.

The next stop appeared to be a supplier of exotic herbs. Maggie could see the sign of the shop two or three businesses down the boardwalk, but she was in no hurry to reach that milestone. Instead she paused to study each bright window with appreciative eyes, studying the wares they offered as if she possessed the means to purchase anything she saw and needed only to make her choice.

Suddenly the bright sunshine dimmed and an explanation of the phenomenon presented itself in the form of the great billowy figure that pressed against her.

''Miss Landers. So delightful to meet you. Doing some shopping, are you?''

It was the owner of the Greenleaf Employers Agency, whispering his high, nasal tones into her ear, caressing her unwilling form with his moist eyes.

Maggie looked around her in confusion.

"Oh, sir," she gasped. "You startled me." She tried to step away from him, though there was hardly room on the boardwalk to do that.

"Didn't think to find me downtown?" he asked, a smile oozing onto his lips. "I enjoy looking in shop windows as much as the next fellow, my girl."

"Yes. Well." She smiled weakly, her eyes darting left and right, giving every impression of a timid woodland creature, trapped and without cover. "I suppose I had better hurry along. Mrs. Denton wanted me to pick up these things before I leave for Dover."

"Dover?" the man repeated eagerly, and Maggie winced, regretting the disclosure. "I was about to ask how things are going for you in your new position, but it would appear they are going very well." He inspected her person again, this time taking in the quality of the dress she wore and the bulging bag that hung from her arm.

"I suppose you could say that . . . that is, the situation is very nice and I am getting along fine . . . learning my duties, that sort of thing." Once again she tried to edge past the massive figure. "I must be going now," she said. She fumbled clumsily with the shopping list and hoped the impression she gave was deep concentration on the list of shops and house goods.

A large, pale hand reached for her arm and encircled the slender black sleeve with startling whiteness.

"Now, girl, I think there would be nothing wrong with stopping in here." He indicated the little tea shop situated right next to the herb shop. "I want to hear all about your position, and how you are finding city life, and what is the latest you hear from . . ." He paused and struggled with the recollection for a moment. Maggie offered him no assistance. "Huntingdon," he produced at last, his voice rising several notes in triumph.

He pushed Maggie in front of him into the little restaurant and she had no choice but to stumble through the door. The man chose a table set far back from the window; the pallor of his skin suggested that he avoided sunshine whenever he was able. They sat across from each other and the man nodded toward the plump waiter, who brought them a teapot, cups and a plateful of delicate little cakes with colorful sugar icing.

"The Dentons... nice people?" he asked the girl, taking one of the cakes and studying it appreciatively before popping it whole into his mouth.

"Oh, yes," Maggie said.

"And the house? Large?"

"Yes. That is to say, large to me. But not *too* large, if you understand my meaning," she replied, quick to qualify her claim.

The man inclined his head and sipped at his tea. He held the porcelain handle of the cup gingerly, presenting the comic appearance of a full-grown adult trying to manage a child's play tea set.

"And the work?" he asked, putting the cup down and reaching for another cake.

"It's fine."

"Not too strenuous? Not making too many demands on you, are they?"

"Oh, no, sir. The work is just... housework."

"I try to take care of my girls," the man said, sounding as if syrup had just been poured over his tightly stretched vocal chords.

Maggie put her own cup to her lips to hide the frown that was pulling at them. She did not need to be taken care of; she did not want this man's heavy solicitousness. But it was not real concern for her well-being that prompted him, she knew. The terms of their business agreement were not yet fulfilled. Maggie was just beginning to see what a relief it would be to meet her obligations and get out from under his suffocating shadow.

"I am sure we all appreciate that, sir," she said. She had drunk two-thirds of the tea in her cup and nibbled without much enjoyment or saliva in her mouth at the cake he had placed on her plate. Now she put the cup on its saucer resolutely and grabbed for the bag at her feet. "But really, I must be going. So much to do. I cannot hope to keep this position if I fail to perform my duties. I am sure you understand."

She put her hands on the table, but before she could push herself to her feet, the man laid one of his hands on top of hers, where it lay like a cold, damp, whole ham.

"Have you anything else to tell me?" he asked.

"No," she said.

"Nothing?"

"I—I haven't . . ." She had been struggling to free her hand and now finally pulled it loose, knocking it against her cup and saucer and spoon, creating a clatter that was amplified in the close quarters of the little tea shop. The few other customers looked around, startled by the noise, and the waiter hurried to the table.

"*Qu'est-ce qui se passe?*" he asked uncertainly, feeling the tension crackling between the lovely young lady and the *gros âne* who had the audacity to share the table with her. The girl turned to the waiter with more gratitude and relief than his simple inquiry seemed to warrant.

"Oh, thank you," she murmured.

"It's nothing," the large man told the waiter impatiently.

The waiter liked looking at the young woman much better and turned to her again, raising his eyebrows in innocent inquiry.

"And the bill, mademoiselle?"

"Charge it to the Denton account," the man at the table said, rising to his feet and pushing the little table back to cause another rattling uproar that attracted considerable attention. The waiter, like everyone else in the shop, looked at the man. The girl gasped. The waiter looked back at the girl.

"Ma'm'selle?"

She had that look of trapped innocence again, but at last she produced her letter of credentials and confirmed that their tea should be charged to the Franklin Dentons. She told herself, and prayed she was correct, that tea was surely not an unforgivable indulgence on her part after a day of shopping, and her employer might not receive this bill for several weeks, by which time this excursion would be forgotten and the modest charge paid without question.

Nevertheless, as the dear little waiter accompanied her to the door and stood watching as she turned one way and her dining companion turned the other, Maggie knew that her pleasure in the day was irremediably marred and her uncertain affection for the city in general was cooled.

She would be relieved to get out from under his nagging claim and away from the ceaseless uproar of London to the restful quiet of the English coast. She would also be undeniably happy to spend the day alone with Mr. Michaels on their journey to that coast.

A hollow appeared in either of her cheeks at that thought. Perhaps her enjoyment of the day was not completely lost, after all.

Chapter Seven

"Did the boxes from the sitting room get loaded?" Mrs. Denton's voice sounded almost panic-stricken, as if the success of this venture depended solely on the boxes from the sitting room.

"Caroline, you didn't send my razor, did you? If you sent my razor I will be a hairy ape by the time we get to Dover. Mrs. Bern, check that bag and see if my wife packed my razor."

"You'll need to wipe down the stove, clear the flues, and look through the cupboard," Ethel hissed into Maggie's ear. "The missus says they cleaned out everything when they left last year, but I don't want to find any nasty surprises."

"We need to be leaving. We won't get there until midnight if we leave right now," Michaels warned.

"Midnight!" Mrs. Denton shrieked.

A soft, slender hand fluttered to rest on Michaels's coat sleeve and a soft voice tickled his ear.

"How terribly grueling for you, Mr. Michaels. And will you be in that horrid coach the entire time?"

"Most of the time, I am afraid, Miss Christian."

"The trip for me will be frightfully boring, and I had so hoped it would not." Miss Christian smiled her slow smile. "You must promise to be careful, Mr. Michaels, and meet us when we arrive."

"I shall hail your carriage the moment it turns into the lane. If there is a lane. Mrs. Denton?"

Maggie hadn't shrieked like Mrs. Denton or lodged her pretty complaints like Miss Christian, but more than either of them, she was horrified to think that after her exhausting day yesterday and her very few hours of sleep last night, she would be jogging along in a carriage until midnight tonight.

"Did you bring blankets, Franklin?" Mrs. Denton called to her husband over the heads of servants and guests, failing to respond to Michaels's question.

"Clean what you can and straighten things." Now it was Mrs. Bern issuing instructions to Maggie. "We will be there in two or three days and I can help you with what you don't get finished. The rooms will need to be aired out, of course, and fresh linens."

"They have to go, Caroline. We can bring the blankets ourselves," Denton said.

"I'm not sure I understand, ma'am...." Maggie was understandably confused by the rapid exchange of questions and orders that was becoming chaotic as their departure approached.

"Start with the main rooms and the kitchen, then go through what bedrooms you can—" Mrs. Bern began, but Mrs. Denton cut the housekeeper's admonitions short.

"I am sure Maggie can manage, Mrs. Bern," she said. "Mr. Michaels, I am sorry you will not be making the trip with us. We all are. Please do not think that it is necessary that you leave this morning with our girl. I do believe Maggie could go on by herself and take care of things."

"Oh, no, ma'am!" Maggie cried.

"Do you think, Mrs. Denton?" Mrs. Bern asked, the barest hint of concern in her voice.

"Certainly not, Caroline!" Denton exclaimed, with a good deal more than a hint of concern in his. "I won't hear of it."

But Michaels's quiet assurance seemed to calm the threatening storm.

"As I told you, Mrs. Denton," he said, "I have a little business to attend to in Dover and this will give me a chance to get that out of the way before the houseguests arrive."

"Do you think?" Mrs. Denton asked.

"Absolutely," Mr. Denton confirmed.

"Quite reasonable," Mrs. Bern agreed.

"Oh."

From the reactions by the various busy occupants of the room Mrs. Denton might have been summoning a firing squad and Mr. Michaels arriving with the nick-of-time reprieve. All the responses, that is, except Maggie's final soft gasp of "oh" as she looked up to find Michaels's dark and disconcerting gaze on her.

"Well, it is very good of you, Mr. Michaels," Mrs. Denton conceded, graciously allowing her entourage the loss of one very handsome young man, partially because his absence would only be temporary, and primarily because he was going to relieve her of a great deal of worry and responsibility.

"Mrs. Denton, Miss Christian." Michaels took each lady's hand and bent over it gravely. Maggie could see, even from where she was standing near the door, that Miss Christian's hand was as steady as a rock and the little maid was quite sure it was as cool to the touch as a garden melon. As delightful as it no doubt was to have those finely sculpted lips murmuring against one's knuckles, Maggie would not have had him take her hand for the world, and wiped her sweaty palm against her skirt at the very thought.

"I look forward to seeing you again, Mr. Michaels," Miss Christian said, slowly raising her long black lashes over her lavender eyes.

"I will count the hours, Miss Christian."

"Maggie, do the best you can. It will be strange to you at first, I know, but I guess you know how to wipe away dust and mop up floors and make beds."

Maggie nodded and somehow felt strengthened when Mrs. Bern gave her hand an encouraging squeeze.

"Now, Michaels, watch out for—anything," Mr. Denton added. He certainly could have used an extra pair of hands for this move which was becoming more heavily laden with each passing year. But of far more pressing concern to him was the importance of seeing that that . . . *creature* was not left alone in his house.

Mr. Michaels's phaeton sat waiting in the driveway, the open baggage rack piled high with bags and boxes full of personal and household items. The two horses that would pull the carriage were big and black and sturdy-looking, not animals built for speed but for strength and endurance. Maggie was surprised when she saw the horses. Mr. Michaels had attained such a dazzle in her eyes that she had assumed his horses would be sleek, beautiful thoroughbreds that would skim over the ground as they raced the winds. She was quick to realize, though, that these two horses were the perfect animals for the job before them—or rather behind them—and what admirable foresight Mr. Michaels had showed in selecting them.

"Have you everything you need?" that very admirable gentleman asked her now.

"I—I believe so," she stammered.

"Very well then, up you go."

And up she did go. Michaels, with his hands at her waist, lifted her into the carriage as if she were a puff of smoke. He came around the wagon, patting the horses on their flanks as he brushed past them, and jumped into the driver's seat.

His exuberance caused the carriage to sway for a moment and Maggie clutched at the side nearest her wildly.

"Oh!" she gasped.

"Something?" Michaels asked.

Maggie shook her head, the dismal realization springing to her mind that she appeared to be stupider with every passing minute.

Michaels dismissed her and her stupidity without a thought and turned his attention to the horses.

"Ho! Up!" he called to them, jouncing the reins. The two horses, too massive to be skittish, leaned forward and the heavy carriage rolled smoothly toward the road, as if it were no more corporeal than Maggie at her most puff-of-smokiness.

They were traveling east, directly into the morning sun. Michaels wore a dark coat and heavy trousers yet appeared to be totally unaffected by the early summer warmth. Already Maggie felt an unladylike dampness at the back of her knees and under her arms. After a few minutes she felt a drop of perspiration inching along her hairline. At last it escaped the meshwork of the yellow strands and started down the side of her face. Self-consciously she brushed at it.

"Warm," she said. It was the first human sound to break the silence of the ride since Michaels's "Ho! Up!" fifteen minutes earlier.

"It is," Michaels agreed.

"Doesn't seem like it gets this hot at home." The pause lengthened until Maggie was afraid she was going to appear foolish again with her unattended remark, but at last Michaels supplied the expected response.

"Where is that?"

"Huntingdon. Well, near Huntingdon. Nearer to Huntingdon than anyplace else, though I wouldn't actually say I am from Huntingdon." She stopped to take a badly needed breath and Michaels drove. "Do you know it?" she asked.

"Huntingdon? I have been there a time or two."

"Have you?" Maggie sounded delighted and Michaels might have just introduced himself as an old friend. "It's very nice, isn't it? The country, I mean. That's not to say the town isn't nice, too, but I'm from the country."

"Are you?"

"Oh, yes. A lovely farm. We raise cattle, dairy and beef, and some wheat. I guess I should say my father and brothers raise them. I know if they were here now Rob and LeRoy would laugh me to scorn for saying I helped with the farming, and Arnold would probably thump me. Papa hasn't warned him not to yet, though he's a great lug of a fellow and I suppose it's only because I am quick that I've avoided what thumps I have. But they needn't any of them be so proud. I've done my fair share of work on that farm."

"Is that why you left?" Michaels asked. Maggie felt inordinately pleased to have elicited a question of honest interest from him.

"Oh, no. I'm not afraid of a little work. I just thought I'd like to see more of the country than the village square every week or so. And not even the Huntingdon square. I guess we don't go into Huntingdon twice a year. But there's a blacksmith shop and a little store—dry goods and yard goods and sundries all together in nothing more than a lean-to shack—about a mile up the road. Folks call it Forkston. I think that's because there was a fork in the road there once. Now all the roads lead into town. Into Huntingdon."

"And from Huntingdon, all roads lead to London?"

"Well, maybe not to London, but certainly away from Forkston. Out into the wide world." She looked around her at the relatively open country they were passing through.

"And if you can think of our island kingdom as the wide world, I suppose that is exactly where the roads have led you. First to London and now to Dover, though from the chalk cliffs you can see even more of the wide world than this." Now Michaels looked around them at the trees that had suddenly, ironically, closed in on them. "It must be very exciting for you."

"It is!" Maggie turned to him and smiled brightly. The ride had loosed a few golden strands of her hair, which floated across her creamy skin and in front of her wide blue eyes. Michaels dropped his own eyes to look into hers. Maggie's smile faded, her dimples disappeared, she felt locked in his gaze, swallowed up in it, her secret self invaded by the dark eyes. At last she turned away and brushed at another droplet of sweat near her hairline. "But it doesn't seem to get this warm at home," she said.

Silence settled on them and Maggie squirmed uncomfortably under its weight. Even in her brief acquaintance with Mr. Michaels she knew he was not the "chatty" sort. He evidently cherished his privacy and nurtured the quiet of his own thoughts.

"Still waters run deep," her father would have said. George Landers did not have the colorful imagination to originate his own pithy sayings, but he did have a true eye as to when someone else's pithy saying was appropriate.

Maggie herself recognized and respected Michaels's reticence. And she made an honest effort to maintain the still tranquillity of the ride, to listen, like Mr. Michaels, to the sound of the wheels or the twitter of the birds or her own unuttered thoughts.

The only problem was that Maggie was, literally, irrepressible. She tried not to be. She would note Mr. Michaels's elegant waistcoat, his masterful handling of the horses, his set, square jaw and finely sculpted profile, and she wanted more than anything else to appear in a favorable light in his eyes. She would determine to be a proper lady, retiring, reserved, at least as cool as the handsome man next to her. She thought of Miss Christian and how refined and aloof that young lady would have been on this ride. Miss Christian would not, Maggie was very sure, have spoken at all except in answer to a direct question from Mr. Michaels. That was how it should be; that was how ladies and gentlemen behaved to one another; that was exactly how Maggie was determined to act herself. And then a brightly colored songbird would flit in front of them, or she would catch a glimpse of a church steeple across a meadow somewhere, and she would find herself launched into a story before she could stop herself.

"We had a beautiful old cow. Best milker on the farm. She gave enough cream to make butter for everybody who trades in Forkston. My brother Randy was sent to bring her up from the field one night and he saw a fox in some brush along the way. Well, Randy took out after the fox, without a gun, without a horse—I'm not even sure he was wearing shoes. But he ran like a hare and finally ran it into the field where Emma—that was the cow—was feeding. Around and around they went, over logs and through a little stream, Randy yelling like a yahoo and the poor little fox spooked wild. Finally the fox ran under old Emma, and there he stood, quivering and panting and staring out at Randy as if he were in his own dark den. Randy was too winded to yell anymore, the fox was too winded to run, and old Emma just stood there, chewing her cud, until she decided it was time to come into the barn. The fox got away and Randy got a cold supper because he was so late milking.''

And so the forenoon passed. Once in a while Michaels would ask a question or offer a quiet comment on her stories, but his encouragement, though welcome, was not really necessary. Story followed story. Life on a little dairy farm with five tormenting brothers may not have seemed very eventful to her while she lived it, but it provided her with an endless supply of homey anecdotes.

"So DeRay sneaked into Ernie Knopf's orchard, thinking he would get himself an armful of apples. But Ernie had his old billy goat tied up to one of the trees, and what DeRay got instead was butted clean across Mr. Knopf's stile. DeRay claims he ran home, but Papa says the billy did more work on that run than DeRay did.''

Maggie laughed merrily and Mr. Michaels allowed his lips to relax into a smile, which they had done an amazing number of times this morning.

"Why, Mr. Michaels,'' she said, breaking off her laughter in surprise. "Whatever are you doing?''

What Michaels was doing was obvious: he was pulling the carriage off the road and coming to a stop.

"I am stopping the carriage," he said.

Maggie's surprise could be understood as she looked around her at the very peaceful, deserted English countryside.

"Whatever for?" she demanded.

"To eat lunch, Miss Landers. I admit that your tales have made the miles pass quickly, but now the sun overhead and the ominous rumbling of my stomach are loudly announcing the fact that it is lunchtime."

By now the wheels had come to a complete stop behind the horses, who, despite their size and strength, appeared as ready for a break as Mr. Michaels.

"Oh. I see. I don't know that I have come prepared..." Maggie began hesitantly, but Mr. Michaels had jumped down from the driver's seat, seen to the horses and now, ignoring Maggie and her weak little apologies, placed his hands once more at her waist and lifted her from the wagon.

"Mrs. Bern saw to the preparations for both of us, Miss Landers. This is a lovely spot, with the babble of a brook nearby, if I am not mistaken. It would appear that nature's own dining room awaits us. Won't you join me for lunch?" Michaels offered the crook of his elbow and Maggie gave him her hand. She was easily as charmed by her companion as the pleasant setting, but after the enjoyable ride and Mr. Michaels's present playfulness, he no longer seemed so forbiddingly elevated from her, so she was relieved to note that the hand she placed on his dark blue sleeve was quite as steady as the hand Miss Christian had given him that morning.

Mrs. Bern had indeed seen to the luncheon preparations. Mr. Michaels pulled a large basket off the back of the carriage. Its contents were covered with a rough woolen blanket, which Michaels spread on the ground.

At his instructions, Maggie seated herself on the blanket
and watched in frank amazement as Michaels emptied
the basket of a long loaf of bread, a bottle of wine, a sizable lump of boiled beef, strawberries, cheese, butter, a
bundle of early fresh spinach and, last of all, a long cigar, which Mr. Michaels passed slowly under his nostrils, inhaling appreciatively.

Maggie may have been ignorant of the ceremonies of
fine dining, but she knew how to assemble a picnic lunch.
Deftly she cut the beef and sliced the bread while Michaels took the little teapot—which Mrs. Bern had also
packed—and went in search of the stream. While he was
away, Maggie broke the dark green spinach leaves into a
makeshift salad and was gathering dried twigs and
branches for a fire by the time Michaels returned.

"Is everything ready?" he asked in surprise. Maggie
proudly displayed her handiwork and smiled.

"Except for the fire and the tea."

"I am surprised you do not have your own tinderbox
with you," he said, squatting in front of the small fire
Maggie had laid and quickly lighting it.

"It's packed away with my things," Maggie confessed.

They passed the sandwiches and the salad back and
forth between them. Michaels picked up the wine and
offered the bottle to the girl, but she shook her head, so
the wine was slipped back into the basket unopened.

Maggie would have understood if Mr. Michaels had
poured himself a glass of wine, but for her part, she could
think of nothing more intoxicating than sitting on a
blanket, under the leafy branches that arched over them,
across from Mr. Jared Michaels.

He had removed his jacket and his light, loose shirt
rippled with his every breath. In the sunlight his hair ap-

peared lighter than under the artificial brilliance of candlelight. But his eyes were as dark and impenetrable as ever.

And yet, despite his occasional unsettling gaze, the half hour the two of them spent over lunch was friendly and easy and still not devoid of talk.

"Mrs. Bern didn't tell me if I should take the plates with the soup bowls or leave them for the dessert. You can imagine my dilemma, Mr. Michaels. And I did so want to make a good impression—on Mr. and Mrs. Denton," she ended in confusion when she realized who it really was she had been hoping to impress.

Michaels commiserated with her over the infinite number of rules and regulations she would have to learn in the next week or two and assured her that she would get along very well.

Soon the teakettle began to whistle and Michaels insisted she remain where she was while he brewed the tea.

"You have already proven your culinary skill. Now allow me to demonstrate the full range of mine," he said, measuring out the tea leaves and moving the pot off the direct flame.

Maggie busied herself with clearing the blanket and packing away the leftovers. She found a little bowl of sugar, but Mrs. Bern's omniscient foresight was marred by the absence of any cream in the hidden recesses of the basket.

The girl placed the strawberries, sugar and cups and saucers in the middle of the blanket, feeling like a child presiding at a make-believe tea party. Except that as a guest, Mr. Michaels easily outshone a whole roomful of the loveliest china dolls.

"Ah, the perfect hostess," Michaels said approvingly, putting the steaming kettle on the grass beside the blanket. "Won't you pour, miss?"

"Certainly, sir," she said, trying to remember all, or anything, her mother had taught her about officiating at the tea table. Afternoon tea was not a luxury often indulged in at the Landers home.

Now she held the cup out to Mr. Michaels and was dismayed to see that her hand was no longer steady and the dark liquid sloshed over the sides of the cup. Michaels had the good grace to ignore the spill. He took the cup, put in a teaspoon of sugar and took a sip.

"You no doubt would have done better," was his verdict. "But this is not bad for the poor concoctions of a benighted bachelor."

Maggie was sure she was drinking the nectar of the gods, but she allowed a simple "Nonsense, this is delicious," to suffice.

A heavy silence fell upon the two of them at last as they finished their cups. It was as if the dark shade of the trees were stifling not only their words but their thoughts, as well.

With determination Maggie swallowed the last of the lukewarm tea and brushed at her skirt.

"Well," she said, "I guess these things had better be packed away again so we can get on our way."

"So soon?" Michaels asked lazily. Contrarily he sat back, snipped the end off the cigar that had so thoughtfully been included in the basket and lighted it with a coal from the dying fire. "It has been a strenuous day for ourselves and the horses. I thought perhaps a few more minutes of relaxation would do us all a world of good." He inhaled a lungful of the rich smoke and exhaled slowly, allowing a thick trail of fog to ascend from his mouth toward the blue sky.

"It has been a long day, hasn't it? And last night! Why, Mrs. Bern kept me up past midnight, telling me this and that, making sure I understood Mrs. Denton's instructions, when what I understood most clearly was that I was tired. Tired and—"

"A little relaxation and quiet," Mr. Michaels stopped her. "Quiet," he repeated softly.

"Oh. Yes. Well, of course. We wouldn't want—"

"Shh," Michaels murmured. "Listen to the brook."

Self-consciously, Maggie stopped again, and then, following Mr. Michaels's directions, she strained her ears to listen for the burble of water.

There it was. Like the distant voices of busy, happy children. Climbing trees, perhaps. Or planning a forbidden raid on a pantry or a neighbor's garden. Maggie remembered enough of those. She was usually given the danger-fraught assignment of scout because of her small size and greater agility. She smiled slightly.

She wasn't really aware of it, but she was almost reclining on the blanket by now, pushed down by the still air and the warm sunshine. The rough blanket and hard ground had somehow been transformed into a down-filled comforter—on a feather bed.

Like her mother's feather bed. The one she helped make up occasionally, the one the boys were never allowed near. She sighed at the memory.

Somehow in that sigh she was carried away from this unfamiliar glade to a place she knew. She looked around her in disbelief.

She was on her family's farm.

She told Michaels it wasn't as warm in Huntingdon, and it wasn't, yet the sunlight here was somehow more brilliant. Everything before her sparkled: the dew of the grass, LeRoy's hoe in the garden, the few small panes of glass on the windows of the house in the distance. Even the cows sparkled.

Maggie smiled at the idea of those dirty old cows sparkling, cows that were stubborn, contrary, sometimes out-and-out mean; cows she had heard her brothers cuss until the air was blue above them. Now the dairy herd stood patiently watching her. Gleaming.

The fields were bright green. The rain must have been good for the crop to be up so far so soon. Why, some of the vegetables in the garden looked ready to eat.

She followed the path that meandered to the house. She could hear men singing out in the barn. Her father, of course, and probably Randy and Rob. Not DeRay, though. His voice was changing and he didn't sing with the family anymore. For a while, anyway. But in another year he would once again add his voice, this time a clear tenor, to "The Highwayman Outwitted" and "Robin Hood and the Merry Friar" and the other songs her family liked to sing around the fire of a long winter evening.

A little sob surprised her as she walked toward the house, listening to the song.

"Go to Joan Glover and tell her I love her,
And by the light of the moon I will come to her."

She was thrilled by the close harmony the round produced, harmony she couldn't hear when she joined the singing herself.

In the time it had taken her to walk the path the sky had darkened and a deep rose sunset was now reflected in the window panes. A candle was placed in the window for the milkers. Another sob escaped. That was usually her job.

And now the back door opened. It was her mother who stood in the doorway, her dear, beautiful mother, the gray somehow gone from her hair, the wrinkles on her cheek smoothed away.

"Who is it?" she called.

"It's me, Mama," Maggie said. She meant to call out, but she realized she had only whispered it and her mother couldn't possibly have heard her. She was stricken to see the door begin to close.

"Oh, don't shut me out, Mama," she sighed.

The sunset had darkened into night with remarkable speed, and she could no longer see the house. Only the light shining in the window. A tear fell from her lash and splashed against her cheek.

Now the light from the barn poured out as her father and brother opened the door and allowed the light from their lantern to guide them to the house. It was Rob and Randy who accompanied their father, the two oldest boys, who had graduated from milking duties years before. Now, though, it was right that they should be by their father. Now that Maggie was so far away.

She strained to see them clearly, a bitter loneliness in her throat. But they were so far away and the light was so dim. A feeling of utter abandonment enveloped her.

Suddenly, out of the darkness, a butterfly, with black velvet wings, fluttered against her cheek. The wings flicked delicately at a tear that had slipped beneath her lid. They were deliciously soft, but somehow the airy playfulness only made her sadder. Weakly she brushed at them, but her fingers encountered not butterfly wings but other fingers.

With a startled jerk she opened her eyes, and instead of the Landers farm, she found herself in a glade on a blanket. Not walking but lying, her head resting on a firm white surface. A surface that was rising and falling with a steady regularity. She realized the fresh country smell of rain and clover were not coming from the fields around her home but from her pillow, against which her nostril lay. And at last the horrified realization struck her that her pillow was the shirt-clad torso of Mr. Jared Michaels.

"Oh! Oh, my goodness!" she gasped, as in confusion she pulled away from her headrest and struggled to sit up straight.

Michaels, who had so tenderly brushed away the tear she shed in her dream, now watched her efforts to sit up with an amused light in his eyes, which Maggie failed to detect in her fluster.

"I am so sorry," she babbled. "I can't imagine whatever came over me. That is, well, of course *sleep* came over me. But I assure you it was not my intention, it is not my *habit,* to be so inexcusably familiar with a man. With a gentleman. With *any* man!"

"It is quite all right, Miss Landers," Michaels said quietly. He had gained his own feet during her embarrassed apologies and now stood beside her, donning his coat. "I am sorry you were taken unawares, but you had made yourself so terribly comfortable I didn't have the heart to disturb you. Here, allow me to help you up."

He offered his hand, and to avoid looking like a cow, Maggie took it and was pulled to her feet. But she resolutely kept her eyes averted, refusing not only to meet his eye but to acknowledge his person. If she had seen his face at that precise moment she would have caught him in an appreciative smile. But Michaels's smiles were of very short duration and this one was long gone by the time her eyes had risen to the level of his neck, which was as close to his face as they would rise.

"I really do not know what to say, Mr. Michaels," she said with at least as much frost in her voice as Miss Christian could have managed, if Miss Christian had been guilty of such an unforgivable gaucherie, which, of course, Miss Christian would never be.

"I do. Let us be on our way. We have stopped rather longer than I had planned. I hoped to be on the Denton property before midnight, but we will never make it at this rate. Up you go, then. The blacks appear to be as impatient as I am."

Again Michaels deposited the girl on the seat cushion, but Maggie clung to the far side of the wagon, finding it much more difficult than Mr. Michaels to throw off the hot shame of her familiarity. Not, and this was one of the considerations that tightened her grip and brought the pink to her cheeks every time she thought of it, that resting her head on Mr. Michaels's thinly clad chest was entirely unpleasant.

They had passed by Maidstone before they stopped for lunch, and now traveled the almost fifteen miles to Ashford in stony silence. The first third of the trip had flown by on Maggie's busy tongue. This third of the trip dragged like a long, boring sermon on a hot Sunday afternoon. A sermon dealing with some minor sin that has never tempted one, and even dressed in its most lurid colors would hardly be interesting. And about which, for the sake of the impressionable youth, the good pastor is being purposefully bland.

Maggie stared out at the countryside until her eyes burned, but she absolutely refused to close them. She became mesmerized by the dark, slowly passing trees and the sound of Mr. Michaels's soft, airy whistle, which was evidently his way to stay awake. The phaeton passed a few fellow travelers—other carriages now and then and the occasional walker—but nothing more was exchanged than polite nods.

Finally they reached Ashford and Maggie was stirred from her revery at last as Michaels stopped the carriage in front of a modest wayside inn.

"What are we stopping for?" she asked.

Michaels turned to her with a look of transported wonder.

"Good heavens! I thought you were dead," he exclaimed. "Well, I don't need to tell you that this eases my mind. I was afraid that I would forget some of Mrs. Denton's instructions for opening the house."

In spite of herself and her sternest self-imposed restrictions, Maggie couldn't help but giggle the tiniest bit.

"No, I am not dead. But that still does not insure that all of Mrs. Denton's or Mrs. Bern's instructions will be remembered. Why have we stopped here, though?"

"Food and rest, Miss Landers. The standard interruptions in any trek."

"I am not..."

"And even if your bread and boiled beef are still with you, our trusty livestock have long since walked off their midday meal."

"I see. Well, of course," Maggie was forced to agree.

"And a bowl of soup always restores the weary traveler. Especially a weary traveler who has spent the afternoon hovering at death's door." He had climbed out of the wagon and now stood at her side. "Shall we let bygones be bygones, Miss Landers?" He offered his hand and Maggie found the invitation in his voice irresistible.

"Very well." She smiled again, allowing him to help her down from the carriage. She waited the few minutes it took Michaels to see to the horses and then they entered the inn for their supper.

The soup was hot and the bread was fresh. Maggie still felt constrained and by now she was thoroughly fatigued, so her conversation was a good deal less sparkling than it had been earlier in the day, but at least there was no more need to worry that she had expired.

"When do you think we will get there?" she asked plaintively as the hostess took away the soup bowls and climbing back into that wagon to resume their journey loomed imminent. Michaels gave her a brave, encouraging look.

"Probably no more than four hours," he said.

The only thing lacking in the distress of her expression was a quivering chin.

"So long?"

"I am afraid so. The horses are nearly as exhausted as you are and they cannot be pushed any faster."

"I see," she said. Like a good soldier, she squared her shoulders determinedly. "I suppose we had better be on our way, then."

"I suppose so." Michaels wiped his lips on the frayed and grayish napkin that had been provided and then stood. Maggie followed him to the door, her feet dragging like two heavy granite stones.

Mr. Michaels saw to the bill for the meal and gave instructions for his horses to be brought around and rehitched to the phaeton. He and the innkeeper exchanged pleasantries while the innkeeper's wife, a little maid and another guest, a woman whose unremarkable appearance had been skillfully enhanced by powders and creams of various hues, all admired the tall, handsome gentleman with the dark eyes who had stopped in for supper.

Maggie was only peripherally aware of all of these things. She might have taken more interest in the money Mr. Michaels had spent on her or felt more pride to be with a man who was the center of so much female interest, but she was simply too tired.

The only real attention she could summon was focused on the unpleasant contemplation of the ride still before them in the cool night air on the carriage cushion that a hundred years ago, this morning, had seemed comfortable to her.

"Miss Landers?" Michaels interrupted her sluggish thoughts. "The carriage is ready." He preceded her out the door and was at the side of the wagon, busy with something by the time she left the inn. When she came close to the carriage she saw indistinct shapes, lumps and mounds, on the smooth seat she had so recently quitted. Michaels turned to help her up again.

"After your long day and now that night has fallen, I thought I might make things a little cozier." He had lifted her up onto the seat before she could distinguish the blankets and lap robes he had arranged on her half of the cushion.

"Oh, thank you," she breathed as she sank back into the warm folds of material.

"And I understand your reservations, Miss Landers, but you are entirely welcome to rest your head against my shoulder."

"Thank you, but that will not be necessary," she mumbled.

Yet, despite her maidenly discretion and her most solemn vows of self-control, when she heard Mr. Michaels's next words, "We have arrived, Maggie," she had to raise her head from his shoulder to peer at the dim outline of a gray stone, two-story rustic-looking house. More than a cottage yet less than a manor. It was her responsibility to have this cold, dark, grim abode cleaned, freshened, warmed and lighted by the time the Denton party arrived in two days.

With a little moan she dropped her head to rest it on the shoulder that had already been supporting its slight weight for many miles.

Chapter Eight

Mr. Michaels had refused to listen to her protests of "things to be carried in" and "messes to be cleaned away" of the night before. Granted, her little protests were weak and unconvincing and an even less strong-willed man than Officer Jared Michaels would have had no trouble ignoring them.

She did insist that one particular box be carried in, and with genuine warmth she lodged her protests concerning the sleeping arrangements that Mr. Michaels proposed. He carried the box, but the protests he stoutly ignored—per Mr. Denton's instructions.

"Where will you be staying tonight, then, Mr. Michaels?" she inquired innocently.

"I presume we can find a guest room in tolerable repair."

"Here?" she cried.

"Of course," he replied.

"But, Mr. Michaels!" she sputtered.

"What is it, Miss Landers?" he asked coolly.

If the shameless thoughts had not occurred to Mr. Michaels, that the idea of the two of them spending the night together, alone, conjured up, Maggie certainly hated to be the one to introduce them. Yet, like her mother, Maggie was absolutely certain that shameless ideas very seldom had to be explained to a man, young or old, pure of heart or black of soul, dead or alive.

"But, Mr. Michaels, I shall be in the maid's quarters."

"I understand that. You may think my room will be more luxurious, but it will probably only be draftier."

"We shall be alone in the house, Mr. Michaels."

"Separated by two flights of stairs and several long, dark hallways, Miss Landers."

"I don't believe this is a proper arrangement, Mr. Michaels."

"And I don't believe I have the energy to care, Miss Landers. But put your mind at rest. Even if you feel that you will be unable to restrain yourself, I shall lock and bolt my door against your nocturnal prowlings."

Maggie blushed; Michaels gave her a candle and her carryall and left her fuming on the landing.

Morning dawned much too early for Maggie. When the first shaft of light struck her eyelids she groaned, turned to her other side and resolutely pulled the coverlet over her shoulder.

It was an hour later that the sun warmed the room enough to entice her to throw back the blanket entirely.

"Miss Landers?"

"Mmm?"

"Miss Landers, are you awake?"

Maggie, who had been sprawled on her stomach, gasped, flipped herself over like a pancake on a hot skillet and sat up in confusion.

"Mr. Michaels? Is that you?" she cried hoarsely, pulling the heavy woolen blanket over her, just as if a three-inch-thick panel of dark oak was not guarding her flannel-nightgowned figure from prying eyes.

"It is. I wondered if you would be interested in break-fast?"

"Breakfast?" Good heavens! Was it time for break-fast? Had she kept Mr. Michaels waiting for his break-fast? How long could she hope to keep this position if she lounged in her bed until—she glanced at the window and the bright blue sky, the sun long since risen above the level of the glass.

Good heavens! she cried to herself again. Eight o'clock at least!

"Yes, breakfast. I have looked through a few rooms and I suspect you will need some strengthening suste-nance today."

Maggie, it may be imagined, had not been sitting like a bump on a log listening to Mr. Michaels's morning pleasantries. She had sprung from her bed, splashed some cold water from the pitcher she had filled the night before into the bowl, and from the bowl onto her aston-ished face and neck.

"Certainly, Mr. Michaels. I will see to breakfast im-mediately," she called as she scrubbed the rough towel over her face and fought her way out of the long night-gown.

"No, no, Miss Landers. I don't believe you under-stand me. I have boiled a few eggs and I thought you might..."

The door was suddenly flung open, interrupting Mi-chaels and his patient explanation to reveal surely one of the most hastily clad women he would ever see. Though a miracle of speed, her two-minute dressing had not been accomplished without some sacrifice. Her fine hair flew wildly about her face, looking much as it had when she first sat up in bed. Her skirt was askew and her poor apron hung from her shoulders any and every which way. She hadn't taken time to tie her sturdy shoes on properly and even the chill water that had forced her awake had not erased the oriental slant to her eyes that a heavy sleep gave them.

"Boiled eggs?" she asked. "Certainly, Mr. Michaels. I can have some eggs boiled for you in five minutes. Would you like anything else? Ham? Porridge? I am not familiar with this kitchen, you understand, but I am certain I can find—"

"I did not mean to wake you, Miss Landers," Mr. Michaels said gravely.

"Wake me?" Maggie cried indignantly. "Certainly you did not wake me. I have been awake and up—"

"And throw your morning into confusion..." Michaels still spoke gravely, but the curve of his lips was beginning to betray him. "But, Miss Landers, if you hurry out to the kitchen and begin to boil *more* eggs, we shall be eating boiled eggs until the Denton party arrives, by which time they will have begun to age. And aging, Miss Landers, does not sit well with a boiled egg."

Maggie was a bright and spirited lass who had long since mastered both offensive and defensive weapons of wit, since they were the only weapons she could employ with any efficiency against her brothers. But Mr. Michaels had her now at an unfair advantage and she could only stand and stare stupidly at the man whose intimidating good looks did not appear to be altered by either his careful toilet or lack of same.

"Come, Miss Landers. A single gentleman who hopes to survive in this savage world must master certain skills. I have boiled some eggs for us myself. There is also the remainder of Mrs. Bern's loaf of bread, and if the house contains no other provisions, I imagine there are fruit preserves somewhere in some pantry, don't you think?''

Breakfast was delicious. More and more Maggie was amazed and delighted by the charming bits of personality that slipped past Mr. Michaels's careful guard.

By the end of the meal Maggie was honestly bright-eyed and alert. Her extra long sleep had been just what she needed to provide the steam for the ordeal that faced her.

Mr. Michaels offered to bring the boxes and packages in for her, but more often than not she found his efforts too slow and the boxes manageable if she got the right leverage on them.

Finally, everything carried in, she threw open the main sitting room doors and smiled grimly. *Now* she was in her element.

How many times had Randy, DeRay and Arnold left a mess like this for her to clean up? Mrs. Bern had said in the confusion of her leave-taking, ''I guess you know how to wipe away dust and mop up floors and make beds.'' Feeling only half-conscious at the time, Maggie had not replied, but she could have told Mrs. Bern that she guessed she did!

With a mop and a pail and a handful of rags, she attacked the room like a whirling dervish. And not just the main sitting room. Soon she began to torment Mr. Michaels relentlessly.

He had left her to her sitting room, thinking he had half a day at least in the library. But before noon the door to the library was pushed open by the girl, herding in sloshing buckets with long poles poking out of them, her arms swathed in cloths, some dry, some dripping. The loose strands of hair around her face were damp now and clung to her cheeks and brow, yet the thought obtruded

itself upon Officer Jared Michaels's orderly conscious-
ness that the girl was absolutely adorable. That was, of
course, before she thumped him smartly on the shin with
that pole of hers, which, it turned out, was attached to
another clump of rags and was probably a mop. Michaels was not so very accomplished a bachelor that he
had a working relationship with mops.

"I am sorry, Mr. Michaels, but you will have to move
to another room," she said, sounding not one bit sorry
for his throbbing shin.

"Is there anything I can do to help?" He grimaced as
he stood.

"Yes. You can leave," she said. So he left.

He tried the kitchen next, since it was light enough to
read in there, but the girl invaded that sanctuary not
thirty minutes later, a veritable nemesis.

Finally he retreated upstairs to the room he hoped was
a guest room, the one he had claimed for himself the
night before. Yet he had barely relaxed on the bed when
he heard an ominous clatter on the stairs.

"Mr. Michaels!" she cried as the bucket pushed the
door open and the gentleman scrambled to his feet.

"Miss Landers!"

Maggie looked around her at the quarters, which had
suddenly been made close by the steamy water and the
long mop handle that swayed first this way and then that,
and sighed.

"Mr. Michaels, it was my understanding that you had
business to transact in Dover," she said hopefully.

Michaels, though he did not stare at her stupidly, kept
his gaze carefully oblique until he remembered that
"business in Dover" had been the story he and Denton
had invented to explain his accompanying the girl.

"Business in Dover," he repeated at last. "Correspondence. I do not have to make any personal calls."

"So there is no reason for you to leave the house?"

He shook his head.

"A ride? A nice brisk ride in the fresh air?"

Jared Michaels's gaze was always dark and intense, but Maggie realized suddenly that it had turned completely black and had focused on her like a ray of cold sunshine under a convex glass.

He made no reply to her suggestions of a ride, and finally, in desperation, to break the frosty silence, she burst out with, "Do you want to go anywhere?"

He shook his head. "As I said, I believe I will stay in and write letters this afternoon."

Maggie nodded and sighed, pushing the sloshing bucket of water before her. Now it was Michaels's turn to sigh.

"But perhaps I will find another room in which to write my letters," he said. Maggie, still disturbed by the cold, hard glare, mumbled some monosyllabic agreement. Michaels stepped gingerly around the cleaning paraphernalia and went in search of another short-lived solitude.

He left without taking any writing materials.

Chapter Nine

The girl was a marvel of ingenuousness. Michaels was the first to admit that. But she had played that last hand, trying to drive him from the house and leave her here alone, with a lack of delicacy that surprised him. And speaking of hands, he didn't believe he had tipped his yet, but if the girl was as clever as she was purported to be— and indeed, as she had shown herself to be since he had known her—he could not hope to maintain his false identity under her careful scrutiny much longer. Certainly not if the best alibi he could provide for himself was writing letters. A healthy young man on a last hurrah before entering the banking world would not really fill his days and nights with writing letters.

He hoped he had not aroused her suspicion, because he wanted to catch her unawares, red-handed. But if worse came to worst, he could at least protect Denton's property, and if he wasn't able to catch the thief in the act, he would busy himself collecting evidence against her.

Officer Michaels, who justly prided himself on his objectivity, failed to consider that it was much easier to think of the girl as a thief and a villain when she was not in the room.

Downstairs and alone once again for the time being, Michaels began to consider that Miss Landers had acted very suspiciously about that box she had insisted he carry in last night. It was there that he would begin his investigation.

The night before, though willing enough that the other boxes remain in the carriage, she had insisted that that box, something with frilly material peeping out the top, be carried in, and not just into the house but back to the servants' quarters and her room.

He might not have thought a thing about it if Miss Landers had not shown such studied nonchalance toward the box herself, directing him to, "Oh, bring that one box, if you would," and following him closely, tucking carefully at the material whenever she had the chance.

Even then she might have been merely an innocent country girl, embarrassed by exposed lingerie, except it was obvious to Michaels that the box held something a good deal heavier than frilly lingerie, packed ever so tightly as it might have been.

Now as he heard the migrating noises of bucket and water being moved to another room overhead, he decided it was his chance to inspect that box and whatever else of a suspicious nature he might find in the girl's room.

The Denton summer cottage, though not a cottage by the fairy tale definition of the word, was considerably smaller than their London townhouse and had only two rooms beyond the kitchen: one for the cook when she arrived and another little cubby hole for the serving girl. Mrs. Bern, naturally, would be in one of the larger bedrooms upstairs.

Michaels, keeping one ear on the faint sound of cleaning overhead, made his way through the kitchen and past the cook's room. The door to the maid's room, at which he had already stood once this morning, opened easily under his touch, which surprised him a little. If the girl was hiding something, she was taking no great pains to do so, he thought. But then he allowed himself to be reassured by the obvious fact that she didn't suspect him. Yet.

The room was small and Michaels was forced to smile at its shameful state of disorder. Posing as a simple country girl, she had not brought with her many personal items, yet each of those items, pulled from its drawer and strung across the small bed, made a considerable array. Michaels, it must be remembered, had been on the other side of the bedroom door as Maggie was running her madcap race to get up, washed, out of her nightgown and into something closely resembling a maid's working uniform that morning or he would more readily have understood the condition of the room.

But the box he had come to inspect was not to be seen amid the clutter. As Michaels looked around for it, he was surprised to think the slight girl had taken it anyplace else by herself. Despite her officious hauling and carrying of boxes this morning, the box he had carried in last night really had seemed too heavy for the girl.

At last he noticed that the long, faded and worn flannel nightgown that he had seen and dismissed a half dozen times as he scanned the room was crumpled in a surprisingly square-cornered, geometrically perfect shape in the far corner.

Unceremoniously he flung it aside to reveal—voilà!—the box underneath it. The length of flimsy material that had been folded on top was now half folded and draped over the edges of the box in an obvious attempt to disguise it further. Michaels paused for a moment to locate Maggie Landers and her active mop overhead before he plunged his hands into the folds of the material. There were several squares of light gauzelike material on top. Under that were other lumps of heavier, denser material. Linen, he decided. Ah, but under the linen, what was this?

His hand closed around a cool metal handle just as he became aware that the noises he had mentally registered as overhead were not. They were in the kitchen. The bucket had stopped in the kitchen, at the sink, but the sound of small feet in sturdy work shoes was approaching the door. Swiftly he pulled the item from the box and, without looking at it, plunged it into his pocket.

He whirled around.

The door opened.

"Mr. Michaels?" she asked, as if distrusting her own senses.

"Miss Landers," he said. His eyes were bits of coal in the gloom of the room. His tall, broad-shouldered frame gave the illusion of brushing the walls on either side of the small space. In the dim light his extreme good looks assumed an almost diabolical air.

All he could think was that this was getting harder and harder. And underneath that thought, without his official consent, the very unprofessional thought plagued him that a girl with hair that blond and eyes that blue could not possibly be a hardened criminal.

She really had thought the box contained some of the mistress's lingerie. The embarrassment of her afternoon nap was not forgotten, even after the pleasant supper and his evident dismissal of the episode. She was, therefore, acutely sensitive anyway and was absolutely appalled when Mr. Michaels helped her down from the coach on their arrival and she saw the white, filmy material fluttering in the breeze for all the world, and more specifically for Mr. Michaels, to see. She could not bear the thought of unmentionables being exposed that way, Mrs. Denton's or anyone else's, but she knew the gentleman would not allow her to carry the box herself, and how could she—delicately—ask him to bring it in, into her room, where she could unpack it, fold the clothes and put things away properly?

The night hid her blush as she designated the box, but it was her maidenly reserve that roused Michaels's suspicions. When he pulled the box from the wagon a fluttering trail followed him, which she hurriedly gathered into her hands and then stumbled behind him until she could clumsily push it into the box.

Puffing, he asked her to open the cottage door, which she did, but then hurried back to his side and the box, to tuck and poke and direct him.

"It's this way, I believe," she said. She was wrong, and back they went the other way in search of the servants' quarters, Maggie poking and Michaels panting.

Maggie was not unaware that she was acting very queerly and wondered what Mr. Michaels must think of her. She would have been stunned to find out what he actually did think of her.

And then it was all for nothing.

Having found her room at last, Michaels put the box on the bed, making a great show of manly prowess over a box of ladies' lingerie, she thought at the time. It was then they had returned to the main hall, where Michaels had delivered her carryall and they had their discussion concerning the sleeping arrangements. When Maggie finally returned to her little room with her one candle, which lighted the room completely, she found that her embarrassment and the whole grand production of getting the box down here had been a waste of time after all. The material was not lingerie material, it was not fine and silky and lacy. It was rather coarse, a yellowed white and square-hemmed all around. If she had been wider awake and less exhausted it wouldn't have taken that much inspection for her to recognize the curtains she and Mrs. Bern had taken down and folded the day before.

Only the day before yesterday? It seemed like a fortnight ago. Relieved of the responsibility of seeing to Mrs. Denton's personal wear, Maggie had lifted the box from the bed to the floor, discovered Mr. Michaels had not been exaggerating the effort it took to move it, wondered briefly what was packed in the bottom of the box and pushed it into a corner, where it sat forgotten. Forgotten even now when she opened the door to her room and found Mr. Michaels standing in that corner of her room, confronting her with all of his diabolical beauty and nailing her in place with his daggerlike eyes.

She stood in the doorway, helplessly gaping at the tall man who filled her little room. His shoulders expanded and contracted with every heavy breath he took. He took several as the two of them stood silently facing each other.

"Mr. Michaels," she repeated at last in a weaker, breathier voice, as if looking him in the eye had drained her strength.

"Miss Landers." His voice was a tense, emotion-fraught whisper. He removed his hand from his pocket, abandoning his nonchalant stance. It may have been only the freeing of his hand, but now he seemed to positively loom, and made the girl think of a mighty beast of prey, poised to spring upon her.

"What are you doing here, Mr. Michaels?" she asked softly, the tremble of her shoulders transferring itself to the halting words.

"I knew you would come," he whispered, now moving one of his feet toward her. Unconsciously, even, it may as well be admitted, against her will, she took a step back.

"Of course you did, Mr. Michaels." She did not quite attain the calm, reasonable tone she was hoping for. "This is my room."

"Maggie!"

"Mr. Michaels!"

In two steps Michaels crossed the room and took her two arms in his hands. The long fingers completely encircled her arms and she looked up, and up, into his face, startled half out of her wits.

Now his breaths were rapid and his chest pushed at her urgently with every inhalation. It was just as well that he was holding her arms because she was not at all sure that her knees would have supported her through the giddy heat that emanated from him and swirled around the two of them and now filled her head.

"You are a great temptation, Maggie Landers, a very great temptation," he murmured fiercely, his breath stirring the hairs along her forehead. "With the face of an angel and a body that would tax the resolve of Saint Jude himself."

"Mr. Michaels!" Poor Maggie was like a lost little mynah bird who knew only one phrase.

Michaels looked deeply into her eyes, pulling her to him by his will alone, though he might have been employing chains and ropes for all of her ability to resist him. Then his eyelids lowered and he bent his head and captured her lips with his.

Being a modest, proper, well-brought up young lady, she was perfectly aware that at some point she ought to lodge a protest: cry out; struggle to free herself; run from the room. Something. Instead, when Michaels pulled her toward him—"crushing her to his bosom" was how she would always think of it—bent and kissed her, though not as savagely as she might have hoped—that is, expected—she leaned into the embrace willingly and raised her lips eagerly for the kiss.

The kiss should have been long and lingering, immersing her in a pool of sensuality, from which she would struggle valiantly to free herself and call a halt to his reckless passion. But while she was still frankly enjoying the feel of his lips against her own and the pressure of his tense muscles along the length of her body, before her maidenly reserve had a chance to assert itself, Michaels pulled back and pushed her away.

"Miss Landers!"

"Mr. Michaels!"

"This is not right," he said. Maggie's one phrase didn't seem appropriate so she made no reply. "What have you done to me? What spell have you cast over me?" She continued to stare at him speechlessly, and now Michaels became aware of her soft breasts pushing at him ever so slightly with her own quick, shallow breaths. "I am a gentleman, Miss Landers. I have never given a young woman cause for alarm before in my life, and I assure you, you have none now. Forgive me. Let us forget that this episode ever occurred. We have been friends, Miss Landers. Can we return to that innocent relationship?"

Maggie, still speechless, gazed into his face with robin's-egg blue eyes that filled her face and threatened to consume Michaels.

He released her arms and took a step back from her.

"There," he said. "Nothing happened. I shall be in my room when lunch is ready." He took another step around her and was at the chamber door, where he turned and faced her once again. "Believe me, Miss Landers. The moment of madness is past. You are as safe here with me now as in your mother's arms." He opened the door and was gone.

Maggie stood where he had released her.

"Oh my," she whispered, her vocabulary doubling itself at last.

Chapter Ten

"Mr. Michaels, what a pleasant welcome at the end of an arduous journey."

"Not too arduous, I would hope, Mrs. Denton. Allow me to help you down from there."

Michaels offered a strong hand, which Mrs. Denton gratefully took.

"Ah, thank you. Don't worry about any of these things. Franklin can bring them in later. Mrs. Bern!" Caroline Denton released Michaels's hand and turned in search of her housekeeper, leaving the young gentleman free to assist Miss Christian, who had been sitting quietly in the carriage.

"Miss Christian," he said, leaning into the dark passenger alcove. "The time has passed on leaden feet. It is such a pleasure to see you again."

She smiled a slow, appreciative smile and held a slender, gloved hand out toward him. He took the hand and steadied her descent from the carriage.

She wore a bright yellow traveling coat, which had completed the dry journey practically dustless. She brushed delicately at its folds and smoothed back her raven black hair.

"And I hope *you* did not find the journey too arduous, either, Miss Christian. I might go so far as to say I particularly hope that you did not find it arduous," Michaels said.

"Not at all. Dear Mr. Denton was very careful to keep the traveling segments short, broken often by rest stops and stops of interest." She smiled up at Mr. Denton, who was still fussing with the reins and the driver's paraphernalia that surrounded him. His fussing suddenly became very confused as he returned Miss Christian's smile brilliantly with a pink glow in each cheek.

"Oh, tosh," he mumbled.

"I am relieved," Michaels said.

"And have you been frightfully bored, waiting for us?" Miss Christian asked softly.

"Frightfully. I passed my time principally in reading in the library until the serving girl forced me to retreat to my own room, where I must confess I more often napped than read. It has been as quiet, and every bit as thrilling, as a deserted graveyard here."

"Why then, Mr. Michaels, did you not go riding or visiting or seeing any of the sights for which Dover is so famous?" Miss Christian was making the same suggestions Maggie had, but Michaels did not skewer her with his black look.

"Ah, Miss Christian, where is the pleasure in pursuing such pastimes alone?"

"Well, then, Mr. Michaels, it is fortunate indeed that we have arrived. Mrs. Denton was just saying how she would love to see the cliffs and hoping for an escort. She will be terribly pleased."

Miss Christian spoke so seriously that Michaels wasn't sure she was teasing until she had turned toward the house with a low laugh.

The company arrived the day after Mr. Michaels's passionate outburst in Maggie's room. The remainder of that day had seen the two occupants of the house self-consciously separated, always in different rooms, always totally immersed in the activities they were pursuing. Both spent the day in deep and troubled thought.

When it came time to retire, Maggie had stood for a long time at her chamber door, agonizing over whether to lock the door or not. Mr. Michaels had assured her she was as safe alone in the house with him as in her mother's arms. But Mr. Michaels was obviously a man of un-bridled passion—the very thought made Maggie almost pant—and his calm renunciation at midday could hardly be trusted at blackest midnight, in a quiet, deserted house; her heart pounded wildly in her breast. Yet she hesitated throwing the bolt. Her mother would have been aghast at her hesitation. Her brothers would have been uncomprehending. In a body they would have pounded the stuffing out of poor Mr. Michaels for his single kiss that afternoon.

Finally, with more than a little regret, she threw the bolt. Wrought up as she was, she slept very lightly all night long. Her doorknob never rattled.

She was up with the dawn, hastily gulped down some bread and milk and hurried from the kitchen. Mr. Michaels had made it abundantly clear that he could fend for himself in the morning, and after not even a door rattle last night, Maggie didn't see how she could face him today.

The house party arrived before noon. Maggie had spent the morning emptying the boxes in the kitchen and the pantry, putting just a touch of home around the clean rooms.

She stayed in the kitchen after she heard Mr. Michaels fling open the front door to welcome the Denton party. She could hear many of his hearty remarks and recognized, even from the kitchen at the back of the house, Miss Christian's throaty purr.

Eventually, Mrs. Denton and Mrs. Bern made their way into the kitchen.

"The house looks very nice, Maggie," Mrs. Denton said distractedly, looking around at the gleaming cupboards and counters. "Yes. I believe Ethel will be pleased." She turned to Mrs. Bern. "When will she be arriving?"

"In time for a late lunch, Mrs. Denton. But after our extravagant breakfast at the inn today a late lunch will, perhaps, be welcome."

"Certainly, certainly. Well, carry on. I have a house party to organize." She waved her hand vaguely. "Oh, Mrs. Bern..." she said, turning at the door.

"Ma'am?"

"We will have to...talk...later."

"Of course, Mrs. Denton."

The lady left the kitchen, still honestly believing that she joked when she said she couldn't do a thing without Mrs. Bern.

"Maggie, I am *very* pleased."

Maggie smiled gratefully to receive finally a word of honest appreciation for the work she had done. The Dentons, in their separate little world of superior position, expected their house to be always this spotless; could not, honestly, imagine anything less. In other years, though, they had sent two or more girls ahead, perhaps a week early. With their sudden guests and reduced staff this year, they had sent Maggie on alone only two days ahead, and yet when they arrived at their summer cottage, it was in a perfect state of repairs. As always. No wonder the Dentons believed this was the natural and universal order of things.

But Mrs. Bern had a firmer grasp on reality and looked around her, frankly amazed that the frail-looking girl in front of her had accomplished so much so quickly.

"The upstairs?" she asked.

"Pretty good, though I am sure you will find places I missed," Maggie told her modestly. "But all of the beds have fresh linen on them. I wasn't sure which rooms would be used, so I prepared them all."

"All of them?"

"There are only seven bedrooms upstairs. It only took a few hours. I must tell you, though, that the laundry is piling up and I haven't had a chance to—"

"I am sure it is, and I can certainly understand if you have been unable to address it. Well, I came prepared to roll up my sleeves and work," Mrs. Bern said, removing her bonnet and actually rolling up her sleeves. "I was fearful for a moment that you had left me nothing to do, but let us see what can be done about the laundry."

Miss Christian had left Mr. Michaels momentarily confused on the steps, and before he could overcome his inertia to follow her into the house, Mr. Denton had finally climbed down from the coach and now stepped quietly to Michaels's side.

"Well?" He spoke in an ominous whisper into that unsuspecting gentleman's ear. Mr. Michaels gasped and jumped, which was a sight that would have amazed most of his fellow runners on Bow Street.

"What?" he sputtered, turning toward Mr. Denton.

"Anything?"

"Anything?" Michaels repeated.

"The girl? Did she try anything? Did you find something?" Denton was still speaking in a loud whisper, spitting into Michaels's ear every now and then, presenting the very picture of intrigue.

Michaels brushed impatiently at his ear and found himself in the totally unfamiliar position of being unwilling to disclose evidence. It was his job, his livelihood. He had always considered it his noble calling to catch criminals, to put an end to wrongdoing, to rip the masque from villainy and expose it in its most hideous guise. But the masque Maggie Landers wore was so delicate, so beautiful, that for the first time in his life he could hardly bring himself to rip.

"I did find something," he said.

"Something that she—"

"Well now, we cannot know that she is responsible, though all the evidence would seem to point..."

"Oh, enough of your legal equivocations. Show me what you have. I think we all know who is responsible."

"Very well." Michaels glanced around him and put his hand carefully in his pocket. In a moment he withdrew his closed fist and slowly opened it under Denton's hawklike gaze.

"A butter knife?"

"A piece of sterling," Michaels amended.

"It would take two hands to wield that horrible thing."

"It *is* very heavy."

"And ugly."

"And valuable."

"Valuable? Who would buy something that hideous?"

"You would. Or perhaps one of your ancestors. Don't you recognize the set, Mr. Denton?"

Denton looked up quickly at the police officer and then back down at the piece of silverware, studying it carefully.

"By gad!" he cried at last. "Is that from that terrible old set Caroline's grandmother gave us as a wedding present? Caroline hid it away. Her grandmother said it had been in the family for a hundred years and Caroline had it boxed and in the basement before her grandmother was out the front door, saying it would be another hundred years before she brought it up again. 'Wedding gift indeed,' I remember she said. 'It is a wedding curse and I'll not have it anywhere where it can be seen!' How did you get a hold of it, old man?"

"It was in a box that was sent down with us. A heavy box about which Miss Landers appeared to be very concerned. I suspect the rest of the set is in that box, Mr. Denton, and regardless of the aesthetic beauty of this particular set of sterling, its intrinsic value in silver ingot must be considerable."

Denton gasped, at last viewing the ugly old butter knife with a banker's eye.

"And you say that girl stole it all from our town house and brought it down here?"

"I said it was in a box that was sent with us."

"About which the girl acted very suspiciously," Denton was quick to add.

"Well, yes," Michaels agreed reluctantly.

"Then we have her, man! Nab her, or do whatever it is you police chappies do to stop a thief."

"We don't 'have her,' Mr. Denton. This knife, or indeed the whole set, can do nothing more than direct our suspicion. No, it is too early to make an arrest. But the incriminating evidence should accumulate quickly, now that we know what to look for."

"And *whom* to look for. Very well, as long as you are on your guard and will not let anything escape you, I shall wait on your professional expertise."

"You needn't worry, Mr. Denton. The girl will get away with nothing while I am watching her."

Mr. Denton nodded his hard-won approval and went up the stairs into the house to join his wife and their lovely young guest. He might not have left Mr. Michaels with such a sense of security if he had taken the time to examine that young man's heart of granite and the little chips of it that had been stolen away by the nefarious Denton maid already, even under Officer Jared Michaels's most careful scrutiny.

Chapter Eleven

This was the most fun Caroline Denton had had on one of these summer hiatuses in years, since she and Franklin first started coming and hosting their summer balls or picnics or arranging outings of one sort or another. But the Dentons hadn't been able to afford this vacation until the thrill of summer outings was growing cool and a nice hot roast on the dining room table almost always sounded more enjoyable to Franklin than a cold picnic. Then, too, most of the neighbors that they could invite to any gala his wife might devise were at least as old as the Dentons and at least as careful of their creature comforts.

This year, though, she had two young people who could be prodded and driven and from whom any protests of being tired, of preferring to stay in, of feeling a little peaked, could be ignored. Caroline Denton was a great little planner, and as Franklin Denton could have warned the young people, she would not be gainsaid in her predetermined idea of what constituted fun.

"Well," she said as soon as Mr. Michaels and her husband had joined her and Miss Christian in the front parlor. "I understand Ethel won't be here until later this afternoon, so we can expect a late lunch. I suppose that precludes any possibility of driving over to the cliffs or the castle today."

Mr. Denton heaved a sigh of relief and noted that the young people had been caught off guard and didn't know how lucky they were that the cook would not arrive until late in the day.

"But it is so lovely over there that we simply mustn't put off a visit another day. So we will spend the rest of today 'settling in,' as they say, and then bright and early tomorrow morning it is off to Dover with us. We will have Ethel make up a nice lunch and just make a day of it." She beamed at the faces around her. Michaels and Miss Christian returned careful smiles and Franklin groaned inwardly.

Egad! he thought. The woman is determined to be gay—perhaps, heaven protect us, all summer long!

He wasn't sure he was up to this.

Despite the fact that Maggie was still extremely troubled by Mr. Michaels's strange, passionate outburst, and that she was living, as Ethel had warned her, the other side of the vacation coin, she was having fun, too.

She was still enjoying the glow of Mrs. Bern's approbation when Ethel Cranney arrived and expressed surprised approval at how good Maggie had made the kitchen and pantry look.

"Well now, look at this!" The cook beamed, putting her hands on her ample hips and turning all the way around. "You've put everything out where it was in London. I won't have to go looking for anything. Good job, Meg."

Ethel immediately began luncheon preparations and Maggie rejoined Mrs. Bern in the laundry.

The room appeared to be shrouded in a dense London fog, even though the window and door were both open and theoretically the current should have cooled and cleared the air.

Maggie was a thorough cleaner and had discovered, in her operations, mounds of soiled linens, towels, bedding and clothing left from at least one summer ago, all of which she hauled into the laundry room. So far, she and Mrs. Bern had barely put a dent in the accumulation. And now when Maggie entered she brought in another armful of dirty things that Ethel had sent down.

Mrs. Bern eyed the additions and sighed.

"It never ends, you know," the older woman told her, pushing a clump of damp hair with her forearm. "But you learn to get satisfaction out of a job well done. No matter how many times the job has already been done, or will be done again."

"I know," Maggie said, receiving one of the sheets from Mrs. Bern and plunging it into the rinsing basin before she churned it through the wringer.

"How clean can the laundry be. How good can the house look." Mrs. Bern smiled wearily at the girl, who ducked her head, conscious of the praise intended. "How well you can serve. It may seem hard, sometimes, that you can't have anything to do with the family or their guests, being in the same house and all, but you learn to see them as a different sort after a while and you don't yearn for the association anymore." Mrs. Bern spoke for the girl's edification.

Mrs. Bern, who had been in service here for nearly forty years and who spoke from vast experience when she warned that there was a real separation of the classes, even Mrs. Bern had noticed Mr. Michaels's good looks and knew, with the wisdom of age, that little Maggie had certainly noticed him, admired him and would inevitably become infatuated with him. Mrs. Bern just wanted to warn Maggie from the outset that the situation was hopeless, so the poor girl could weather the summer with her heart as whole as possible.

Mrs. Bern was not offering any advice that would help Maggie ignore an unprovoked fiery kiss, though, so the girl, who gave full credence to Mrs. Bern and her experience, nevertheless felt herself *un*edified.

"Yes, ma'am," she said simply. She pulled the sheet through the wringer and was aware of the little tingle she still felt in her stomach when she thought about that kiss.

The two women finished the laundry and had it hung out to dry by the time Ethel had lunch prepared. Maggie splashed her face with cold water in an attempt to prune the roses that were blooming in her cheeks. She put on a clean apron, set the table and was ready to carry in the first course of cold soup when Mrs. Bern announced to Mrs. Denton, "Luncheon is served."

This was the first time since The Kiss that she would confront Mr. Michaels. What would he do? What would she do?

What they did, respectively, was eat lunch and serve lunch. Maggie brought in the salad and the fish and cleared away the dishes, and Michaels was either eating or carrying on a quiet conversation with Miss Christian. As far as Maggie could gather, they were talking about the Continent and comparing notes on Paris. Miss Christian also mentioned Lisbon and Venice, but Mr. Michaels, she assumed, and it surprised her, was not as widely traveled as the beautiful young woman. Mr. Denton, though, had traveled extensively in his youth and he demanded all sorts of updates from Miss Christian about some of his most fondly remembered locations. Miss

Christian produced the information, but in an unexciting style that left Denton wondering what he had found so entrancing about the spots.

Maggie would have shown more interest in the conversation herself, but as she put the teapot down, Mr. Michaels finally looked her in the eye. No one else at the table noticed or would have attached any special significance to the glance if they had seen it. But Maggie read into the opaque, inscrutable look all sorts of intimate understanding, troubled questions and suppressed longing. And Mr. Michaels, the only other person at the table even aware of the glance, would have been embarrassed by the interpretation Maggie gave the look, and even more embarrassed by the fact that he could not completely refute that interpretation.

Lunch was finally over and the guests excused themselves to "settle in." Miss Christian, it was understood, was nursing "just the tiniest bit of a headache after the trip" and was left strictly alone in her room. Mr. Denton had gone outside to inspect the land and the outbuildings, to see how everything had weathered the winter. He invited Michaels to join him, but that young gentleman informed him gravely that he had "things to do inside." Slowly Mr. Denton dropped an eyelid at the detective and left him to do what he needed to do.

Mrs. Denton, thrilled by the prospect of the next few weeks, twittered and fluttered about the house, keeping Mrs. Bern in tow.

Maggie had dutifully helped Ethel with the meal, directly after which the cook retired to her room and Maggie was left with the cleaning up. Finally, dishes done, kitchen sparkling and Mrs. Bern occupied, Maggie found herself, for the first time since she had knocked on the Denton door in London, with nothing to do.

She looked around the kitchen. There was nothing else to do in here and Mrs. Bern had given her no further instructions about the laundry. Anyway, those clothes, she knew from twenty years on the Landers farm, were not dry yet.

What did the serving girl do when there was nothing to be done, she wondered. She looked longingly out of the little kitchen windows. Might she be allowed to go outside and breathe a little fresh air?

She took another look out of the window. The sun was shining so brightly out there, but she had heard that with the proximity of the sea, it never got too hot here. She put a little hand against her hot cheek.

Yes, she decided. When serving girls had nothing to do they *could* go outside for a walk. Quietly, so as not to alert anyone in authority who might hold an opposing view, she opened the kitchen door and carefully closed it behind her.

Officer Jared Michaels had assumed that an investigation would become geometrically more difficult with the number of people in the house. But not a half hour after lunch he found himself completely alone in a house that seemed nearly deserted, except for Mrs. Denton's endless planning to Mrs. Bern in the parlor. He knew Miss Christian was in her room with a headache, and since he could not find the Cranney woman, he decided that she, too, was resting in her room. Then, bounty of bounties, from his upstairs window he saw Maggie slip from the house. Now was his chance.

Silent as a disembodied spirit, he sped down the stairs and through the kitchen. The cook's door was shut, and though he paused for a moment he heard no sound: not the snore he was hoping to hear, nor even a heavy, measured breathing. She was either a very quiet sleeper or she was not in the room.

Passing the cook's door, he came at last to the maid's quarters. As he opened the door on the little room he could fully sympathize with the girl and her desire to get outside. The afternoon air was stifling in the closed room, the gray walls cheerless, the ceiling low, somehow threatening. The poor girl...

Sternly he drew himself up short and reminded himself that he was not to sympathize with the girl, her blue eyes, blond hair or deep and darling dimples anymore; such sympathies were interfering with his investigation. He was at the Denton summer home to catch a clever thief, not indulge himself in any foolish romance.

He pushed the door all the way open and turned to the corner where the box was. He had come to find out once and for all how much of the Denton silver the girl had stashed away for herself. He could then confront her with that accusation along with the rest of the evidence he would soon have.

The room had been carefully tidied since the last time he was here and was now in an orderly state. There was no nightgown to fling aside, no mounds of personal goods camouflaging the box. There was also no stack of white gauzy material covering what was packed underneath. Because there was no box.

Michaels turned all the way around and easily inspected every inch of the room. The box was gone. The evidence had been removed. The girl had somehow gotten rid of her booty. Now Michaels had nothing on her but his word and one ugly butter knife.

It should have been dire wrath that consumed him and bitter gall that he tasted. But even Officer Michaels recognized relief when he felt it.

Chapter Twelve

"Oh, Mr. Michaels, you quite take my breath away! Step back a ways, do." Miss Christian called to the man from the safety of the little phaeton she and Michaels had shared on this ride out to the cliffs.

Mr. and Mrs. Denton were in the heavier carriage and had stopped a half mile back at a pleasant little hillock that afforded a misty view of the ocean and was "a perfect site to set out lunch." Franklin Denton, having determined to swallow the bitter pill, merely smiled pleasantly at each of his wife's little chirps and did his best to aid and abet her. Now Caroline directed her husband where to place the roasted chicken, the fresh raspberries, the cake Ethel had baked that morning. Mr. Denton did so dutifully, only now and then allowing his eyes to stray beyond the hillock to the phaeton off in the distance.

Michaels smiled back over his shoulder at the lovely figure in the little buggy.

"Nonsense, Miss Christian. There is no danger. These cliffs have stood here since time immemorial. I suppose they can hold my weight while I throw a few stones." He picked up another rock and threw it out as far as he could in an attempt to get it into the water below. The water was at ebb tide and there was little hope that he would accomplish his goal. If, that is, his goal was to fill the ocean with small stones. If, on the other hand, his goal was to elicit a gasp and cry from the young woman in the carriage every time he raised his leg, threw his arm back and let sail with a rock, he was accomplishing it admirably.

"Oh, Mr. Michaels," the young lady called now. "If you are very sure that one has nothing about which to be alarmed, I think I should enjoy a closer look myself." A slender arm was thrust from the confines of the phaeton and Michaels bounded back to help her down.

"Indeed not, you needn't be alarmed, Miss Christian. Take my arm and prepare yourself for a magnificent view."

Franklin Denton could see Michaels help Miss Christian down from the wagon from the prominence of his position and suppressed a sigh as his wife handed him a dish of sweet relish and pointed out a spot on the blanket where he could put it—very nearly the only vacant spot left on the blanket.

Even from a quarter of a mile away, Mr. Denton could admire the lavender bonnet and skirt that Miss Christian had worn that day. Standing by her side, her hand firmly grasping his arm, Mr. Michaels was able to admire the bonnet and dress, too, and a great deal else about Miss Christian, as well.

"Straight across from here is Calais. Some people claim they can see it on a clear day, though I never have myself," he said conversationally.

"I was in Calais only two summers ago. Charming little resort. The dear locals put forth every effort to amuse one. And to think it is only a day's boat ride across. How delicious." She turned to look at Michaels and smiled, though her eyes lacked any sparkle of genuine joy. Joy one associates with innocence and inexperience. The beautiful Miss Elizabeth Christian, as Michaels could have freely attested, was many admirable things, but it had been a long time since she was innocent or inexperienced.

"I am afraid this is the nearest I have ever gotten to Calais, myself," Michaels admitted. Miss Christian laughed her soft, silky laugh.

"Really, you would think from our conversations that I gad madly about, from country to country, continent to continent. My travel experience has been relatively restricted, actually. One would have expected a young gentleman of your station to have traveled at least as extensively as I."

"Of my station?" Michaels asked.

"Certainly. Well situated. Prosperous. Of prominent social position. A young man of finance about to be launched into the banking world."

Michaels gazed at the ivory profile near him for a moment with his most unfathomable look.

"Ah, yes, my somewhat elevated position."

"I suppose your travel was curtailed by your schooling. You are so very serious, Mr. Michaels. Your summers and vacations were doubtless spent studying and filling that lovely head of yours with information that has not been required yet of dear Mr. Denton after all his years at the bank." Miss Christian laughed ever so slightly, but Mr. Michaels did not seem to share her amusement.

"You are correct about one thing, Miss Christian." The girl turned to admire the sea view. "A young man of my station must be totally committed to his schooling."

She purred softly.

"That, I am afraid, is the trouble with travel on the Continent. All the men one meets are portly counts or pallid princes of exhausted capital. All the men one wishes one could meet are back in the universities."

"Then how fortunate we are to have been drawn together accidentally this summer," he offered in a slightly flat tone.

"I do not believe in accidents, Mr. Michaels," the young woman said, turning her eyes seriously toward the gentleman; eyes, he noted, that nearly matched the deep lavender of the bonnet that surrounded them.

"You do not?"

"No, sir, but I do believe in fate, in predestination." She spoke with the earnest sincerity of the true believer. "In my travels I have been exposed to certain Eastern religions that have convinced me meetings between two souls of depth and strength are never accidental."

Michaels smiled into her sober face.

"Karma, Miss Christian?"

The young woman opened her eyes wide in surprise.

"I have not traveled, but reading can take one around the world. Very well, I concede, and thank whatever mystic power drew us together." He patted the hand hooked through his elbow and turned back toward the phaeton.

Franklin Denton, finished with the dinner preparations, had not, like his wife, been able to lose himself in a very slender volume of very inferior poetry. Instead he had watched the two young people, filched a few raspberries and one roll, been stopped from relieving the chicken of one of its legs by his wife's ominous "*Franklin*," and now waited impatiently for the two lovebirds to finish their cooing at each other and come and address this very passable feast. He was feeling out of sorts. Not just because his wife had insisted on this little outing or because he was hot and hungry. His ire, though he would not have admitted it even to himself, was attributable to a schoolboy jealousy over Miss Christian's preference for Michaels's company.

He saw Michaels help Miss Christian into the phaeton and with relief saw it draw close to the laden hillock at last.

"These outings can work up a healthy appetite, can't they?" he cried, springing to his feet to help the young lady down almost before Michaels had pulled the wagon to a stop.

"It's the sea air," Mrs. Denton said, closing her book.

"It's a happy combination of both," Michaels called from the driver's side of the carriage.

"I must admit I am simply starved," Miss Christian said, taking one of the raspberries between two slender fingers and nibbling at it delicately.

Maggie had paid dearly for her few minutes of free time the night before. Mrs. Bern had her up at four-thirty in the morning the next day.

"They are going on an outing today and Mrs. Denton wants a picnic lunch. You need to help," the house-keeper had told her, once she was sure Maggie was awake enough to understand.

The water from her pitcher was like a snow-fed mountain stream at four-thirty in the morning. But it woke her, and it didn't take a quarter of an hour before she was out in the kitchen, where Ethel, she could only assume from looking at the mess around her, had already been hard at work for an hour or more.

As soon as the sky began to turn gray, Maggie was sent out to the garden with a bucket for the raspberries with which Miss Christian was to revive herself a few hours later.

By the time she returned with a full bucket, the smell of baking bread and roasting chicken filled the kitchen.

Maggie ran and fetched and carried for Ethel until Mrs. Bern claimed her to run and fetch and carry for her.

The second-best china was to be used and it and the glassware had to be carefully cleaned and packed. By six-thirty, they started to put the food into the baskets, as well. Maggie thought she had already seen a picnic basket filled to repletion by Mrs. Bern. She and Mr. Michaels, she soon discovered, had merely limped along on survival rations. *This* picnic included everything Maggie could possibly imagine, from apple butter to candied yams. And everything was packed with an eye for beauty. Mrs. Bern even considered briefly including a sprig of wildflowers but decided they would wilt and fade long before the picnickers reached the cliffs of Dover, which were, at this season of the year, covered with wildflowers anyway.

Finally, at eight o'clock, the Dentons and their guests assembled for an informal breakfast of sweet rolls and coffee, and by nine, with an occasional yawn as a result of their early rising, Mr. and Mrs. Denton in one carriage and Mr. Michaels and Miss Christian in a lighter carriage had embarked on their adventure.

Maggie, carrying a bucketful of slop out the back door, had seen the carriages bound away and caught a glimpse of Miss Christian's purple outfit. Maggie knew, clear across the courtyard, that the outfit was worn specifically to complement the young woman's eyes.

Maggie, too, was yawning and felt an unfamiliar twitch of discouragement when she faced the kitchen that Ethel had abandoned. Evidently the cook felt it was her job to

dirty as many dishes as she possibly could and create as
big a mess as seemed humanly possible, after which her
job was done. Maggie could hear snores issuing from the
cook's room from the kitchen door.

Like an angel of mercy, Mrs. Bern suddenly appeared, and as was always the case with Mrs. Bern, the
job was tackled and completed before one had a chance
to draw a breath.

"Now, Maggie," she said, turning to make sure no pot
or pan had escaped her vigilance, "I know you have been
working long and hard, but you need to straighten Mr.
and Mrs. Denton's room and the guest rooms before you
take a rest. Nothing elaborate. Just make the beds, bring
any soiled garments down for the laundry." Maggie
groaned. "Tomorrow," Mrs. Bern assured her. "And
dust a bit."

Maggie nodded dumbly and slowly climbed the stairs,
her work shoes dragging heavily across each step.

The Dentons' bedroom was a reflection of the couple.
Mr. Denton's side of the bed was carefully smoothed. His
coat and vest were hung in the closet and his soiled small
clothes were left in a neat pile near the dresser. Mrs.
Denton's half of the bed looked like a herd of gazelle had
romped through it during the night. Her dressing gown
lay on the floor, along with the dress she had worn to
supper the night before. Maggie carefully inspected the
dress, sponged off one small bit of gravy and draped it
carefully over a hanger, pulling at the folds, flattening
some of the wrinkles with her hand.

It was not a marriage of similarities, but whether
Franklin Denton would admit it or not, he needed the
touch of chaos his wife brought into his life.

Maggie entered Mr. Michaels's room with a certain
familiar boldness that pleased her. Oh, yes, Miss Chris-

tian had ridden out with him in her oh-so-purple dress and hat, but had he ever boldly taken her in his arms to immolate her lips with a kiss? In Maggie's vivid imagination, Mr. Michaels's kiss had gained considerable vivacity. She was mildly disappointed to see that the bed was made, his clothes were picked up, and he evidently washed out his own things—an extremely bacheloresque habit of his.

Miss Christian's room was last. When she opened the door she felt the air of expectancy in that room. The covers were flung back on the bed, expecting someone to fold them into place. Her dress of yesterday afternoon and her gown of last evening were laid across the chairs, expecting to be hung up. The lingerie was in a neat little bag, waiting for someone to take it downstairs and see that it was washed; scraps of paper and bits of cloth and hair were scattered about the floor, ready to be swept away.

With a scowl settling between her brows, Maggie pulled on the bedding, hung the dresses, used a rag to gather the scraps on the floor. She looked around her and seemed to feel a satisfied complacency settle over the room. Her scowl deepened.

"Well, perhaps Miss Christian didn't expect the shoulder of this dress to slip off the hanger," Maggie thought, pulling at the shoulder of a very elegant and heavy gown that would soon be dragged by the weight of the material off the hanger and into a heap on the closet floor. "And I don't suppose she was expecting this little hole in her dressing gown to settle around the head of this nail," she continued, carefully working the eyelet over the head of a nail that rose from the flat wood of the chair, which would leave a gaping tear if Miss Christian pulled at it unthinkingly. "And just what were we ex-

pecting here?" Maggie asked as she pulled open the deep
drawer in the dressing table, hoping to find an expensive
scarf she could sabotage in some way. There were a few
scarves, a writing tablet of some sort, some hair combs
and at least one hat pin Maggie found as she pawed her
way to the bottom of the drawer. There in the back,
though, under everything else, was a small, sturdy box.

What have we here? Maggie thought, pulling the box
out, expecting something more elegant than the rough,
unsanded wood that met her fingers. She pulled the top
off the box, then stood staring at it with eyes that still
glittered cattily.

"What have we here?" she whispered aloud. It was a
brilliant, gaudy bracelet, encrusted with precious and
semiprecious stones in no particular pattern or color
scheme. Maggie recognized it immediately.

Mrs. Denton had carefully overseen the inclusion of a
few "good pieces" as she called the jewelry she selected,
that she would take down to Dover with her.

"Oh, good heavens, no. Not that horrible thing. I forget from year to year that I still have that," she said with
something like disgust when Maggie drew it from the
jewelry box.

Maggie had seen the bracelet returned to the box,
which Mrs. Denton carried away to her room to await
Mr. Denton, who would return the box to the vault in the
bank.

What was that bracelet doing here, in Dover, in this
box? It had somehow been mistakenly packed, obviously, and the rough wooden box crammed in any old
where when the unpacking began. Miss Christian, she
was sure, wasn't even aware of the box's contents; perhaps she wasn't even aware of the little box, tucked so far
back in a drawer not frequently opened.

Maggie returned the bracelet to the box and slipped the box in the pocket of her skirt. She would return it to Mrs. Denton. Or, even better, she would give it to Mrs. Bern, who would certainly see that it was returned to her mistress.

Maggie closed the dresser drawer and hurried from the room. It no longer had a feeling of expectancy or complacency. Now the feeling was something like accusation and guilt. Whatever the feeling, she knew she didn't like Miss Christian's room. Her sense of escape was real as she closed the door behind her.

Real, but perhaps premature.

Mr. Denton detained Michaels when the two carriages returned late that afternoon.

"Michaels, old man, come take a look at this fine equipage. Don't get a chance to show it off often," he called loudly.

"Oh, come along, Elizabeth, my dear." Mrs. Denton gathered the young woman's hand under her arm. "Our gentlemen are going to indulge themselves in some dreary manly amusement. The best amusement I can imagine for myself is a few quiet moments in that wonderfully comfortable chair in the sitting room."

Denton watched the ladies' departure out of the corner of his eye, all the time holding up the leather and metal that constituted his collection of reins and harnesses. When the women were out of earshot he dropped the Spanish bit he was holding and all pretenses.

"I trust you have been enjoying yourself," he commented sourly, "but have you made any actual progress on the robbery?"

"Some," Michaels answered vaguely.

"How much did the girl get?"

"I don't really know."

"I thought you were going to check the box last night. Didn't you have the opportunity?"

"Well, yes. But it seems the box is gone."

"Gone!" Denton's jaw dropped and his eyes popped.

He had felt an oppressive sense of doom ever since Jeremy in his office had announced an Officer Jared Michaels of the Bow Street police to see him. Michaels's authoritative manner and his own frantic self-assurances that this was the finest police force in the kingdom had never dispelled that feeling of doom. Now the officer sent to protect him and, more importantly, his, and catch the notorious thief—whom he had frustratingly within his grasp—had let property of considerable value slip through his fingers. The sense of doom darkened.

"You must calm yourself, Mr. Denton," Michaels said. Which, it should be noted, had little effect. Mr. Denton's world had become a gray and dreary place and it would require something more than Michaels's cheery words to bring the sunshine back; real, personal property was what was needed now. "The box is no longer in the girl's room, but nothing has been taken from this property, so the box is still here someplace. It has only been moved."

"You don't know that," Denton moaned.

"Well, I am reasonably certain," Michaels said. "And assuming that it is on this property, and Miss Landers is the one hiding it, I will find it. I plan on keeping a very close watch on your maid, Mr. Denton. The girl will not make a move that I don't know about. I am good at my job, and I have no intention of letting this girl get away with anything. Else, that is."

Michaels smiled encouragingly and clapped the other man on the back, but Denton only moaned wordlessly.

"I believe we had better rejoin the ladies now, don't you?" Michaels asked.

The two men walked slowly up the drive to the house. The afternoon sun was shining brightly on Michaels's face, but Denton walked under a black cloud.

In the time it took Maggie to leave Miss Christian's room and return to the kitchen with the bracelet in her pocket her mind had become racked with doubt and uncertainty. What had she done? How could she explain herself? Even to Mrs. Bern, who was very fond of her. She was suddenly in possession of a very valuable piece of jewelry.

Where had she gotten it?

Out of the back of one of the drawers in Miss Christian's room.

How had she happened to run across it? Whose was it?

The mistress's.

Oh, really? And was there only one bracelet like this in the world?

One could only hope, of course, but was there no possibility that Miss Christian owned one like it? The coincidence would be fantastic, granted. This was so like the bracelet of Mrs. Denton's that she had seen.

For one brief moment.

A week ago.

Maggie really didn't know what to do. There was no justification she could give for finding this bracelet in Miss Christian's room. And removing it from that room, she had decided, was possibly the most foolish thing she could have done. She might have *told* Mrs. Bern about a bracelet she had happened upon in her cleaning, and then her duty would have been fulfilled, she would have been burdened with no responsibility, and she would defi-

nitely not have in her possession an incriminating piece
of evidence.

She didn't speak to Mrs. Bern. Instead, she went to her
room, put the box first on the bed, then on the night table and finally in her drawer. In the back of her drawer,
behind her writing materials and the little Bible her
mother had given her when she left the farm. Between
each of these moves she paced the small area of her bedroom and wrung her hands.

She would put it back, she decided at last, though in
her heart of hearts she knew it was Mrs. Denton's bracelet. She didn't know how it had come to be in Miss
Christian's scarf drawer, and she would love to return it
to her employer, but she just couldn't afford the risk.

Back and forth she paced. Back and forth. She would
return it to Miss Christian's room and *then* tell Mrs. Bern
about it. No, no, she couldn't do that. She would still
have to account for finding it among Miss Christian's
personal things. Perhaps she could confront Miss Christian herself with it; explain that she had happened upon
it in her cleaning and would the young lady like her to see
that it was returned to Mrs. Denton? No, it just *might* be
the Christian girl's.

Back and forth, back and forth. There was nothing she
could do but put it in the back of that drawer again.
Soon. Now. While she had the chance. Before . . .

She was startled by a loud rap on her door. She jumped
violently and whirled around.

"Maggie, they're back. You need to come and help put
things away." Mrs. Bern opened the door and poked her
head into the room. "Maggie. Did you hear me?"

"Yes, ma'am. I heard you fine."

"Come on, then. We need to clear things away before
Ethel starts supper."

Maggie looked wildly toward the little stand by her bed, half convinced that the glow from the bracelet would alert the housekeeper like a beacon of alarm on the dark sea.

"Maggie?"

"Yes. All right. I'm coming," the girl said. She left the room and followed Mrs. Bern into the kitchen.

"What do you need?" she asked Ethel. The cook, without a glance, pointed to the picnic basket on the table. The contents were somewhat depleted and in total disarray compared with the neat basket Mrs. Bern had sent out that morning. Maggie removed the leftover food, throwing most of it away. She placed the dirtied dishes and glasses on the counter, upset to find one of the dishes cracked. The soiled linens went to the laundry room, the cutlery was carefully wiped and put away. Slowly but surely, Maggie was making her way down to the bottom of the basket.

And accompanying her every action was the thought, *I waited too long. What will I do now?*

The evening was long. The minutes ticked by with galling deliberation. A seemingly immense block of time would pass, which the grandfather clock in the corner of the sitting room reported as five minutes. Mrs. Denton, bless her heart, was trying to engage her guests in lively conversation.

"Weren't the cliffs lovely today?" she asked.

"Yes."

"They were indeed."

Thirty seconds of silence passed while Mrs. Denton waited for one of them to elaborate on their agreement, to specify what it was about the jaunt to the cliffs they had particularly enjoyed. Finally she threw another pebble into the still pond of the room.

"There did not seem to be as many gulls as there are sometimes."

"The early season, I suppose," Michaels offered.

"Do you think so?" Mrs. Denton asked. Evidently the young man did think so, but he offered no further verification of his judgment.

"Perhaps we can go again when the tide is in. The ocean is quite spectacular with the waves pounding against the base of the cliffs. I am afraid that effect was completely lost today. Isn't the ocean spectacular when the tide is in, Mr. Denton?"

"What? Oh, yes, my dear. Breathtaking."

Denton was reading one of his financial papers and not assisting in this effort whatsoever.

Mrs. Denton cringed beneath her suspicion, but it was beginning to appear to her that these two beautiful young people were the dullest creatures on the face of the earth.

That was not fair, nor entirely accurate. Miss Christian was quite exhausted and perfectly willing simply to admire and be admired this evening. Being beautiful was not as effortless as Mrs. Denton seemed to believe.

And Michaels, for his part, was deep in meditation on a subject that would have startled and deeply wounded both his hostess and the lovely young woman. To begin with, he was not thinking about Miss Christian at all, how she had looked earlier in the day with the ocean at her back, nor how she looked now, almost recumbent on this maroon divan.

Instead, Michaels's mind was troubled as he considered the thievery, dishonesty and skulduggery rampant in the Denton home.

Assuming that Maggie was a thief, was the notorious and widely experienced thief he was after—and Michaels did not assume that as readily as Mr. Denton would have liked or as readily as he had come into the Denton home expecting to assume the guilt of the new maid—how was he going to apprehend her? Did he *want* to apprehend her?

The thought startled the young man and he jerked his head involuntarily.

"Is anything wrong, Mr. Michaels?" Mrs. Denton asked hopefully. Naturally she did not hope that something was ailing the young man, but the ills of the flesh to which mankind is liable was a voluminous subject. Surely they could talk about their health.

But Mrs. Denton was thinking from her station in life, when one's aches and pains are of consuming, and it is supposed, universal interest. Michaels merely shook his head and mumbled, "Nothing."

At last the serving girl came into the room, bringing a silver bowl of the hard candies Franklin favored and inquiring quietly of each of the occupants if there was anything she could get for them. Mrs. Denton asked for another bowl of the cherries they had brought with them from the London market. Maggie regretfully informed her that the cherries were all gone. Of course.

Last of all Maggie bent gingerly over the seat that Mr. Michaels occupied. Mrs. Bern had instructed her to ask everyone if they wanted anything, and it would look awfully queer if she asked everyone else and ignored Mr. Michaels, but her daydreams—and night dreams, too—had been filled with replays of his kiss, and Maggie had worked herself into a dither over its meaning and his intentions.

"Nothing," he said again, this time in answer to the girl's query. But when he said it he raised his eyes to hers, and for the first time since she had opened the Dentons' town house door and greeted the gentleman standing on the step, his eyes were not veiled, were not shrouded in mystery, hiding his thoughts behind a fog of ambiguity. There was a clear, honest message in the look. Mr. Michaels appeared to Maggie as he had never appeared to anyone but his mother, and that not for a decade or more. He looked bewildered and defenseless.

"Are you sure there is nothing I can do for you?" she repeated sincerely.

In an instant the defenses were up again, the man was lost behind the shutters of his dark eyes.

"I don't think so, Maggie," he said, a smile resting on his lips that appeared ironic and bitter. "But I shall certainly let you know if I think of anything. You are the very one, I am sure, who will be able to help me."

Chapter Thirteen

Michaels had given his word to Mr. Denton that the little maid would not make a move of which the runner was not aware. And both Officer Michaels and his word were very good. For the next two days Maggie did not make a move without that gentleman observing and chronicling it. In fact, she hardly drew a breath that Michaels did not jot down in the small, work-worn notebook he kept in his coat pocket.

"Up before dawn," the notations began under the date and location that Michaels faithfully recorded. "Busy in kitchen until breakfast served." Then, in a neat column along the left-hand margin, was a detailed schedule of Maggie's day.

Kitchen duties: cleaning, scouring, etc. 9.00-10.30
Housecleaning: downstairs guest rooms. ?
                   10.30-12.30
Luncheon served:
                change of clothing
                (length of time in room not unusual)
Afternoon activities varied:
                assist Mrs. Bern, laundry.
                silver, windows.

Mrs. Denton, bring writing materials
from bedroom.?
carry messages to household members
pick up after family and guests in each
room.
free moments, darning stocking. ?

Evening: help in kitchen, preparing supper
sent to garden, cellar, pantry, dining
room, linen closet, to guest rooms, to
parlor
Served supper
Cleared table
Kitchen, 8.00-9.30
Retired

Michaels marked the entries of her morning cleaning
in the guest rooms, Mrs. Denton's errand and Maggie's
afternoon free moments with question marks, indicating
that those activities were suspicious and would merit an
even stricter inspection by him.

The girl was allowed to enter the bedrooms alone and
unattended to clean them in the mornings. What was she
finding in those rooms? What was she planning as she
smoothed the coverlets on the beds and hung up the
clothes?

Again, in the afternoon, was her every moment filled
with domestic industry? Michaels shook his head disbe-
lievingly. The girl was clever, he would give her that. She
gave every appearance of being compliant and hardworking. To the untrained eye she might have seemed the
ideal, farm-grown serving girl.

Ah, but Officer Michaels was not one to be fooled so
easily. He had done all in his power to be unobserved in

his surveillance, but he was willing to acknowledge that he was not invisible. There was the chance that the girl had noticed him noticing her. Certainly if she was suspicious of him, he must give her the impression that she was alone and unobserved. Give her enough rope and she might hang—

Michaels drew his thought up short. The trouble was, the girl was so very good, so very convincing. He usually prided himself on the superior insight his years with the Bow Street police had given him into the characters of people. For the first time he found himself regretting that insight. He would like nothing better than to believe the girl was exactly what she presented herself to be: a sweet, innocent, honestly hardworking farm girl. A pretty girl who drew one to her with her trust and gentleness of spirit.

Michaels shook his head resolutely, trying to dislodge the sentimental thoughts that insisted on plaguing him. His job was to stop the girl, to catch her and bring her to justice. To give her enough rope . . .

He surprised himself with a low, angry growl.

For two days Maggie watched for an opportunity to put the little, unsanded wooden box back in Miss Christian's drawer. But Mrs. Bern had her busy every moment: up before dawn, working in the kitchen, cleaning the bedrooms, helping with and serving lunch, and then, in the afternoon, when one would think she might have a minute to herself, either Mrs. Bern had her polishing silverware or washing windows or Mrs. Denton called her to fetch and carry and convey messages all over the house. At the only time in the two days when she had a minute and she was sure Miss Christian was in the parlor and would not surprise her if Maggie went up to the young lady's room, Mrs. Bern put a stocking and a darning needle into her hands, for goodness' sake!

At night she could hardly sleep with the guilty image of that bracelet spinning in her head, and the morning found her groggy and red-eyed. If Miss Christian would only leave the house again, for even a little while, long enough for her to snatch a spare moment and race up those stairs, pull open that drawer and shove that blasted box into its nether regions. But having shepherded her little flock to the white cliffs, Mrs. Denton seemed willing to let everybody remain stationary long enough to send down roots now, and for her part, Maggie had the uncomfortable feeling that she was a prize retriever being kept on a very short leash.

Then, on the afternoon of the second conscience-stricken day...

"Miss Christian, I must request your kind aid in saving my sanity," Michaels said to the young lady.

Miss Christian looked up from her indifferent needle-point work in mild surprise. The warm afternoon had been stealing away softly, much as the afternoon before. Mrs. Denton was busy writing up menus and lists of one sort and another: special cleaning projects to be addressed, people in the neighborhood to whom either cards must be sent or visits made, provisions Franklin would have to pick up on his first trip into town.

Mr. Denton was reading the London dailies he insisted be delivered once a week. He was perusing the close columns of tiny figures on the financial page with every appearance of understanding what the coded entries meant.

Bankers, it should be noted, do not take vacations; they only transfer interest.

Mr. Michaels had not been in the parlor and Mrs. Denton and Miss Christian had assumed he was in his room, writing letters. As usual. That was how the young man had explained his absence for most of the day before. Mr. Michaels either had a great many correspondents or was surely the slowest letter writer on God's green earth.

Now, though, that gentleman entered the parlor, surveyed its occupants and sighed heavily.

"Whatever do you mean, Mr. Michaels?" Miss Christian asked, raising her thin, black eyebrows.

"I mean that I shall go out of my mind if I do not get out of these rooms and into that glorious sunshine immediately."

"Oh, that would never do, Mr. Michaels. You losing your mind, that is."

"That is exactly the way I feel. Sunshine and fresh air is the perfect remedy for what ails me."

"And you needed my aid to...?"

"Why, to share it with me," Michaels said brightly.

Miss Christian smiled slowly and put aside her needlework.

"You have the delightful talent of making one feel positively noble about abandoning one's duty, Mr. Michaels."

The gentleman took Miss Christian's hand and pulled her to her feet.

"It is a trick I have learned," he said. "It guarantees an unhurried stroll of an otherwise unconscionable length. Mrs. Denton, Mr. Denton, you will excuse us?"

Mrs. Denton looked up and smiled absently.

"By all means, children. Enjoy yourselves."

Mr. Denton did not have to look up. He had been watching the whole syrupy scene since Michaels entered the room and now barely hid a disapproving frown before Miss Christian turned her sleepy smile in his direction.

He was sorry his wife had chosen to address the two of them as children, because now it seemed ludicrous for Denton to invite himself to join them, as he would have liked. Instead he watched the two of them leave as the frown settled itself onto his brow again.

Mrs. Denton pulled the bell rope at her side without looking up. Momentarily Mrs. Bern would appear. Mr. Denton folded back the sheet of his newspaper and shook it angrily.

"Oh, what is it?" Mrs. Bern murmured impatiently, glancing up at the bell over her head. Immediately the housekeeper smoothed away her exasperation and handed Maggie the damp rag to add to the girl's considerable collection. "You can finish these mirrors yourself, Maggie. This one and the one in the receiving hall are the only ones left downstairs. Check upstairs when you finish here."

By the time Mrs. Bern had swished through the door, her serenity intact, Maggie had given the mirror that stood over the sideboard in the dining room a final swipe with the rag and turned toward the door and the receiving hall herself. Like the short mirror above the sideboard, which was evidently meant to reflect the food and give the illusion of luxuriant bounty to every meal, the mirror in the receiving hall was narrow, affording little practical use as a looking glass but, again, lending the illusion of added space and grandeur to the room.

The mirror also reflected the light from the small windows on either side of the front door, and Maggie was surprised and relieved, though not entirely pleased, to see

Miss Christian and Mr. Michaels walking together along
the drive that led from the Denton property. Miss Christian's parasol was hoisted, its dainty ruffles brushing the
young lady's back. The young lady's shoulder was
brushing the gentleman's shoulder, and a disapproving
frown with which Mr. Denton could have sympathized
settled on the little maid's face as she scrubbed at the
mirror.

Finally the couple turned onto the tree-lined lane and
Maggie reminded herself that now was her chance. Dear
Mrs. Bern had even left instructions for her to go up-
stairs when she was finished here.

Maggie gathered the rags that lay about her feet and
hurried through the kitchen and into her room to get the
hellish box. Ethel stood at the sink and looked up in dull
surprise as the girl rushed into her room and then back
through the kitchen.

"Where are you going?" she asked.

"Upstairs while Miss Christian's away," Maggie
panted. At the door she remembered her alibi and called
back over her shoulder. "Mirrors."

She had grabbed the box from her drawer and jammed
it into the front pocket of her apron. Now as she hurried
up the stairs the weight of the wooden rectangle slammed
against her thigh with every step she took, like the short
whip cracks of an anxious jockey, spurring her onward
and upward.

Her arms were full of cleaning rags and her hair was a
mass of disarray. She stumbled along the upstairs hall,
perfectly aware that if stealth was her aim she was failing miserably.

At last she came to the young lady's door, but with her
hand extended to open it, she heard Mrs. Bern call up the
stairs.

"Mrs. Denton says to get the mirror in her room. Maggie?"

"I heard you," the girl called back. She looked at the door in front of her and then at the other door at the far end of the hall. If Mrs. Bern was still at the foot of the stairs she would hear her open this door and would think it awfully strange if Maggie went into this room when the housekeeper had just given her instructions to go to the master bedroom.

All right. She would hurry down there, clean that mirror first, just in case Mrs. Bern could hear her, and then come back to this room.

"To check the mirror in here," she could say.

Maggie scurried down to the Denton's room, wiped distractedly at the big mirror with a wet cloth and then tried to find a dry corner on another cloth with which to shine it. The job took longer than Maggie meant for it to, but she still felt safe when she finished it and returned to Miss Christian's room.

She pushed the door open carefully, feeling as if her hair were standing at attention on top of her head and down along the base of her skull. Once inside the room, she closed the door behind her just as carefully, glanced around the room in an automatic check to make certain she was alone, then hurried to the dresser where she had discovered the box with the bracelet. There she dropped to her knees.

On cue, with impeccable timing, the door slammed open.

"Maggie!"

"What are you doing there, girl?"

Michaels and Miss Christian entered the room together, but Miss Christian left the gentleman's side and hurried to the dresser to stand, it seemed on guard, in front of the drawers.

Maggie looked up at the two of them, looming like the Sanhedrin over her, and gulped convulsively.

"Cleaning," she whispered.

"You cleaned my room this morning." Miss Christian spoke down her nose imperiously. Maggie gulped again.

"Mrs. Bern told me to clean the mirrors," she said.

"Down there?" Michaels asked from the doorway.

"I dropped my cloths," the girl said, grabbing for the rags, which surrounded her like the petals of a daisy.

"Well, never mind about the mirror, girl," Miss Christian said.

Maggie, her arms full of rags again, the box still banging against her legs, stood and nodded, looking from one to the other of them, her eyes brimming with fearful supplication. When Michaels considered the girl's cold-blooded machinations he might have remembered that look and reconsidered.

"Certainly, miss," she mumbled.

"Well, Mr. Michaels, I really do not see the book you were talking about. Are you certain you saw me carry it up here?"

"I thought you did," he said, moving only slightly so that Maggie had to squeeze past him in the doorway. "But it appears I called a premature halt to our little walk unnecessarily. We must venture forth another day, and I promise not to remember a poem, passage or inscription from any book that I feel you must see."

His lips curved upward apologetically. It had been another weak excuse, but at least it had returned them to the young lady's room in time. Nor had he claimed that he had to finish writing a letter, which he felt was a great flight of creativity on his part.

Maggie was halfway down the stairs by the time Michaels and Miss Christian left her room. The gentleman could hear the girl's heavy shoes on the steps. He was surprised, therefore, by the hint of motion he caught out of the corner of his eye. He glanced quickly down the short side hall and was puzzled to see Ethel Cranney's unmistakable bulk moving down to the dead end of the hallway.

Curious, he thought. He might have asked himself more about the incident, for example, what was Ethel doing up here? Why was she so anxious not to meet them? Where had she been when Maggie went into Miss Christian's room? But at that moment, at that precise moment, on cue, with impeccable timing, Miss Christian put her arm through his, rested her hand on his sleeve and leaned her raven black head against his shoulder.

"It was unfortunate that our walk was so very short. You are a very pleasant companion, Mr. Michaels. On a walk."

His close attention was called to something entirely different from Ethel Cranney's departing figure in the short side hall.

Chapter Fourteen

"Anything new?" Denton asked, looking over the top of his book.

The ladies had retired, with Denton assuring his wife that he would join her in a moment, as soon as he finished this thrilling chapter. If the chapter was as thrilling as he claimed, demanding every bit of his attention, it was curious that he would know the exact moment when the women were out of earshot.

"I have been noting her every move," Michaels said, pulling out the raggedy little notebook.

"And?"

"Nothing unusual . . . until this afternoon."

"Yes?"

Michaels was speaking slowly, imparting his information only piecemeal, as if he regretted parting with it at all.

"Curious," he said.

"What?" Denton's whispered questions were getting louder and more demanding.

"We, that is, Miss Christian and myself, surprised her in her room. In Miss Christian's room."

"What was she doing?"

"Kneeling on the floor."

"Kneeling on the floor?"

"She said she went in to clean the mirror."

"On the floor?"

"She had dropped her cleaning cloths."

"And that was curious?"

Michaels paused to replace his notebook. He reminded himself that it was his job to investigate these robberies and his responsibility to report on his investigations, at least the one going on in the Denton home, to Mr. Denton. Michaels also closed the book he had allowed to fall into his lap and lifted it to the reading table at his elbow.

"I purposefully gave our Miss Landers a free opportunity this afternoon when I left with Miss Christian. You may remember?"

Denton remembered.

"I then invented an excuse to return early, unexpectedly, from that walk. As I had foreseen, Miss Landers was busying herself in one of the rooms." Michaels's voice did not reflect any of the triumph or satisfaction his statement seemed to prompt.

"She was stealing something?" Denton gasped. Michaels nodded. "Then you caught her."

"The girl did not have anything in her hands. Though that is not to say she hadn't secreted something about her person."

"You didn't search the girl?"

"I did not want to cause Miss Christian any distress. She was with me, you recall."

"Yes, yes. Well, of course not, I suppose. But is Miss Christian missing anything? What did the girl take? Where is it?"

"Miss Christian, though justly alarmed to find the girl in her room, did not mention to me that anything of hers was gone."

"Nor to me," Denton said in answer to Michaels's implied question.

"Nevertheless, if the girl *did* take something, I believe it must be in her room."

"The silverware is not in her room," Denton reminded him.

"Yes, but it was. The girl may be stashing her booty in another part of the house, but I believe she must first leave it in her room until she gets a chance to transport it. And as far as I have been able to see, she has not had that chance."

"What do you propose, then?"

"I need to search the girl's room again. And to do that, I need Miss Landers to be occupied someplace else. Out of her room, away from that part of the house."

"I think I can arrange that," Denton said thoughtfully. "Tomorrow afternoon, shall we say?"

Michaels nodded. "Your housekeeper sees that the girl is busy all morning. She won't have a chance to move anything before tomorrow afternoon."

"Providing she doesn't move it during the night," Denton warned.

"Providing that," Michaels agreed. Denton expected him to describe the elaborate safeguards he had taken against that eventuality; something complicated and thorough. Instead the police officer sat in his chair nodding.

Denton humphed impatiently and pushed himself to his feet. You would think the boy hoped the little wench *would* shed her ill-gotten gains during the night.

"Tomorrow afternoon, then," he said at the doorway.

Again Michaels nodded and Denton went to bed.

"Mrs. Denton, don't you think things in this room ought to be, oh, I don't know, rearranged or something, to signal our return this year?" Denton looked round the room slowly, pausing to signal Michaels with a raised eyebrow.

The house party had just finished a luncheon of cold fruit, hot bread and some concoction Ethel had described as "a good way to get rid of remaining roast beef," though if it actually contained any of yesterday's roast beef, Mr. Denton could not identify it. They had all returned to the sitting room with some vague hope of afternoon entertainment, though nothing of an amusing nature actually manifested itself.

Miss Christian called to Mr. Michaels to examine some illustrations in one of the lovely old books in the Denton bookcase, but the book was short and the illustrations were few, and eventually Miss Christian had yawned, delicately of course, and excused herself.

"I don't remember ever growing so fatigued in the afternoon," she said. "It must be this salt air, don't you think?"

Michaels said it must be, though some people actually found the change of air invigorating.

"Do they?" Miss Christian asked.

After the young lady left for "just the tiniest bit of a nap," Michaels turned his ear toward the door and was interpreting the faint sounds he heard coming from the kitchen. The serving girl was still there, cleaning up after lunch. Until this assignment, Mr. Michaels had not been aware of the amount and hours of work the serving staff of even a moderately well-to-do household was called upon to perform.

Mr. and Mrs. Denton had remained in the room, but Caroline Denton joined Miss Christian in spirit, at least. In fact, she had been teetering on the brink of a restorative afternoon nap herself when her husband spoke.

"It seems like some change ought to be made. What do you think, my dear?"

Caroline Denton suddenly brightened, like a parched desert flower receiving a generous watering. There was nothing in the *world* that Mrs. Denton loved more than rearranging things. It was a ceaseless bone of contention in her not-altogether-tranquil married life. Franklin liked things where they were supposed to be. If it had been left up to him, nothing in his world would ever have been moved, replaced or put to rest. Now, for him to suggest that she rearrange the parlor was little short of staggering and was a boon that Caroline Denton would not stop to examine. If Franklin wanted things rearranged in here, by george, things would be rearranged. With a vengeance.

"Mrs. Bern! Maggie!" she cried in an excited, screechy voice. Those two women hurried into the room as Michaels quietly excused himself.

Ethel Cranney was already busy with supper preparations. Michaels started into the kitchen and quickly backed out when he saw the cook bustling about. Actually, "bustling" suggests small, frantic business, and Ethel did nothing small, nor was she quick enough to be frantic. Instead, she moved constantly about the kitchen, emptying this pan, dirtying that.

Michaels stood impatiently on the other side of the wall, listening to the constant motion. Eventually, the

smell of cooking tomatoes permeated the wall. Suddenly
he heard the kitchen door open and peeked around to see
Ethel going outside, most probably after some pungent
herb from the flourishing herb garden next to the wall of
the house.

Not one to allow opportunities to go begging, Michaels scuttled into the maid's room, shutting the door
quickly behind him. Once again he carefully studied
every corner to see if the box was really gone. It really
was. No matter. As he had assured Denton, if the girl was
letting no grass grow under her feet, and from what Michaels knew of this particular thief she would not be,
chances were very good that he would find something else
in here. Somewhere.

He went first to the small wardrobe, inspecting its few
contents completely in a single glance. He lifted the thin
mattress from the bed and checked the floor for loose
boards. Adept in his line of work, he left no trace anywhere that anything had been touched. At any point,
Miss Landers might have confronted him again and he
could have gotten himself out of the situation the same
way he'd saved himself last time. Which quickly devised
ploy, incidentally, had not only kept his identity intact but
at the same time had not been entirely unpleasant.

The maid's room was so sparsely furnished that, naturally, it didn't take him long to come to the night table,
to open the drawer, to notice the writing materials and the
Bible pushed to the back. The rough wooden box was
speedily extracted, the top removed, the stunned moment of study afforded that the hideous bracelet always
demanded. Michaels allowed himself another moment to
acknowledge the bitter unhappiness he felt at finding in
this room what he knew he would find.

The two moments past, Michaels slipped the box and the bracelet into his coat pocket. He put his ear to the door. He could hear no commotion as he opened the door a crack. He couldn't see the cook in the kitchen, or at least the portion of the kitchen he could see through the doorway at the end of the hall. Her bedroom door was closed, though, which it had not been when he entered this room. Evidently Ethel Cranney was not a woman of extravagant initiative. With her duties caught up, she allowed herself a rest.

Carefully Michaels stepped into the hallway, closed the door behind him and hurried through the hall and kitchen as quickly and quietly as he could. With one hand in his coat pocket, his fingers never losing touch with the unsanded wood, he returned to his spacious room. The girl, he knew, entered these rooms every day, though he was aware that he left her little to do. But she had free access to his things, his small supply of cash, his more valuable watch. He shook his head. Nothing of his was missing. Miss Christian had reported no losses, and other than a heavy box and an ugly butter knife, nothing of the Dentons' was gone. And now this.

He drew the box from his pocket, though he didn't remove the lid. Where had she gotten it? Was it Mrs. Denton's or Miss Christian's?

In the year of our Lord eighteen hundred and twenty, the penalty for the theft of twelve pence and above was death. The glittering bracelet in this box was worth far and away more than twelve pence. It was worth as much as he would ever earn as a Bow Street runner. He was holding in his hand the life of a beautiful young girl with golden hair and robin's egg blue eyes and two deep and darling dimples. A soft-spoken girl who listened with wonder, whose aim in life seemed to be to please, whose red lips were soft and warm and willing.

He bounced the box from one hand to the other as he stood in the echoing spaces of his room.

"Mr. Michaels, sir?"

There was a soft tap at his bedroom door and the muffled words he heard could easily have been manufactured by the face and figure that kept revolving inside his brain.

"Mr. Michaels? Are you there?"

No, the words were real; the voice was real; the girl was real.

"Yes? Certainly. Come in, Maggie."

The door opened a crack and Maggie peeked in. It was the first time she had seen this room with Mr. Michaels actually standing by the bed. She gulped nervously, repeating to herself that she had been sent up here and that, really, there was nothing indecent about Mr. Michaels standing in his own bedroom.

"Mrs. Denton wondered if you and Miss Christian wouldn't like to take a walk through the apple orchard."

"The apple orchard?"

"Yes, sir. It's quite lovely. The trees are a perfect mass of pink and white, and the hum of the bees is wonderfully calming. Though you wouldn't think it would be, would you? Them working their little hearts out, busy and buzzing and gathering every drop of honey they can. And yet, it's so peaceful seeing them work like that. I guess it makes you believe all is right with the world as long as there is such industry going on."

Maggie would have self-consciously stopped her babbling with any other member of the household, but Mr. Michaels had already indulged her chatter all the way from London to Dover, had seemed to enjoy it, in fact, and somehow, even troubled as she was by his advances, the young gentleman drew the words from her.

"If I were to take a walk through the orchard, you would seem to be the companion ideally suited to accompany me, Maggie," Michaels said. "Why, I can almost hear the bees from here when you speak."

He didn't smile, only watched her closely when he spoke, and Maggie blushed slightly at his words.

"Oh no, sir. Not me. Why, I look a fright." She glanced down at her soiled apron, which really did look a fright, unaware of the sparkle of light through her silken hair or how charming the play of her hands was as she described the activity of the bees. "Miss Christian, though, would look beautiful beneath those trees, what with her black hair and all."

"Yes, I suppose she would, wouldn't she? But Miss Christian is asleep, I am afraid, so we may never know."

"The young lady came down into the sitting room not five minutes ago, sir. Looking for...you, I believe." Maggie spoke softly, reluctantly. She was an honest girl and felt compelled to tell him the truth, though in this one instance she would rather have not.

Michaels patted his coat pocket, like an old man checking to make sure he had his spectacles with him, and then looked into Maggie's eyes again.

"Then there is no need for us to speculate. Let us find out once and for all how Miss Christian looks in the apple orchard. Shall we?"

Maggie mumbled a "yes," but she knew she would not be joining the two of them under the trees. Nor would she want to.

The walk under the apple trees was very pleasant indeed, and Miss Christian was nothing short of a vision.

The diaphanous gown she wore matched the apple blossoms in both color and delicacy; her little bonnet put just a touch of shade and mystery on her face without actually confining any of the black tresses that flowed out from under it. And she spoke of faraway places and things she'd seen, of which most people could only dream. But she did not talk about the bees buzzing around the blossoms or describe the inner peace their industry evoked.

Eventually the two of them returned to the house to find Mrs. Denton still making a few, final changes.

"No, no, Mrs. Bern, I thought we had decided that vase would look better under the window. No? Didn't we? Oh, you are correct. It was the tray we were going to put there."

The room had indeed been rearranged with a vengeance. Michaels bruised his shin against a hassock that had not been in front of that chair when he left earlier this afternoon. When he left to search Maggie's room. His successful search.

The box was small enough that he had slipped it into the breast pocket of his coat, and the wood was rough enough to stab his chest with a sharp sliver occasionally. He didn't mind the pricks. In his present mood he rather enjoyed them.

Mr. Denton had claimed Miss Christian the moment the two young people had returned to the house, and now Michaels sat alone in the parlor, turning the pages of one book after another, reading a sentence here and there, connecting them together with a train of thought that resembled the buzzing of a hundred, a thousand bees and had a lot to do with crimes committed and courts of justice and his unswerving efforts to see that the twain met.

"Dinner is served." Mrs. Bern disturbed him at last, and with the rest of the household, Michaels trudged into the dining room to sit down to a plain dinner of tomato something or other, which featured boiled beef and cabbage and wasn't as good as any one of the ingredients alone would have been.

Mrs. Denton did her best to maintain a lively conversation, but considering that her efforts were largely unaided, she was not entirely successful.

"I think we ought to go out to the castle. What do you think, Franklin? Don't you think our guests would find that fascinating?"

"Absolutely, my dear," Denton said around a mouthful of salty beef.

Mrs. Denton smiled at the two young people, but they did not respond and she was forced to abandon the subject of the visit to Dover Castle for the time being.

"I hope you and Miss Christian enjoyed your walk today, Mr. Michaels," she said instead.

"Oh, yes," Michaels replied.

Miss Christian offered nothing more, though Caroline looked at her invitingly.

"Both of them, in fact. Didn't you go out together earlier, as well?"

"We did," Miss Christian said.

"But that was rather a short walk, wasn't it?" Mrs. Denton said.

"Rather," Michaels agreed.

"And the apple trees?"

"In full blossom," Michaels said.

"Quite lovely," Miss Christian assured her.

Mrs. Denton looked beseechingly at her husband, but Mr. Denton was at a loss as to what she would have him say, since the trees *were* in blossom and no doubt were lovely, as well.

Finally Maggie brought in a custard that was loose and watery. She couldn't help but watch Mr. Michaels. That gentleman avoided her eye. He was watching, instead, Miss Christian, who was watching the serving girl through narrowed lids. Michaels reached for one of the custard cups Maggie was handing around and was poked in the chest by a sliver from the wooden box.

When the meal ended the jolly little party returned to the parlor. Mrs. Denton was able to talk her husband into a two-handed card game and Miss Christian joined Michaels on the side of the room he had chosen. Taking the seat nearest to him, she, too, picked up a book and thumbed through the pages.

"I did enjoy our little outings today. Hopefully they will not be our last," she murmured.

"What?"

"Our walks. Both of them. Though I might have wished for our first one to be a bit longer."

"Perhaps it was fortunate that we returned when we did," Michaels said.

"Oh?"

"Well, didn't you think it . . . unexpected, finding the maid in your room when we returned?" Michaels ventured softly.

"What?" Miss Christian asked, glancing up from her book. "Oh, not particularly, I suppose. The mirrors, I think she said."

"Yes, of course," Michaels said, and returned to his own fascinating book, which he was relieved to see he was holding right side up.

"Still . . ." Miss Christian said, and Michaels hurriedly gave her his attention.

"Yes?"

"Well, I mean, there she was on the floor, after all. I suppose that was rather queer."

"Wasn't it?"

"I wonder why they keep her on?"

"Keep her on?" Michaels asked.

"That girl. Not very experienced, I don't believe. And a deal too familiar with the house guests, it would seem to me."

"I have thought of it as a sort of country friendliness."

"Do you think?" Miss Christian asked in slightly scandalized tones. "One is fortunate to have received schooling in the city, then, isn't one?"

Michaels, against his training and better judgment, was charmed by Maggie's apparent naiveté and openness and so could not join Miss Christian in her condemnation. He chose, instead, to introduce his most important question at that juncture.

"I hope she did not . . . that is, I suppose you would know if something was missing from your room?"

"There is not, thank heavens," Miss Christian said. "The same thought occurred to me and I can assure you that I checked—" she broke off the sentence short and paused for just a moment before she continued "—everything. I checked everything in my room and nothing had been removed."

"I am relieved," Michaels said, and Miss Christian could not but hear the ring of sincerity in his words. She offered him a small smile of gratitude for his concern that caught him off guard. "We must give the girl the benefit of the doubt, then, I suppose, and assume she had indeed come to clean the mirror," he finished.

"But of course," Miss Christian said.

"Really, Caroline, a loving wife more careful of her husband's self-esteem might allow him to win the occasional hand," Denton grumbled loudly.

Caroline Denton laughed merrily.

Miss Christian looked across the room and smiled slightly.

"It would appear our hosts are in need of an arbitrating voice," she said, speaking loudly enough for the card players to hear her.

Denton, forgetting his ill-temper in an instant, smiled back at the young lady.

"I believe you are correct, my dear," he replied. "My wife is being merciless."

Miss Christian stood and held her hand out toward Michaels, insisting he join her as a spectator at the card table, which did not particularly please either of the gentlemen.

In time, one by one, the occupants of the house retired to their beds. Mrs. Bern came in first to ask if Mrs. Denton had any further instructions, saying that Ethel had gone to bed, she was on her way, but Maggie would be finishing up in the kitchen for a few minutes yet.

Then Mr. Denton yawned and said that "a man must learn to gracefully accept humiliation."

Michaels had returned to his book and looked up to bid the two ladies good-night when they left the room together a quarter of an hour later.

Finally alone in the room, he pushed the book away from him and collapsed back onto the cushion of the chair. He had a beastly headache.

This should not have been so difficult. His next course of action should have been very clear to him. The girl had been surprised in a compromising situation in a guest's room; he had on his person—as the dots of irritated skin and perhaps blood on his chest would attest—a valuable object, stolen by her, found hidden in her room, constituting undeniable evidence.

He had not actually *seen* her take this bracelet, that was true. It was also true that nothing had been reported missing from the Denton home or by guests of the Dentons. Not even the silver set, since he had been the one to show Denton that it had been removed from his London house.

Not even this, he thought, bringing his hand up to his chest and the hard rectangular outline in his pocket.

But it was not Michaels's job to weigh evidence and pass judgment. It was his job to produce the evidence and carry out the judgment of the court. His duties seemed clear and simple; they always had been until now. This shouldn't have been so difficult.

He ran his fingers through his hair and moaned very softly.

There was a rustle of sound at the doorway and his eyes sprang open.

"Oh, Mr. Michaels." Maggie jumped at finding the room occupied, then colored slightly when she realized by whom it was occupied. "I thought everyone had gone to bed."

"I am just on my way, Maggie. In a moment." Suddenly the effort of rising to his feet and climbing the stairs seemed more than he could manage. Instead, he leaned his head against the cushion of the chair again.

"Is everything all right, Mr. Michaels?"

"I am afraid I have a headache."

Maggie bent over him and scrutinized his face, as if attempting to see and study his headache for herself. She laid a cool hand against his brow.

"Here?" she asked. He nodded. "Well, then," she said, stepping behind the chair where he sat, "this is what I always do for my brothers when they have a headache." She began gently to knead his shoulders and the tense muscle at the back of his neck. She smiled dreamily with her slow, soothing actions and began to talk. "Usually after they have been out in the barn milking. LeRoy especially would come in, growling at everyone, cursing the poor old cows if Mama wasn't in the room and tromping up and down until it was apt to give the rest of us headaches. 'Sit down, LeRoy,' Papa would say, 'and let Meg rub your shoulder.' LeRoy would plop into a chair and in no time at all he would ease up and more often than not go to sleep."

Michaels was not asleep, but his headache was undeniably lessened under the girl's gentle touch. He closed his eyes in fatigue until he realized that the girl wasn't talking, and it occurred to him to find that awfully strange. He opened his eyes again, and though she couldn't see his face, Maggie seemed to know.

"And the orchard?" she asked.

"The orchard?"

"Was it lovely?"

"Very."

There was another pause. Michaels was aware that the kneading of his neck muscles was not as gentle as it had been.

"And Miss Christian?"

"You were absolutely correct—she looked spectacular."

"I knew she would," Maggie said. Suddenly she seemed to recollect herself, where she was, what she was doing and how hard she was doing it. Gently she smoothed the skin at the back of his neck and straightened up.

"Better?" she asked.

"Better." He caught her hands in his and squeezed them fondly. "But oughtn't you be in bed yourself? The sun rises awfully early here in Dover."

"And I really believe Mrs. Bern is waiting for it, tapping her foot impatiently if it isn't right on time." Maggie smiled. "I was just on my way to bed," she said, coming around the chair again to face him. "But you looked like a man who needed a helping hand." She smiled at him and turned to go. "I hope you can get some sleep now yourself, Mr. Michaels," she called to him softly from the door.

He raised his hand in a salute and watched the slight figure disappear into the dark house. He twisted his neck experimentally and was surprised to feel no stiffness. At last he stood to extinguish the lamps. He would have to light a candle for himself before he dared traverse this rearranged floor.

In the light of a single candle his frown returned. The question was not that obtuse, his obligation was clear.

He had to admit that it was not the evidence or his duty that was causing the difficulty. It was the girl. And her soft voice. And her gentle manner.

He would sleep on it. Perhaps a good night's rest would clear away the fog that filled his brain and dimmed his determination.

Chapter Fifteen

Even without the headache, Officer Jared Michaels got little sleep that night. He did get a sore back, dark circles under his eyes, and, at last, he made his decision.

"Oh, Mrs. Bern, that's Mr. Michaels's bell. Why don't you go see if he has decided to take some breakfast after all? Or no, Maggie, you go."

Mrs. Denton was explaining the tinkling bell that sounded shortly after breakfast as the dishes were still being cleared away.

There was a network of pull ropes and bells in the guest rooms and most of the rooms down here. Maggie had by now become accustomed to the ring with which Mrs. Denton summoned Mrs. Bern. The sound was brassy, the ring very short and businesslike. The little tinkling alarm she heard now—only just, above the clattering of the dishes and the murmur of Mrs. Denton's and Mrs. Bern's voices—was totally unfamiliar to her. Until now, Mr. Michaels had never called for help from his room and Maggie was surprised by the difference in the bells.

Mrs. Denton, for her part, didn't even need to look at the bells to know that the summons was coming from the gentleman's room and not Miss Christian's.

Maggie replaced her armful of dishes on the table with a jarring clatter and executed a quick bob.

"Yes, ma'am," she said, and hurried from the room before Mrs. Denton changed her mind and decided to send Mrs. Bern after all.

She scrambled up the stairs, her heart beating as loudly as her heavy shoes against each step. Mr. Michaels, self-sufficient, independent, autonomous Mr. Michaels, was calling for help, and Maggie Landers was going to give that help, just as she had the night before.

Oh, he had looked so lone and pitiful, sitting in that great chair last night. She knew that it had been terribly forward of her to offer help and then to place her hands right on his shoulders—his wide, muscular shoulders. Despite her quiet chatter, she had been perfectly aware that there was a grave difference between easing the headache of one's brother and rubbing the neck of an outlandishly handsome gentleman. And then that man, who just that day had been out in the apple orchard with a young woman he frankly admitted had looked spectacular, that man had taken her hands in his. Somehow that gentle gesture had touched Maggie's heart more deeply than his unexpected kiss. What she herself had recognized as a shallow flirtation had deepened in that moment.

She giggled softly to herself as she hurried down the hall. She recognized her foolishness, but like everything else right now, it pleased her.

She knocked gently at his door, suddenly shy to be alone with him again.

"Come in."

When Michaels finally determined to take action and pulled the cord, he wasn't sure that Miss Landers would be the one to answer the summons. She was the logical one, but Michaels was ready with a minor request if it was Mrs. Bern who came to his door, or even an inquiry, just in case Mrs. Denton answered her guest personally. But it was the familiar silvery blond head and wide, questioning eyes that confronted him when the door swung open.

"Miss Landers," he said matter-of-factly.

"Can I help you, sir?" she asked solicitiously from the doorway, not taking his "Come in" literally but assuming it had only been an invitation to open the door.

"Come in and close the door, Miss Landers. You and I need to talk."

Maggie's heart skipped a beat. This was her most glorious dream come to life. Now she would close the door and face him. He would see her longing and submission and would rush to her, taking her in his arms, covering her face with kisses that really were fiery this time, confessing his love, admitting to her, perhaps with a broken voice, which was how she always imagined it, that he could not live without her.

She felt her knees trembling as she stepped into the room. The hands she held out to pull the door shut were shaking. Softly the door handle clicked into place. In the morning hours, this room, on the west side of the house, was dim and shadowy. Maggie took a deep breath, moistened her lips with the tip of her tongue and then turned to him, ready to suffuse her entire being with longing and invitation.

Michaels stood where he had been, his position and attitude unchanged since she opened the door. His face carefully cool, his dark eyes like dull, gray stones that let no light escape.

In his hand he held a box.

Maggie looked at the box, puzzled, and then looked back into his face. She couldn't help but recognize the distinctive box and she felt her cheeks become warm. The faint nod that Michaels made almost escaped her.

"That is correct, Miss Landers," he said. His voice was not just cool, it was frosty. It actually raised gooseflesh on her arm to hear it. What it was not was cracked with emotion. "Perhaps it is time for us to tell the truth, Miss Landers. Allow me to begin. I am Officer Jared Michaels of the Bow Street police, London. I suspect *you* have suspected something of the sort." Maggie's jaw relaxed on its hinges, and if Michaels had interrupted his carefully rehearsed speech for the briefest moment, he would have clearly seen that poor little Maggie Landers barely comprehended what he was saying. She was certainly not facing him with her own crafty suspicion. "You know what my commission has been—to stop you. To end your wave of crime. To bring you to justice." He took a breath and looked down at the box in his hand. "If I were to do that, Miss Landers, do the job that I have never shirked before, to follow the letter of the law, you know what the consequences would be. What would be the consequences of this single theft." He raised the hand that held the box, but this time he did not release her from his flat gaze.

"What...what are you talking about?" she whispered.

"I am talking about the gallows, Miss Landers. The hangman's noose. Surely that possibility has crossed your mind on occasion during your colorful career?" He sneered. All of his masculine beauty was lost in that sneer and the face she had fancied she loved became ugly and threatening.

"I didn't..."

"Come now, Miss Landers. I thought we had agreed to drop our little masquerades. I have been candid with you. And at odds with the justice that I have spent my life upholding, I am prepared to be merciful. The least you could do for the duration of this conversation is to stop your amateurish theatrics."

Maggie closed her lips and stared at him silently out of eyes that seemed to fill her entire face.

"I will now confess to you, Miss Landers—" Maggie knew this was not going to be the confession she had invented in her pretty little daydream "—that I have agonized over my immediate course of action. I was sent down from the Street and retained by Mr. Denton to safeguard his property and to apprehend you. Mr. Denton's main concern, I feel I am safe in saying, is his personal belongings. If we return this, and you retrieve the silver you stole and anything else you have taken from him, Mr. Denton will be satisfied. He is not a man of bloodthirsty vengeance. If I were to suggest the fate that awaits you, he would be horrified. Mr. Read, too, the Bow Street magistrate, could be lenient if an officer of the law were to speak for the accused. What I am suggesting, Miss Landers, is the only alternative we have—exile. The Botany Bay colony, specifically. Not an attractive alternative perhaps, but not the hangman's rope, either."

For a long moment Michaels and Maggie stood and stared at each other. Michaels believed he was prepared for whatever reaction the girl might have to his proposal. He hoped she would be grateful and repentant, ready to accept his offer, in which case he was prepared to be lenient and discreet. A quiet consultation with Mr. Denton, a restoration of that gentleman's property, and then Mr. Michaels and Maggie Landers would simply quit the Denton house party unremarked.

But that was the ideal denouement of this confrontation. The girl might just as well have a strong aversion to the idea of exile, might become desperate, even dangerous. Her life was already forfeit. Perhaps she would see her chances for escape improved if she disposed of a certain Bow Street runner. Michaels was also prepared for the slim dagger or the lady's pistol cached in a sash or under a garter.

What Bow Street Officer Jared Michaels was not prepared for was silent tears.

As they continued to stare at each other, Maggie's eyes filled with great salty drops, which began in a moment to slide down her cheeks, one after another. She opened her lips soundlessly twice, not succeeding in her efforts to speak until her third try.

"What are you talking about? What have I done?"

Michaels had steeled himself for everything else. He had stood in this room, twisted in that chair, tossed and turned on that bed, the irrefutable proof staring him in the face, had finally and firmly convinced himself that the young woman was a hardened criminal, a successful thief who had robbed ten, even twenty, homes. Caught so off his guard, he was not able to screw his face into the sneer again and warn her once more against her theatrics.

In exasperation at her and himself, he flicked the top off the box with his thumb and exposed the sparkling, gaudy bracelet.

"I am talking about this, Miss Landers. I am talking about a box full of sterling you had me carry into your room the night we arrived here, about a certain butter knife I found and the rest I might have found if you

hadn't surprised me in your room. And wasn't that a
pretty scene we created then?'' Maggie, struggling to
comprehend what Michaels was telling her, understood
that remark perfectly and felt her cheeks burn with
shame. But Michaels continued heartlessly. "I am talking about the fact that you have secreted the silverware in
some hiding place, just as you secreted this—'' he thrust
the opened box toward her ''—in the back of your bu-
reau drawer. I am telling you that it is over, that you have
been caught and must suffer the consequences.''

Maggie took two gulping sobs.

"I was going to return it to the drawer as soon as possible. Oh, Mr. Michaels, surely they won't hang me for
that!''

Maggie Landers had one other endearing characteris-
tic, more powerful even than her dimples. Unlike taller,
more statuesque, grander, even more beautiful women,
when Maggie Landers cried she dissolved into an utterly
irresistible morsel of defenselessness. Her narrow shoulders shuddered, her lips grew pale and trembled. Her
poor little face appeared to be drowning in a pool of in-
comprehension. She reminded one of a small puppy more
surprised than hurt by an unwarranted injury.

Michaels, man born of woman, was absolutely help-
less against her merciless onslaught. In two steps he had
crossed the wide space that divided them and folded the
girl into his arms.

"Oh, Maggie, Maggie, what am I going to do with
you?'' he murmured against her hair. The girl, heartless
vixen that she was, ignoring his already painful remorse,
sobbed quietly.

He laid his strong brown hand against the pale yellow
of her hair and gently stroked the silken strands. She took
a trembling breath and Michaels could feel the damp-

ness from her face soaking through the thin material of his shirt.

"Hush now, hush," he murmured. He put his hands on either side of her face and forced her to look up at him. The pleading expression in her eyes had not changed, and perhaps more in an effort to hide that expression from his view than anything else, he bent his head and kissed her.

This kiss did not have any of the studied, manufactured passion of that kiss in her room, the morning after they arrived and he discovered the silverware. This kiss was tender and warm and comforting. Or at least it was meant to be merely comforting, but as the warmth of her lips gave beneath his, as they parted ever so slightly and her breath mingled with his, Michaels felt a corresponding warmth growing within himself.

"What have you done to me?" he whispered, drawing his lips away from hers but transferring them to her chin, to the tip of her nose, to her cheek, where he tasted the salt of her tears on his tongue. No longer compassionately gentle but with a growing urgency, he trailed his kisses along the bone of her jaw and then down the short, soft length of her neck.

He drew his hand around to the front of her bodice, and in another caress he imagined to be only reassuring, he cupped the firm mound of her breast and drew his fingers lightly across the material-covered flesh, feeling its peculiar weight even through the thickness of apron, shirt and layers of underclothing.

Maggie's slender arm had encircled his neck and had, seemingly of its own will, guided and encouraged his kisses and caress. His lips now against the hollow of her throat, he felt another hiccuping sob, and a moan, partly of sorrow and partly of passion, escaped from between her lips.

"It's all right," he assured her. "Everything will be all right."

He buried his face in the crook of her neck and nibbled delicately at the pearly skin. Maggie pushed against his hand and reluctantly he withdrew his fingers and raised his hand to fumble impatiently at the hooks that fastened the clothing at her bosom. As he did so, her moans began to articulate themselves.

"No, no," she whispered.

He paused and looked into her face. Her eyes were closed but tears still seeped steadily under her lashes. When his kisses stopped, a moment of sanity returned to Maggie. She opened her eyes and searched his wonderingly.

"I don't understand," she said.

Sanity was not as quickly restored to Michaels, but the sudden, clear realization struck him that the girl really did not understand.

Even with her tears and his sympathy and the passion that had overcome them both, he had still been convinced that the girl was a thief. A clever thief. It had even occurred to him as he held her that she was manipulating him now.

But the fear and question were so real in her eyes that he stopped and pulled away from her.

"You have been caught, Maggie," he said reasonably, as if explaining where the birds go in winter to a small child. "But I promise that I will do everything I can to help you."

"Caught?"

Now he took a step back and looked at her, his brow furrowed. How stupid did she think he was? How stupid did she think she could make him believe she was? He ran his fingers through his hair and half turned. The girl was clever and could control him in a way he did not like to consider, but surely she did not believe he could ignore the evidence, would trust those eyes of hers to be as innocent as they looked? What did she mean when she said she did not understand?

The chair from the writing desk faced the bed. Putting his hands on her shoulders, he guided her to the foot of his bed and pressed down gently until she sat. Then he pulled the chair closer and sat facing her, their knees nearly touching.

"Maggie, do you know that I am a Bow Street officer?"

"A runner?" she whispered. He nodded.

"I have been commissioned to stop the activities of a certain female thief. We know how she operates, Maggie, and have only been waiting for this chance to catch her."

"To catch her? Do you mean me?" The wonder in her voice rang perfectly true. A less experienced law officer than Michaels would have believed her, could not have helped but believe her. Michaels searched her face carefully.

"We know it is a woman who, somehow, gains ingress to a wealthy home and then relieves the owners of considerable property. Until now we have been unsuccessful in our attempts to capture her, but we received a tip as to where you, that is, *she* would next set up her operations. In the home of a wealthy banker named Denton.

"Now Denton, the banker, informs us that he has just hired a new maid. She presents herself as a fresh young thing from the country, innocent and naive. She is ignorant of the niceties of society, is friendly and trusting.

Perhaps a touch too trusting to be really convincing, but it is such an endearing quality. More importantly, it is also the perfect cover.''

Maggie had drawn in her breath sharply when Michaels mentioned the maid, and a red mantle suffused her face as he described her.

"Denton, careful of his property, sent me along with the new maid to his summer home. His concern was well-founded, as it turned out, but as suspicious as he was, he was still a little late. You had not waited for the move to Dover to begin your operations.''

"That isn't true,'' Maggie protested, still confused but quite certain that she had done nothing to injure the Dentons in London.

Michaels ignored her and continued with his narration.

"You were not as discreet as you might have been about the box that night we arrived,'' he cautioned.

"I thought it was lingerie,'' Maggie said hopelessly.

"It wasn't lingerie,'' Michaels snapped impatiently. "You know what it was. You were so careful of that box and its contents.''

"What contents?''

"The silverware set, Maggie. The set you had me, like a trained monkey, carry to your room.''

"I didn't!'' she maintained stubbornly.

"I am not an idiot, Maggie,'' he told her sadly, almost wishing that he was, that he could ignore the clear evidence and believe, instead, those clear eyes. "You were too concerned about the box to be ignorant of what it contained.''

"I thought it was Mrs. Denton's underclothing,'' was Maggie's weak defense.

"The box weighed thirty pounds," he returned irrita-
bly. "I *took* a silver butter knife from it before you had
a chance hide it. Which reminds me, how *did* you hide
it?"

"I don't know what happened to it. I thought it was
Mrs. Denton's. When I had a chance to inspect it I saw
it was just curtains. I assumed it was the box Ethel
packed for the kitchen."

"And what did you do with the box of 'kitchen-
ware'?"

"I...I...put it on the floor, I remember that. It was
in the corner of my room, I think. I put some of my
things on it..." Maggie's brow furrowed as she tried to
remember. "Until this moment, I swear I hadn't given it
another thought."

Michaels allowed her claim for the moment, improb-
able as it was.

"A heavy set of sterling is doubtless a problem to dispose of, but something like this is much more manageable, I would suppose." He drew the box from his pocket
again, the top of which he had replaced. But both of
them knew what it held. Maggie, whose blushes were
fading in and out in a kaleidoscopic display, turned a dull
red once more.

"I did not steal that. I only took it from the room, but
I was going to return it."

"I'm sure," Michaels said in a tone of voice that
tempted her to slap him across his face, which he insisted on keeping so close to hers. "Perhaps you mean
instead that you took *only* this, before Miss Christian and
I stopped you."

"No! I was trying to put it back when the two of you
came into her room. I found it in Miss Christian's room,

but I thought it was Mrs. Denton's. I thought I had seen it before and I was going to return it to her.''

"Mrs. Denton?"

"Yes. But I have since decided that I may have been mistaken. That is why I was going to put it back."

"When Miss Christian and I caught you in her room?"

"Yes."

"But you didn't put it back then."

"Well, no," Maggie stammered. "That would have been . . . awkward."

"Indeed," Michaels said.

"But I was going to return it as soon as I could do so without being observed."

"And that is why you had it hidden in your room?" Michaels asked ironically.

"Yes," the girl replied simply.

Michaels studied her carefully for a moment, then turned his hands toward her, palms up, in a gesture of hopelessness.

"Maggie, don't you see how hard that is for me to believe? Miss Christian and I surprised you in her room in a very unlikely position for cleaning mirrors. . . ."

"I have explained that," Maggie said, beginning to feel frantic under the dull, relentless throbbing of Michaels's words.

"Yes, of course. I know what you said. Unfortunately, I also know what I saw. Maggie, you acted suspiciously about the box you had me carry in. You were surprised in Miss Christian's room. I have discovered two expensive stolen items in your possession. In the possession of my most likely suspect. How can you ask me to believe that you didn't know what was in that box, that you don't know what happened to it, and that you were going to return this—" he held up the little wooden box accusingly "—as soon as possible?" He sighed.

"Because it's the truth?" Maggie offered timidly. Michaels sighed again.

"I want to help you, Maggie."

The girl narrowed her eyes and pulled at the shoulder of her blouse, which, she just noticed, had been pushed down on her arm at Mr. Michaels's last offer of help. Suddenly Maggie saw herself as a much less willing participant of that offering.

"I know what you want," she said. Michaels was surprised by the accusation in her voice. She was hardly in a position to be accusing him. "And what you are willing to do, or at least promise to do, to get it."

Michaels was taken aback. That was a wholly unfounded charge. Wasn't it?

"You say I am the most likely suspect. Don't you mean the most vulnerable suspect? Let us consider the party that came here to Dover. What about your Miss Christian? Isn't she a new member of the household, being taken to its bosom, being placed in an extremely advantageous position? Why aren't you accusing her of something, or did you fear your offer of 'help' and 'understanding' would be scorned by her?"

"Miss Christian is a friend of the family," Michaels said. He had been caught off guard again, not by her helplessness this time but her indignation. "But as long as we are looking for suspects, do let us examine the house party. The Dentons would not steal from themselves. Miss Christian, as I said, is an old friend of the family. I am an officer of the law and am innocent of any wrongdoing..."

Maggie ha-ed derisively.

"Mrs. Bern has been with the Dentons for thirty years or more, and Ethel is an adequate cook, admittedly a relatively recent addition to the staff, but not as recent as yourself, and lacking, it appears to me, your drive and initiative."

"And because I do the job I was hired to do with a little energy, that makes me a criminal? The standard for judging wrongdoers has undergone something of a change, it seems to me."

The two of them sat silently looking at each other again. Miss Landers's tears had dried and Michaels wondered how he ever could have thought this young woman was defenseless. He felt himself being swayed, entirely against his will, by her arguments.

"Maggie, I was sincere when I told you I am willing to help you."

"As sincere as you were that morning in my room?" she asked.

Now Michaels's face received a rush of blood. He felt like a boy with his hand caught in the biscuit-tin.

"No, not like then. You surprised me...I may have acted out of place."

"Or out of desperation," Maggie said, beginning to feel extremely betrayed. She had embellished that little scene to mean a great deal, to her and to him. To discover now that it was only a stalling ploy of Michaels's was painful indeed.

"Maggie, in my profession it is not always possible to be a perfect gentleman. In certain situations, certain tactics are required."

"And you deemed any action you took excusable, merely by calling me a thief and yourself an officer of the law?"

Everything about this case was complicated: the thief's disguises, his assumed persona in this house, the way this blasted girl fogged the issues and his course of action. Here, now, was a perfect example. Maggie was *supposed* to have been contrite, confessed his accusation was correct and accompanied him to Bow Street, where he was prepared to do all in his power to reduce her sentence. Instead, she continued to claim she was innocent, to *look* innocent and somehow make him look and feel guilty.

"Maggie, it was hardly my personal decision to accuse you of thievery. Mr. Read, the Bow Street magistrate, sent me here to bring a halt to these thefts. Mr. Denton is the one who pointed you out to me as my most likely suspect. But I swear to you I would contest Denton, and even Magistrate Read, if you are guilty." Maggie managed an indignant sputter, but the policeman still didn't let her stop him. "I am even willing to listen to your claim of innocence. I am not sure that I can give it full credence, in light of the overwhelming evidence against you, but at least I have listened to you. Now allow me to put my case. Mr. Denton, considering only your possession of one butter knife, is convinced that you are the culprit, that I am shirking my duty by not arresting you on the spot. I have thought that perhaps he is correct."

"No!"

"But I have forestalled him, have convinced him that we need further evidence before I can take any action. This—" he patted the bulge in his coat pocket "—we both know, he would consider all the additional proof we need. I have not shown him the bracelet." At last he paused at the one point in his speech where Maggie had no denial or indignant outcry to make. "You say," he continued, "that you have had nothing to do with these thefts. That against all appearances, you are as pure as the driven snow. All right. Ignoring my decade of police experience, my careful training, my common sense even, we will allow your innocence for the moment. I am still willing to help. I will continue to make excuses to Mr. Denton, and, as you say, there are other avenues to explore, however unlikely they seem. I can perhaps give myself another week." Now when he paused the unlikely picture of Ethel Cranney hurrying down a short side hall sprang to his mind's eye. "Maybe I *should* ask a few questions of the cook," he murmured thoughtfully. He pushed his chair back at last and stood. He replaced the chair and pulled at his vest to straighten it. At last he looked down at her and offered his hand.

"You may go, Miss Landers," he said.

"Go?" Somehow, when she considered the charges he had leveled and his bullying, walking out of this room freely, of her own accord, had not appeared to be an option.

"You have won for yourself another week. I will see what else I can find out about this workmate of yours, but please—" and the plea was genuine in his voice "—do not make me regret this."

Maggie didn't reply. In fact, she didn't say anything out loud as she walked to the door. Her knees had trembled when she shut that door, and now as she opened it she realized they were trembling again.

She said nothing to the tall, broad-shouldered policeman who was standing almost where he had been standing when she came in. But to herself, silently, she grimly vowed, *That is a week, Officer Michaels, during which can investigate the beautiful Miss Christian.*

Chapter Sixteen

Maggie went directly to her room, shut the door and lay down on her bed. An hour later Ethel looked in.

"Mrs. Bern has been trying to find you," she said.

"Tell her I am sick," Maggie groaned.

"Tell her yourself," the cook said, and shut the door.

It was another half hour before the door opened again. This time the opening was gentler; the door was stopped before it banged into the wall.

"Maggie?" It was Mrs. Bern, speaking in her most motherly voice. Maggie felt like a perfect beast with her invented illness, but she did not feel physically able to meet with Mr. Michaels again today. Or the lovely Elizabeth Christian, who most certainly would not have allowed herself to be taken advantage of the way Maggie had by the unscrupulous Jared Michaels. Of course, Maggie had completely wiped from her memory the way she had pressed herself close to Michaels's comforting hand and the way her arm about his neck had guided his exploring lips. She had a lot of thinking to do. So when Mrs. Bern made her solicitous inquiry, Maggie half turned on the bed and groaned again.

"You are not feeling well, dear?" the housekeeper asked.

"I guess it was going out so early after the berries," Maggie whispered pitifully. Weakly she threw back the covers. "But if you need me . . ."

Mrs. Bern hurried to the bedside and stopped her, pushing her, unprotesting, back down onto the mattress, smoothing the covers over her.

"No, no, you do need the rest, child. Ethel and I can certainly see to supper. I shall tell Mrs. Denton that you are busy elsewhere, if she inquires."

Just as Mrs. Denton accepted the uniform tidiness of her house as the natural and unvarying order of things, in her mind she had also placed the staff beyond the pale of human frailty. To learn that one of her servants was sick would have staggered the woman and shaken her view of the natural order of things. Mrs. Bern, not in the habit of lying to her employer, knew that it would be much easier on everyone if Mrs. Denton was told that Maggie was still working, only out of sight.

"Thank you," Maggie croaked.

"You just get some rest. Tomorrow Mrs. Denton is taking everyone to Dover Castle after lunch, so it will be another long day for us."

Maggie moaned again, and this moan was not only for effect.

Maggie Landers did not have a suspicious nature. Though a bright girl of some imagination, still she naturally credited everyone with her own pure motives. Her wide-eyed, trusting nature was hardly to be believed, in fact, and it is small wonder that Mr. Denton and Officer Jared Michaels of the Bow Street police, jaded by their experience in the wider world, attributed the girl's naïveté to a calculated display.

But finally her suspicions had been alerted, and Maggie lay in her little bed, reviewing some dark thoughts and feeling not a little jaded herself.

She had been a fool and a goat to have trustingly assumed that Miss Christian knew nothing about the bracelet in her drawer. Why wouldn't she be aware of the contents of her dresser? Why had Maggie been so gullible in allowing her the benefit of the doubt?

Maggie flipped over impatiently and lay staring at the blotched ceiling.

And the bracelet *was* Mrs. Denton's. She may have seen it only once, fleetingly, several days ago, but the bracelet was distinctive and she knew what she knew.

A more innocent, charitable Maggie Landers might still have made some excuse, such as Mrs. Denton loaning the bracelet to Miss Christian—as if Miss Christian would ever be caught dead wearing an atrocity like that— but not *this* Maggie Landers.

The girl tightened her lips until they became one thin line above her chin. Not the Maggie Landers who had been accused and threatened—and used disgracefully for the pleasure of an unprincipled "officer of the law." In Maggie's erratic memory, the recent encounter in Mr. Michaels's room had become extremely lurid, with his impassioned kisses and caresses. And though she had grown up in a family of boys, she had an exaggerated perception of how satisfying eager kisses were to a man. *This* Maggie Landers saw the world as it really was, in all its sordid wickedness, and she knew, or at least she was willing to accept the possibility, that Miss Christian had taken the bracelet.

The only consideration hard to justify to herself was that this wealthy, beautiful, old and dear friend of the Franklin Dentons' was a notorious thief. But resolutely

Maggie clenched her fists into tight little balls and whispered, "Well, why not!"

Michaels was not allowed the luxury of solitude and a dark room in which to do his thinking. Mrs. Bern knocked briskly at his door only a few minutes after Maggie left the room. He had the bracelet out again, studying it unhappily when the summons sounded at his door. Quickly he looked around his room and hit upon the bottom drawer of the cabinet against his wall as the best hiding place for the bangle. He opened the drawer, pulled forward the jumble of shirts, trousers and a long nightshirt that had been left in the drawer by the last guest in this room, shoved the little box behind everything and guiltily slammed the drawer shut as the door cracked open and Mrs. Bern peeked in.

"Mr. Michaels?" she asked.

"Yes, come on. What did you want, Mrs. Bern?" he asked, embarrassingly short of breath.

"Mrs. Denton wondered if you wouldn't like to join them in making plans for the visit to Dover Castle tomorrow?"

Michaels was sorely tempted to tell Mrs. Bern that indeed he would not like to take part in the planning session, but from the stony look in kindly Mrs. Bern's eye and the firm set to her upturned lips, he got the impression that a refusal of the invitation was not really an alternative.

"By all means," he said instead, grabbing his surcoat from the back of the chair and following the housekeeper down to the sitting room.

"Mr. Michaels, come and join our happy circle," Mrs. Denton cried gaily as he entered the room. "Do take that chair next to Miss Christian. I was just telling her that

Franklin and I have not been to the castle ourselves for years. This will be a great lark for all of us."

Caroline Denton looked around at her husband and her two young guests, but instead of the scowl, the expression of impatience and the look of boredom, she employed her selective vision and saw exactly what she wanted to see: eager anticipation on every face.

Michaels, with a clearer vision, turned to Miss Christian at his side and raised his eyebrows wearily. Her lips turned up faintly.

"I hope you are quite recovered from your headache," he said.

She aimed another faint smile in his direction.

"Quite," she said. "And you were seeing to personal business?"

"I was?" Michaels asked in surprise, then quickly changed his question to a statement of fact. "I was. Personal letters—" He nearly grimaced as he said it. Surely the beautiful Miss Christian could not find enthralling a man who spent most of his life corresponding with half of the British Empire. Michaels honestly cared for the adorable Denton maid, and his last display of passion had hardly been a sham. But somehow when he sat this close to the dark, sultry Elizabeth Christian, he wanted very much to seem enthralling to her. Mr. Denton, who had long since accepted his prosperous potbelly and allowed his social repartee to deteriorate to comments on the weather and general inquiries as to a person's health, could have wholeheartedly sympathized with the younger man, especially as he sat breathing with difficulty in the too tight waistcoat, cudgeling his brains for a witty remark.

"We can take the big barouche and all ride out together. Oh, I know you young people would rather be alone, but you must indulge your seniors occasionally and allow us the pleasure of your company." Mrs. Denton paused for a moment and Michaels and Miss Christian obligingly filled the break with stout and gentle denials, respectively.

"It won't be another picnic, will it, my dear? I prefer my roast beef hot and my claret cool."

Mrs. Denton gave her husband an exasperated look.

"Of course not, Franklin," she said, using the indulgent tone that drove her husband to distraction. "We went on a picnic *last time*. Surely you don't think we would go on another picnic tomorrow?" She twittered in amusement and so didn't hear her husband's muttered undertone.

"We went to the cliffs last time," he growled softly. "But that is not preventing us from going to the cliffs again tomorrow."

Michaels heard most of the remark and couldn't help but agree. Miss Christian was politely attending Mrs. Denton and her further description of the planned outing and Dover Castle.

Michaels, not being an active participant in that conversation, found his mind worrying at the possibility of Ethel Cranney being the thief he was after. He and Mr. Denton had both automatically dismissed the cook when they started considering suspects. Ethel was the sort of person one does dismiss when one contemplates shrewd, ingenious and inventive plots. The trouble was, Ethel was a good deal like her cooking: bland and solid, with no imagination, no flair and not even much flavor. But as Michaels thought about it—which thoughts were emphasized rather than distracted by Mrs. Denton's flowery descriptions of the scenes they were to view the next day—Ethel's sluggishness could be as much of an act as the grand lady or the vivacious serving girl he had described to Mr. Denton. Why not? Didn't Ethel have access to a fair amount of the Dentons' valuable property in just her kitchen and dining room domain? A certain ugly set of silverware sprang immediately to mind. And with her employers engaged or away, couldn't she have free run of the house? To dispose of the silverware, to hide a bracelet in Miss Christian's room?

"It is settled, then. We will leave tomorrow, directly after an early lunch, Franklin. Then we will have the rest of the long summer day to explore. Doesn't that sound delightful, Mr. Michaels?"

Michaels nodded absently and then collected himself enough to add, "It does indeed, Mrs. Denton."

That would allow him tomorrow morning to make some discreet investigations and still give him the afternoon with the raven-haired young woman at his side.

He turned to look at her automatically with the thought and was as pleased as a schoolboy with his first crush to find her eyes already upon him, a faint smile on her lips.

Chapter Seventeen

"Fit as a fiddle. I can't imagine what was wrong with me last night."

"Simple exhaustion. You have been working yourself to a shadow since you arrived. I am relieved you are feeling better, and you must be careful not to wear yourself out again."

This caution was delivered seriously by Mrs. Bern to the maid in the kitchen the next morning as a leisurely breakfast was being prepared. The breakfast would be leisurely for the Dentons and their guests. Mrs. Bern, Ethel and Maggie were as busy as a swarm of those bees Maggie so admired.

At Mrs. Bern's excuse for Maggie and her warning that the girl not work herself too hard, Ethel looked up sullenly and then down again at the biscuits she was rolling out. Clearly the cook did not approve of Mrs. Bern's leniency, but one might have suspected that was because Ethel hadn't thought of Maggie's little ploy first.

Noisily the cook slammed the pan of biscuits into the hot oven.

"Did you get those eggs?" she asked Maggie. The girl produced the basket with the few eggs she had been able to gather that morning, wondering at the shortness of Ethel's tone.

Maggie had fully recovered her equanimity and this morning she was able to coolly lay out the sideboard with the biscuits, poached eggs, smoked haddock, browned potatoes and all of the etceteras that attend a country breakfast. As she did so the house party filtered into the room, greeting one another, commenting on the favorable weather, crowding close behind the maid to slip an egg or some of the potatoes onto their plates while the food was still hot.

The others were taking their places at the table when Mr. Michaels approached her at the end of the sideboard.

"What kind of preserves are these, Maggie?" he asked, indicating the bowl next to the bread but not looking down at it. Instead he was looking at her. He had been a little careless with his shaving that morning and the extra whiskers on his neck and along his jaw, combined with his dark eyes, gave him a positively swarthy look.

He was thinking that he never had seen such a perfect personification of a summer morning. Every one of Maggie's golden hairs sparkled like a sunbeam; her eyes were as blue as the morning sky, her cheeks as pink as the dew-moistened clover.

At last she tore her eyes away from his gaze and looked down at the table.

"Apricot, I believe, sir," she said.

"Apricot? Ah, good." He leaned toward her slightly and lowered his voice. "I have not been able to..."

"Jared, my boy, come join us," Mr. Denton called. "The ladies want to hear some more of your stories."

"Oh, yes. I had no idea that hooligans and ruffians lived such colorful lives," Miss Christian cooed. "You seem wickedly familiar with your subjects for a banker, Mr. Michaels."

Michaels had turned to face the party at the table with Mr. Denton's first word, failing to tell Maggie what it was he had not been able to do yet. Now he approached his place, shaking his head.

"I have not been a banker my entire life, Miss Christian."

She parted her lips and raised her eyebrows. Michaels shook out his napkin.

"A mysterious past, Mr. Michaels?"

"Hardly. It is only my schooling again, come back to haunt us. It is surprising the strange sorts of stories one retains from one's school days. But perhaps my reading then was more sensational than uplifting."

"Well, do tell us more about that Dick Turpin fellow. A silly, romantic female like myself regrets that he was ever apprehended." Miss Christian spoke to Michaels with a familiar confidentiality that raised Maggie's hackles as she delayed her exit from the room.

How completely that woman captivated Officer Michaels! She reminded Maggie of a spider, spinning her web, entrapping her hapless prey.

Finally Maggie was forced to turn toward the door with a half smile on her lips. The idea of Michaels being a hapless victim of anything or anyone was ludicrous.

Still, Maggie left the room distrustful of the Christian woman. She was a fine one to speak of mysterious pasts. In Maggie's hearing, Miss Christian had discussed the weather, the house, the food, the Dentons, a good deal about Mr. Michaels and his presumed job, his likes and dislikes, her own preferences as to composers, authors, playwrights and fabrics, and the effect of the sea air on her coiffeur, but Maggie had not heard her mention one word about her family. Since she was determined to take exception to everything about Miss Christian, and since she had become hardened and coldly and calculatingly suspicious, it finally occurred to the girl to find that a little strange.

Back in the kitchen, clearing away Ethel's breakfast mess, Maggie infused her voice with as much nonchalance as she could muster.

"Miss Christian doesn't talk much about her family," she said to Mrs. Bern. "Maybe she hasn't got any?" She watched the housekeeper closely under her brow, hoping the older lady would expose a skeleton in the Christian family closet.

"I really do not know," Mrs. Bern said without looking up.

Maggie, still carefully casual, wiped and put away a dish or two before she spoke again.

"Don't you?" she asked. "I thought Miss Christian was an old friend of the family."

"Oh, no."

Mrs. Bern was not being terribly communicative, but the girl forged ahead and nudged her with a mildly interested, "No?"

"It was my impression that the morning she arrived at the London house was the first time the Dentons had ever met her. They are acquainted with the Percy Christians up in Birmingham, but our Miss Christian is not related to that family."

Maggie thought carefully about what Mrs. Bern had just said, and as she did so her efforts at cleaning slowed until she stopped altogether and turned to the housekeeper.

"Neither of the Dentons knew her?" she asked.

"Not when she arrived." Mrs. Bern was preoccupied and didn't notice that Maggie's interest had become avid.

"She is a stranger in this house?"

"Here now, when are you going to be finished with this place?" Ethel's rough voice pulled both Maggie and Mrs. Bern up short. "I wanted to get some pies made before I had to start on lunch."

Mrs. Bern and Maggie exchanged surprised looks. Mrs. Denton had ordered nothing special for today, pies or anything else that would take extra preparation. Pies, of course, would be a welcomed surprise to the diners, either at lunch or supper, but the shared surprise was over Ethel's willingness to put forth the effort.

"We are finishing up now," Mrs. Bern assured the cook, and any other questions that Maggie might have had were hastily put aside.

The pies gave Michaels the perfect opening.

"This is something of a treat," he said when Maggie placed the pie and accompanying coffee in front of him. He spoke with just the right touch of careless enthusiasm in his voice. He was a much more experienced investigator than Maggie, and his assumed tones sounded more natural than the girl's. That was fortunate, since his auditors were more attentive than had been Mrs. Bern.

"Isn't it?" Mrs. Denton asked. She was pleasantly surprised by the dessert Ethel had prepared, but not agog, which her husband was.

"I say," he said, and then, "by Jove, I say."

Miss Christian requested "only the tiniest sliver of a piece," which Maggie reported in the kitchen as a request for a scrag end of mostly crust.

The crust was not the best part of the pie. Mrs. Denton sampled hers and then discreetly scraped the filling out from between the tough, doughy pastry. The men ate theirs; Mr. Denton even ate two pieces, but that was because they were rugged males, not because they didn't have discriminating tastes.

"What a lovely effort for Ethel to have made," Mrs. Denton said, indicating to Maggie that she could remove her plate.

"Rather an effort for us, too," Mr. Denton murmured for Michaels's benefit. The younger gentleman's lips twitched upward, but Miss Christian, who had also heard the remark, frowned and even gave Denton a disapproving look. Mr. Denton was cowed, though he tried not to be devastated, and Michaels was mildly surprised by Miss Christian's concern for the cook. Miss Christian seemed even less aware of the people that constituted a serving staff than Mrs. Denton.

"We must leave before it gets any later," the lady of the house announced cheerfully. Silverware clattered, chairs were pushed back, there was a brief, soft confusion of voices, and then the ladies went upstairs to do whatever ladies do upstairs when a departure is imminent. Michaels and Denton went outside to bring around the carriage.

The Dentons had come down to Dover this year without an outside man, and Mr. Denton appreciated Michaels's help in hitching the team of horses to the formal barouche. He supposed he could still do it alone, in the same way he supposed he could still wrestle. He had done both as a young man and thought he remembered how, but he had no desire to prove his ability.

"I will admit that I have tasted better apple pie." Michaels smiled across the backs of the horses.

"Doubtless." Denton grimaced. "But then I told you from the beginning that Ethel is only a mediocre cook. Even my dear, undemanding wife seemed to sense the shortcoming today."

"And you say Mrs. Cranney was hired shortly before your departure from London?"

"A week or two."

"What kind of references did she bring with her?"

"I do not really know. Caroline hires the servants." Mr. Denton stopped his hitching, buckling and tightening and looked across at the younger man. "What do you mean by these questions?" he asked.

Michaels looked up innocently, or at least as innocently as his dark mane of hair and penetrating gaze would permit.

"I only wondered how a cook could obtain favorable references and make pastry that tastes like clay."

Denton was anxious for an actual thief to be apprehended in this case of robbery that Officer Jared Michaels had come into his home to investigate. And he wanted Michaels to arrest the girl they both knew was the thief. Why was this Bow Street runner asking questions about his cook?

Denton narrowed his eyes.

"Pie has nothing to do with the crook you are being paid to stop. What progress are you making there?"

Michaels snapped one of the harnesses into place before he replied. Mr. Denton saw nothing strange in the delay, naturally attributing it to the other man's deliberate manner. Michaels had found that to be a handy camouflage for reluctance.

"Another piece of evidence has come to light," he said at last.

"What?" Denton asked eagerly. Michaels patted the neck of the horse nearest him and stepped back to the passenger box.

"I think it is best if I keep that to myself for the time being, Mr. Denton," he said, swinging into the box. Denton, still not wholly satisfied, joined him. "And who knows what significance pie will have in this case?"

The ladies, perfect visions of loveliness after their venture upstairs, joined the gentlemen and the party was off. Mrs. Denton was determined that they be gay, and though at times it became a little forced, her husband and guests complied.

The early summer English countryside was idyllic. Through the trees that lined most of the drive, glimpses were afforded of verdant meadowland. Once the heavy coach clattered noisily across a wooden bridge, but other than that, the very weight of the carriage ensured a quiet, comfortable ride. The sun was warm, but this near to the sea it didn't seem too awfully hot.

All of the elements combined provided for a surprisingly delightful ride.

"There already?" Mrs. Denton cried as her husband pulled on the handful of reins he held and the barouche came to a stop. "My, it seems we simply flew here."

Michaels and Miss Christian made the appropriate sounds of accordance, but Mr. Denton, pulling out his kerchief and wiping his brow, rubbing his cramped hands and fighting an almost irresistible urge to jump down onto the ground and massage his buttocks, was not able to agree with his wife wholeheartedly.

"And there is the castle," Mrs. Denton announced.

And there was Dover Castle, its gray stone walls rising to magnificent heights over their heads, blocking out almost everything else.

Michaels and Mr. Denton climbed down, straightened jackets and offered their hands to the ladies. Mrs. Denton and Miss Christian stiffly joined the men, taking just a moment to pull down the veils from their wide summer hats and push up their lacy parasols.

"Come along, then. Franklin, don't lag behind. Oh, Mr. Michaels, lend me your arm over these rough stones, won't you?" Mrs. Denton continued to direct the action, being also determined that they stay together as a group today. She had nothing against couples and was even making serious matchmaking plans for later in the week, but the segregation of her husband and herself made her feel a weight of years that a woman will move heaven and earth to throw off. Being with the young people made her feel young, made her believe she *was* young.

Franklin was not immune to the influence himself. Gamely he offered Miss Christian his elbow for the treacherous trek across the rock-strewn ground that surrounded the castle, picturing himself in a shining suit of armor, having just saved this lovely damsel from a fire-breathing dragon.

The party made its way into the gloom of the interior, stopping occasionally to admire the antiquity that surrounded them, the two oddly paired couples standing far enough apart for quiet, private conversations.

"I have enjoyed my visit, Mr. Denton. You and your wife have been *so* accommodating," Miss Christian said, looking after the other two.

"Tut, tut, my dear. One suspects one knows the part of this visit you have found most enjoyable." Denton leered.

"Ah, what grandeur," Michaels said softly to Mrs. Denton. "But I hope this exploration is not tiring you."

Mrs. Denton looked up at the tall man at her side in surprise at the evident worry in his voice.

"Certainly not, Mr. Michaels," she said.

"You must forgive me. It is only that I noticed you did not eat all of your pie and I hoped you were not feeling ill."

On the other side of the hall Miss Christian lowered her head demurely.

"I fear I have been less than discreet," she murmured. "I hope I have not appeared too awfully bold?"

"Certainly not. Mr. Michaels is a delightful young man. No connections, of course, but delightful nevertheless."

"Oh? It was my understanding that Mr. Michaels was a member of London's society—the sort of enterprising young man who amuses himself with a job and responsibility?"

"I thank you for your concern, Mr. Michaels, but I assure you that I am not ill, though I might have been if I had eaten all of that pie." Mrs. Denton smiled faintly.

For Miss Christian's benefit, Denton shook his head, feeling more wicked pleasure than the honest regret he was trying to show.

"No, I am afraid not. Enterprising, yes, certainly. Why, he may rise to head teller at the bank someday. But

I am afraid this little holiday we are treating him to may very well be the closest he comes to London society."

By now Michaels and Mrs. Denton had their heads quite close together.

"I have tasted more delicate pastry," Michaels agreed. Mrs. Denton smiled at his understatement. "But then, I don't suppose Ethel came to you sporting credentials that claimed she was a pastry chef."

"Ah well, one should be more conscientious about credentials, I suppose," Mrs. Denton admitted softly. She didn't want her husband to hear her confession.

"I was not aware..." Miss Christian said vaguely, again looking off after the other pair.

"Rather informal, were they?" Michaels was saying. He smiled understandingly at Mrs. Denton. It was one of his rare, genuine, upturned lips smiles. A very nice smile. Mrs. Denton wondered briefly why he was so sparing in its employ.

"And of course Mrs. Denton and I are so glad the two of you have hit it off. It has made it rather jolly for the poor boy," Mr. Denton told Miss Christian.

"One must eat, Mr. Michaels. A starving man doesn't stop to ask for references. And it never occurred to me, I am afraid, to ask if the woman could make a flaky crust." Mrs. Denton returned Michaels's smile weakly.

"Poor boy?" Miss Christian repeated softly, a shade of hesitation in her voice. "Yes, well, I am glad he has enjoyed himself."

* * *

"No references?" Michaels asked. Mrs. Denton shook her head guiltily. "Well, one always hopes for an angel in disguise, doesn't one? You simply had the misfortune to hire a devil of a cook."

Mrs. Denton's sudden burst of laughter surprised the dark, hoary chamber. And its occupants. Denton and Miss Christian both looked across at her curiously.

"Caveat emptor," she murmured to Mr. Michaels. "Let the buyer beware." Then she released his arm at last to join her husband, who was leading Miss Christian to the end of the hall and the broad doorway.

"Didn't you tell me last night that this was erected by King John, darling?" she said, claiming her husband's other arm.

"Back in the twelfth century, if my schoolboy history is standing me in good stead."

"It is an excellent example of medieval fortification," Michaels offered, coming up behind the threesome.

"You can see that it still includes both Saxon and Norman handiwork."

Mr. Denton and Mr. Michaels continued offering historical tidbits as the party, now generally clumped together, wandered through the rest of the building. The women "Oh, really-ed" and "Is that so-ed?" politely, and no one looking at them would have guessed how interesting some of them found the information that had been exchanged that day.

Chapter Eighteen

"I found out something very interesting today," Maggie said without any preliminaries.

"As did I." Michaels shut his bedroom door behind the girl and the two of them stood challenging each other.

The travelers had returned, but not until it was almost dark. The ride back had been less interesting and so considerably longer. Everyone was unusually quiet, and back at the Denton place they had gathered in Mrs. Denton's sitting room, waiting wearily for supper to be announced.

Lamb chops didn't offer the challenge that pie crust had, and shortly after their arrival Ethel had a passable dinner of lamb chops and turnips prepared and Maggie had it on the table.

Accompanying her service, she participated in an interesting dumb show with Michaels. Maggie caught his eye first from across the table. She opened her eyes wide, then squinted them together, then turned her chin toward the end of the room, though she meant to direct the gentleman's attention to Miss Christian, who was sitting there.

Michaels, for his part, waited until she came to pour his wine, then looked up into her face, pointed with his fork and knife at the lamb chop on his plate and then looked up at Maggie again and shook his head.

Neither was conveying any information at all to the other, and yet their nods and stares and head jerks continued through the entire meal.

After the diners finished, they gathered once again by mutual consent in the parlor and stumbled somehow into a game of whist. Mr. and Mrs. Denton teamed as partners and proved themselves, even after an exhausting day in the country, a formidable duo.

The play continued for an hour or more, well past the point where the outcome of the game was questioned or the skill of any of the players, though the conducive influence cards have on the general pleasantry of a house party might well have been questioned.

"That does me in," Michaels said, throwing down his cards after yet another sound trouncing. "Miss Christian, I am afraid you were most unfortunate in the partner you drew tonight." He and Miss Christian exchanged dry smiles. His was one of apology, hers was one of agreement. "Rather than shackle you longer, I believe I shall say good-night." He rose and Mrs. Denton gathered the cards fussily.

"It has been a long day for all of us, I suppose. But what an enjoyable time we had!"

It was an indication of how familiarity was callousing them when the air did not immediately fill with fawning seconds to Mrs. Denton's statement. Instead, "goodevenings" were offered, Mr. Denton remarked that his back ached, and Miss Christian suggested that she not be called for breakfast the following morning.

Maggie, up hours earlier than the Dentons or their guests, had been struggling to stay awake until the card players went to bed. She hadn't been entirely victorious in her effort and might have missed the event entirely if Miss Christian hadn't come into the kitchen, where Maggie was dozing.

"Oh!"

"Oh!"

Both girls jumped and looked about them furtively.

"I was just—"

"I had to do—"

"—looking for..."

"—something...finish..."

"—that is, I wondered if I might get a little something to eat."

"—cleaning. Just a spot or two I wanted to get at before morning."

Now they stood studying each other, seeing how effective their excuses were.

"Yes, well, I suppose I am not hungry after all," Miss Christian said, breaking the deadlock first. Maggie ran her hand over the gleaming counter and then bobbed her head.

"Good night, miss."

"Yes."

Miss Christian left the kitchen and in a few seconds Maggie thought she could hear her footsteps on the stairs. Her heart still beating rapidly, and now wide-awake, she waited a few minutes longer and then peeked out of the kitchen doors. All was dark and silent. She slipped the heavy, sensible work shoes off her feet and scurried through the dining room and up the stairs in her stockings. At last she came to the wide door, like most of the other doors in the house, but holding special significance to Maggie, looking darker and more massive than the others.

She looked quickly up and down the dim hallway and then tapped softly.

"Yes?" The voice was muffled and surprised, but Maggie assumed it held an invitation to open the door and come in.

"I found out something very interesting today," she declared as soon as the door had opened wide enough to disclose Michaels standing at the foot of his bed in his shirtsleeves.

As she stepped into the room the gentleman returned his, "As did I." And then before Maggie was aware of what was happening, he closed the door behind her and there they stood. Again. Alone. In Mr. Michaels's bedroom.

She turned quickly and found herself standing so close to Michaels she could feel the heat of his body. Anyway, she felt the heat of somebody's body.

"What?" Michaels asked.

"Wha...?"

"What is it you think you have discovered?"

"Oh." She took a step backward. "Yes." Another step, and now her vision cleared and she thought petulantly that Michaels didn't need to sound so condescendingly indulgent. "I have discovered, Officer Michaels, that when she arrived, Miss Christian was a stranger to both of the Dentons."

Michaels did not appear to attach great significance to Maggie's statement.

"Don't you see? The Dentons didn't know her. She never talks about her family or her background. She never mentions important people she knows or illustrious ancestors in her family tree. Don't you find that peculiar?"

"Not necessarily," Michaels replied coolly, and Maggie felt like stamping her foot or, even better, stamping *his* foot. "Miss Christian has spent a good deal of time abroad. I suppose most of her family is located somewhere on the Continent. We would therefore have no mutual friends, and Miss Christian is a very reserved young woman who doubtless considers my acquaintance too new to merit personal disclosures." He waited for the girl to abandon her position, but when it didn't appear that she was going to, he proceeded with his own, weightier, discovery. "Ethel Cranney was hired without references."

His statement fell into the room like a heavy rock in a puddle of mud.

"And?" Maggie finally supplied the cue..

"And she was not recommended to the Dentons by anyone they knew. She was hired off the street, as it were. Though I do not believe her attainment of this post was that haphazard. Oh, no. Ethel Cranney was very much aware of the seasonal hiring in the Denton household, waited for the proper moment and then appeared, claiming to be a cook. A cook, I might add, who makes a piecrust not distinguishable from chalk paste!" Michaels made his final proclamation triumphantly and felt like striking a pose and crying, "Eureka!" Maggie looked at him blankly.

"Piecrust?"

"I found that curious."

"Piecrust. And you don't find it curious that Miss Christian is a stranger in this house with evidently no familial ties?"

"Not particularly."

"Then I suppose I must continue to investigate," Maggie said thoughtfully. Michaels looked at her determined, adorable face and his lips twitched treacherously.

"You have decided to become a sleuth?" he asked. "I fear the Bow Street runners are facing serious competition."

Suddenly Maggie's clear blue eyes were blazing.

"I'll not have you taking that tone with me!" she cried. "And if you would cease being a conceited ass for one brief moment, you would see that my discovery is every bit as valid as your own."

Now Michaels was offended.

"You expect me to seriously consider the fumbling efforts of a . . . a *child* and discount my own years of criminal experience?"

Maggie raised her eyebrows at the gentleman's questionable phrase but refused to answer him. He stood frowning down at her, breathing heavily through his nostrils.

She thought he looked dangerous, frightening.

He thought she looked haughty, infuriating.

She knew he didn't have the sense he was born with if he refused to listen to her, and he knew he was not going to listen to the ridiculous ramblings of a giddy schoolgirl.

Suddenly, completely without warning and seeming to come as a surprise to them both, Michaels grabbed the narrow shoulders under her worn muslin blouse and pulled the girl to his chest. He bent his head and roughly kissed the lingering jeer off her taunting red lips. She threw her arms around his neck and ardently returned the kiss. He lifted her into his arms and carried her to his bed, their lips still locked. He sank with her onto the mattress, and then, supported by the bed frame, he was free to let his hands rove over her body. Which they did.

"Maggie!"

It was Mrs. Bern, calling from downstairs. Maggie and Michaels pulled away from each other and shared a look of complete surprise, as if neither one of them knew where they were or what on earth they were doing.

Quickly Maggie sat up, then Michaels sat up; then Maggie stood up and smoothed her hair, and Michaels stood up and carefully tucked in his shirttail, which had, somehow or other, come loose. Maggie reached up to his collar and tugged on it to make it lie straight, and Michaels brushed a few strands of hair off her cheek.

"If you make any other startling discoveries, please feel free to report them to me," he said, which seemed to surprise him as much as everything else.

"I certainly will," she said coolly, then hurried to the door to answer Mrs. Bern's summons before, heaven forbid, that worthy lady came looking for her.

"Tomorrow night, then?"

"After dinner."

She stepped through the door, Michaels closed it behind her, and they stood on either side of it, both with heaving chests, neither understanding exactly what had just happened.

Chapter Nineteen

Having picnicked at the cliffs and toured Dover Castle, all that was left for the Denton house party to do was to exchange house calls with their few neighboring vacationers.

Mr. and Mrs. Pasley took the cottage immediately to the north of them. Mr. Pasley was the retired owner of a dry goods store. The little store, which had barely provided the necessaries of life to him and his growing family, would hardly have allowed Pasley the generous retirement fund that gave him comfortable chambers in town and the cozy Dover cottage he and his wife summered in from late April to early November every year. But a cousin of his had died, leaving behind a lot of money and only a few blood relatives. The inheritance came at a time in his life when both of his daughters were married and living half the kingdom away and his son had joined the navy. The money, which a few years earlier would have gone to his children, he was able to keep for himself and his wife now.

The Pasleys were common people. Commoner even than Mr. and Mrs. Denton, though Mrs. Denton would have been scandalized to have it suggested that she was common. They were not coarse, certainly, but having

come into their money late in life they knew nothing of
the theater, the music hall or any travel other than from
London to Dover and back again. They were also advanced in years, with failing hearing and eyesight and
sedentary habits. The Pasleys were not, in short, acquaintances who would contribute measurably to the
gaiety of the Dover locale for Mrs. Denton's guests.

To the south was a modest little house that a certain
knight of the realm loaned out to poorer relations. The
people who took that place tended to be a much livelier
group, sometimes consisting of a whole houseful of
young people. Though not well-to-do themselves, they
usually knew people who were, and they were always
wonderfully informed on all of the scandals in the peerage.

The only trouble was that they were new people every
year, and the intricacies of introductions, calling cards
and exchanging formal visits had to be observed anew
every year before any sort of friendly intercourse could
be established. When, and even if, the house would be
taken each summer was also uncertain. When the Dentons arrived in the middle of June the house was still
closed, and Caroline watched it fretfully, hoping for signs
of life soon.

Of course, there were the Lennins, the Barkers and
Widow Trevor beyond the Dentons' nearest neighbors,
but they were all rather colorless people of the Dentons'
maturity. Mrs. Denton had never objected to them before, had even looked forward to the exchange of winter
news and the several evenings of card playing she and her
husband could look forward to every summer, but this
year she wished she could offer more to her guests.

Ah well, one works with what one has. There was always the hope that Sir Averly's house would fill with amusing people later in the summer.

"I have sent a note across to Stanley and Geraldine Barker inviting them in for tea."

"Today?" Mr. Denton asked. They sat alone in the dining room. The windows in here were in the east wall, and in the morning the room was quite cheery. With the shadows of afternoon it became gloomy and ever so much more formal.

Mr. and Mrs. Denton waited now for either or both of their guests, neither of whom had made an appearance yet this morning.

"Yes," Mrs. Denton answered. "Oh, that reminds me, I shall have to speak with Mrs. Bern."

Mrs. Denton need hardly have announced that she would be speaking to Mrs. Bern and Mr. Denton didn't bother to reply. Besides, they were interrupted at that point by Mr. Michaels.

"Up rather late, aren't you?" Denton asked. His wife was surprised by the tone of accusation in her husband's voice.

"I had some things to do last night." Denton looked up sharply, but Michaels was directing his attention to his wife by then. "And what a charming picture you present, Mrs. Denton, sitting in that pool of sunlight. Scones this morning? Ah, and sliced ham. I might prefer coffee, if there is any?"

Mrs. Denton, pleased, flattered and hoping to atone for her husband's rudeness, hastily assured Mr. Michaels that hot coffee was certainly attainable in the Denton house and gave the service cord a healthy yank.

Maggie hurried into the room, received the order and hurried out again, avoiding Michaels's eye but struck by his presence nevertheless, as if by a splash of cold water.

"Coffee," Ethel grumbled. "And what's wrong with tea, I should like to know? Always making more work for me to do. 'What is it we can have Ethel do now?' they asks themselves. So it's coffee this morning."

By the time her complaints had faded out, the beans were ground and the coffee was brewing. When Maggie returned to the dining room with the coffee urn, Miss Christian had finally joined the party. It was she talking as Maggie entered the room.

"A tea party. How very pleasant, I'm sure. Barkers, you say? Friends?"

"Acquaintances would be a more exact description."

"I see." Miss Christian nibbled at her scone and Mr. Michaels stood, offering to bring her a cup of coffee. "No, thank you. If I decide to have coffee I believe I can get it for myself."

Maggie tightened her lips at Miss Christian's cool dismissal of the gentleman yet still refused to meet his eye when he presented his cup for coffee.

"And where is it the Barkers hail from?" Miss Christian asked.

"Oxford, I believe," Mrs. Denton said. "Would you take a little marmalade?"

Mrs. Denton summoned Mrs. Bern for a prolonged conference directly after breakfast, leaving Maggie to clean the kitchen alone. Working unsupervised, her thoughts all atumble, Maggie was slow and inefficient. Two hours later she was still not finished with a job that usually took thirty minutes.

She was going over and over the scene in Michaels's room yesterday evening. She was no longer trying to make sense of it; *that* she had given up as hopeless. No, she just enjoyed thinking about it, to think about the fire of his kiss, his strength as he carried her effortlessly to the bed, and then, well, the actual activity on the bed. As chaotic as it had been, Maggie could still feel the warmth of his hand everywhere he had touched her.

Dreamily she was rewiping the counter that she had wiped a dozen times, while on the other side of the room another counter was still dirty, though she had passed it with her damp rag a dozen times.

"Maggie."

The girl recognized his voice and spun around to face the doorway, where Michaels had stopped, surprised to find the room occupied, his thoughts and purpose thrown into confusion when he saw by whom it was occupied.

"Mr. Michaels," she said, just as surprised.

"I didn't expect to find you in here," he said.

At that innocent statement, for some perverse reason, no doubt having something to do with the mysterious nature of women, Maggie chose to take offense.

"Oh?" she asked, her brows arching to match the tone of voice. "And whom did you expect to find here in the kitchen, Mr. Michaels? Miss Christian, perhaps? You were hoping for a private, secluded meeting with her now, I suppose."

Michaels scowled at her for her temper and then at himself for having been made to feel guilty.

"I am investigating your allegations, Miss Landers," he said, his voice stern in an attempt to cover his embarrassment at the excuse he felt compelled to offer her. "I wondered where the cook spent her days. I am, in case you had forgotten, attempting to clear your name and

reputation before you are brought before the magistrate
on certain charges.''

"*I* haven't forgotten," Maggie said. "Though I think
you are wasting your time."

"We had both better hope that I am not wasting my
time, Maggie," Michaels said quietly, jarring the girl
from her petty jealousy. "You wouldn't like Botany Bay.
And I don't think I would, either."

Maggie's eyes opened like a morning glory and sharply
she drew in her breath.

"Mr. Michaels?"

"We will discuss it later. But we should cease to work
at cross purposes, don't you think?"

"Yes." Maggie was stunned by what Mr. Michaels had
so casually suggested and doubted that she understood
him entirely. She didn't dare allow herself to understand
him, in fact.

"Then where *does* Ethel Cranney spend her days?" he
asked.

"What?" she said distractedly.

"Ethel. Where does she spend the day?"

"In her room."

"All day?" Maggie nodded. "Where is her room?"

"Down there." She pointed down the hall past the
kitchen. "The room right before mine."

Michaels passed the girl as he made his way to the hall
and she fell in behind him, directly on his heels.

The hall was dark, especially after the bright kitchen.
Michaels would have passed the door if Maggie had not
laid her hand on his shoulder. She meant just to touch his
shoulder, to alert him, but it was such a broad, muscular, terribly *nice* shoulder that she laid her hand flat
against its warmth, nor did she remove her palm immediately.

Michaels stopped, more electrified by the slight weight on his shoulder than he would have liked the girl to know, even after his partial confession. He turned to look at her, her face a pale beacon in the twilight of the hall, and raised his eyebrows questioningly. She nodded. He put his ear against the door and she held her breath. In a few moments he straightened.

"I don't hear anything," he whispered.

"She may be asleep."

"I don't even hear any breathing." He pressed his ear to the door again and then shook his head. "Are you sure she is in there?"

Maggie looked surprised but shrugged her shoulders. Unless Ethel was cooking she was never in the kitchen, and Maggie had never stopped to question before where the cook went. When Maggie had returned to this room after breakfast and found it empty, she had simply assumed Ethel was in her usual retreat.

Michaels raised his clenched fist, and before Maggie was sure what he was doing, he rapped his knuckles against the wood directly in front of his face. They waited silently for a moment or two, Michaels with his ear almost against the door and Maggie stifling her breath against his arm, which neither of them found unpleasant. There was no reply, so Michaels knocked again, a little louder this time but hardly pounding on the door even yet.

Still no response.

Michaels dropped his hand to the latch and pulled. The catch disengaged and the door swung open.

The room was a duplicate of Maggie's small room: the bed, the two-drawer dresser, the small window looking out onto the back lawn. Yet there was a subtle difference that clearly marked this as the room of a heavy, middle-aged woman rather than that of a slight young girl.

The bed was unmade, the covers piled sloppily at the foot. The area of bed mussed was broader, the impression in the mattress deeper. A brown homespun skirt was laid across the chair, a considerable expanse of material. There was still water in the basin that sat atop the dresser, cold, with a film of soap over it. Water had splashed out onto the floor and had not been wiped away. Everything was somehow dingy looking, from the dusty floor to the foggy window to the cobwebs in the corner of the ceiling. Maggie had put a cheery little sampler on her wall from her room at home, one that announced with daisies and bluebirds that Charity Begins at Home; these walls were bare and somehow grayer for it.

The room smelled faintly of onions.

But as evident as it was that this was Ethel Cranney's room, Ethel was not there.

"Where is she?" Maggie asked.

Since it was the question Michaels had been about to put to her, he had no answer for her.

The mystery of what Ethel did with herself when she was not in the kitchen remained unsolved. Michaels hastily searched the room, opened a few drawers, pawed through the dull wardrobe, but no stolen Denton loot was uncovered. Someone approaching the open kitchen door triggered his and Maggie's hasty return to that room, which they did only just as Mrs. Bern entered the other door looking for Maggie. She found the girl in the still not entirely clean kitchen, along with Mr. Michaels, concerning whom Mrs. Denton had just inquired. The two of them conveyed the distinctive aura of guilt and Mrs. Bern tightened her lips. Mr. Michaels, no doubt, casually dallied his way through the serving staff of every home he visited, but Maggie was a sweet young thing, unaware, the housekeeper was sure, that these breathless assignations had no meaning to a gentleman of quality. The girl must be put on her guard, and if she refused to be, then it was fortunate indeed that henceforth Mrs. Bern would be on hers.

"Maggie, there will be guests for tea, so you need to tidy the sitting room. And Mr. Michaels, you are wanted in the garden, I believe." Mrs. Denton had not actually summoned the young man, but she had wondered aloud where he had gotten himself—gotten something *for* himself, anyway, Mrs. Bern thought censoriously, choosing one of the few times these two young people had been alone together when there was nothing for which to censor them—and that lady was now in the garden, a safe distance away.

Maggie looked up quickly at Mr. Michaels and then hurried away to the sitting room. Mrs. Bern waited, with lips pursed, until Mr. Michaels quit the kitchen, too, and then she went to join the girl with much motherly advice, which she knew, just from Maggie's last look at the gentleman, would fall on deaf ears.

Maggie dusted and swept up the sitting room, pretending to listen to Mrs. Bern's warnings but hearing instead Mr. Michaels tell her he would not like Botany Bay, either. She sensibly tried to put all sorts of meanings to the words: no thinking man would like the penal colony on the desolate continent half the world away, including Michaels; she wouldn't like it any more than he would if he was the one sentenced there for robbery; there were any number of places where Mr. Michaels would not like to be, Botany Bay among them. But she always heard his quiet voice in the back of her mind, and her initial impression remained that if she was exiled, he would go with her.

The idea made her heart thump against her breast. It also distracted her from her cleaning and more than once Mrs. Bern was forced to interrupt her lecture to point out a place Maggie had missed.

When the two ladies returned to the kitchen they found Ethel there, murmuring unhappily over the formal tea party that had been sprung on her for that afternoon, and which she evidently saw as another deliberate swipe at the cook and her hard lot.

She inquired sullenly of Mrs. Bern if they would expect tarts at this fancy tea, but the housekeeper hastily assured Ethel that tarts, in fact pastry of any kind, would not be required.

Maggie volunteered timidly to make the sugar cookies her family had enjoyed in Huntingdon, and was relieved when Ethel, far from being offended by the suggestion of an invasion of her kitchen, seemed to welcome the offer of the little maid to share the labor. Mrs. Bern had no objection, either, and Maggie was soon stirring, rolling and cutting out the wafers.

The cookies, sandwiches, pickles, bread and butter and jelly, thinly sliced ham and the few fresh summer vegetables Mrs. Bern and Maggie had been able to find in the garden were prepared and on dainty serving plates when the Barkers arrived at four o'clock.

Maggie was in her stiff white apron and answered the door.

"Mrs. Denton, Mr. and Mrs. Barker," she announced woodenly to the gathering in the parlor.

That Mr. and Mrs. Barker were tall was Maggie's initial and most forceful impression of the couple. Mr. Barker was taller even than Mr. Michaels, who stood for the introductions. Mr. Barker's shoulders, however, were narrower than Michaels's, though Mrs. Barker's shoulders nearly matched those of the policeman in their width.

"Geraldine, Stanley. Come in. It's been simply ages since we saw you last. But you are looking as lovely as ever, Geraldine."

Geraldine Barker was a long-faced woman with heavy eyebrows, a nose that approached a length where it might more descriptively have been called a proboscis, and absolutely colorless lips. Yet studying her face discreetly, Maggie could see that Mrs. Denton had not been offering merely empty flattery; Mrs. Barker was very likely as lovely now as she had ever been.

Mrs. Denton sent Maggie after Mrs. Bern, whom she was sure would want to say hello to these old friends. Mrs. Bern left the kitchen issuing final instructions for the serving of the tea, which commenced as soon as the housekeeper returned.

The pickles and condiments went out first, while introductions were still being made.

"Mr. Barker, what a pleasure to meet you. Mr. Denton says that you are retired? From what noble calling, if I may be so bold as to ask?" Miss Christian was saying. Barker and the young lady stood near the table, so Maggie could hear them clearly.

"Investments. This and that, my dear. If a man is canny enough or lucky enough he may do himself a lot of good occasionally. 'Making a killing' is the rather grim phrase for an extremely happy event."

"And did you make many of these 'killings'?" Miss Christian asked as Maggie deliberately straightened and repositioned the dishes she had carried in.

"My fair share. Or rather more than my fair share, in point of fact," Barker remarked cheerfully.

Maggie returned to the kitchen for her next armful.

"Put the sandwiches and fresh vegetables to the left of the center of the table," Mrs. Bern cautioned. Maggie nodded and hurried back into the sitting room. Mrs. Bern was interested only in the serving of tea, but Maggie, concerned with that, too, of course, was also trying to carry on a criminal investigation.

Mrs. Denton was now beginning to lead the migration to the tea table, making the socially correct remarks concerning the pleasantness of afternoon tea and what a convenient excuse it provided for friends to meet.

"We do indeed make the same annual trip Caroline and Franklin make, though we've a ways farther to come," Barker was saying, offering the young lady his arm.

"Oxford, did Mrs. Denton say? What lovely country." Miss Christian smiled.

Maggie left the room again, to return moments later with the bread and ham and the plate of her cookies that Mrs. Bern had arranged so beautifully. Now Mr. Denton was inviting Mrs. Barker to sit, and though Mrs. Denton and Mr. Michaels had taken their places, Miss Christian detained Mr. Barker.

"Oh, yes, the Barkers have been accused of being scholarly more than once, I am afraid." Barker laughed. "One is practically required to be if one lives in Oxford, I suppose. And now our son, Claud, has made it international by attending the University of Paris."

"Really? Oh, how thrilling. I have traveled a little on the Continent myself..."

A little? Maggie thought in surprise as she carefully deposited the plate of cookies almost directly in the middle of the table, leaving room only for the teapot, which she would bring in last of all. From what she had heard Miss Christian tell the Dentons, you might have thought Miss Christian annually guided tours through Europe.

"...but have never had a chance to actually *study* abroad."

"Caroline, why don't you ask Mrs. Bern to join us for tea?" Mrs. Barker said as Maggie prepared to leave again.

"I think that would be lovely, if you are sure you don't mind?" Mrs. Denton said. Mr. Barker looked across to his hostess and heartily assured her that Mrs. Bern would be a welcome addition to the tea party.

So it was Mrs. Bern who took out the teapot and the hot water, and Maggie was left to wonder what else Miss Christian was learning about Oxford, the Barkers, his comfortable income and their son, Claud, studying abroad.

Even her distaste for Miss Christian's nosiness—which a more callow, confiding Maggie would have termed, "polite interest"—might not have blossomed into another full-blown suspicion if the young lady had not called for a cup of hot milk before she went to bed.

Miss Christian, with a delicate temperament, did occasionally request warm milk at night and Maggie usually provided the service. Tonight was no exception.

The tea party had lasted well past eight o'clock. The Barkers and Dentons had winter reports to make to each other, which were retarded by Mrs. Denton's attempts to interest and involve her young guests in the conversation. Then Michaels was called upon for more of his lurid crime stories. Mr. and Mrs. Barker hung upon his every word, horrified and delighted by this rare glimpse they were allowed into the wicked London underworld.

They, too, commented jokingly on Michaels's apparent familiarity with his subject.

Finally someone suggested cards. The someone was Mrs. Denton, who really did have a passion for the game, and though a six-handed game might have been played, Miss Christian had captivated Mr. Barker for the evening. Mr. Barker, not surprisingly, did not find his captivity chafing.

More sandwiches were called for. As soon as it was decently dim in the room, Denton lighted the lamps and served drinks to the men. More tea was served. Mrs. Denton asked if there wasn't any cold chicken left. There was. It was produced.

Michaels was partnered with Mrs. Barker and their team was having much better luck than the Christian-Michaels match. No one was anxious to leave the card table, and Mr. Barker was certainly not anxious to leave the fascinating side of Elizabeth Christian, primarily because this beautiful young woman appeared to find him fascinating.

"Oh, Mr. Barker, how perfectly scandalous of you." Miss Christian laughed, tapping him gently on the back of his hand with her porcelainlike fingertips. "And you needn't try to look as if you cannot imagine what I mean."

"Well, Lady Farnsworth *does* enjoy her evening sedative, and it should come as no surprise to learn that its purchase without a doctor's approval would be illegal."

"Mr. Michaels, you deceived us, I am sure," Mrs. Denton cried, watching the pile of cards being drawn to the other side of the table. Again. "I thought you said you did not play often."

"I don't, Mrs. Denton, but everyone is allowed a run of luck occasionally."

On the other side of the room, Mr. Barker leaned toward the young lady. "Well, tell me, Miss Christian," he said, "how is it you find yourself single? I would have thought some eager young puppy would have snatched you up some time ago."

"I am looking for something more substantial than a 'young puppy,' Mr. Barker. I would like a husband with judgment, understanding. And, naturally, a respectable education. I am afraid a young woman without family must be extremely cautious in these matters. Unlike more fortunate girls, concerned only with their maidenly pleasures while responsible adults watch over their futures, I must look for a gentleman who will sustain my welfare through life. It becomes a lengthy search, I have found."

"You've no family, then?" Mr. Barker asked solicitously.

"I've a dear aunt living on the Continent, but she, I am afraid, is my nearest relative."

Mr. Barker "tsked" sympathetically.

The minutes ticked away as the contestants and conversationalists continued to enjoy the evening. Mrs. Denton was absolutely in her glory, at last having gathered a convivial company and hosted an honestly lively social function. In fact, the evening would have been perfect if she and Franklin had won just a few more hands of cards.

It was Mrs. Bern and the Barker coachman who finally broke up the party.

"Your driver has returned, Mr. Barker. Shall I tell him it will be a bit longer still?"

Even then Stanley Barker might have sent his driver away again, and who knows how long the evening would have lasted, if Mrs. Denton had not chosen that moment to win at last a hand and so the current game.

"Perhaps a little longer..." Barker started.

"Oh, no, Stanley. Don't have Phillip make the trip again," Mrs. Barker called. "Or worse, tuck himself away someplace with a bottle of liquor."

Mrs. Denton protested warmly, saying what a pleasant time they were having, and how they hadn't seen one another for months, and what a delight it had been to get together, and all the time being positive that at last the tables had turned and she and Franklin would start to win.

"Oh, thank you, my dear. It has been lovely, but we had better go. It will be pitch-black before we get home as it is. Now, Caroline, we girls must get together sometime next week. Let us definitely plan on it."

"With Claud in Paris, Mrs. Barker and I thought we would make the crossing to visit him later this year. It would be smashing if you could join us," Mr. Barker was saying. He had risen by now, too, and pressed Miss Christian's fingers. Though not given to gallantry normally, he might even have kissed her hand if his wife hadn't pulled him away.

"Maybe we can do some shooting this week or next," Mr. Denton said to Barker.

"Even though we were handicapped with me as a partner, I thought we were formidable," Michaels told Mrs. Barker.

"Franklin, their driver is waiting. You and Stanely can plan your lethal assault on the local game another time," Mrs. Denton scolded.

And, "Your invitation sounds delightful, Mr. Barker," Miss Christian said. "I will consider it."

Finally the visitors were away and a peaceful quiet descended on the room. Michaels picked up one of the few remaining slices of bread, dried out by now, and put a piece or two of the chicken meat against it. He contentedly stood munching as Mrs. Denton surveyed the room.

"Should I have Ethel fix us some supper?" she asked as Miss Christian sank into one of the sprawling, overstuffed chairs.

"Not for me," the young lady sighed.

"Michaels and I can make do with what's left here," Denton said, joining that gentleman at the tea table and quickly claiming the last crisp cookie on the plate before the younger man saw it.

Mrs. Denton sat on the sofa across from Miss Christian.

"Good," she said, relieved that she did not have to face another meal that evening. Instead, her eyes slowly closed and she dozed.

Michaels and Denton, of whom either one alone might have fared well on the scraps, were finding the pickings lean. Unexpectedly the air filled with a soft humming, a gay folk tune, and Maggie entered, carrying a plate of sliced bread and ham. Denton, who distrusted the girl and honestly believed she was blatantly robbing him blind, was tempted to kiss her on her pretty red lips, which were pressed together to produce the hum.

Michaels, for his part, could barely restrain himself.

Maggie smiled up at both of them, and then, catching the look in Michaels's eye, she blushed ever so slightly.

"Might I take these things?" she asked, stacking several of the empty plates.

"A fair enough exchange, it seems to me," Denton said jovially, having personally relieved her of the burden with which she entered the room.

The remainder of the evening went slowly, quietly, flowing like an all-but-stagnant pool of water until Mrs. Denton finally roused herself and announced that she and Mr. Denton would say good-night. Denton, who had been reading a mildly interesting book of history—his interest in history had been revived with his visit to Dover Castle and Miss Christian's flattering interest in him and his historical facts—was surprised by his wife's decree, but the book was not so very interesting, and now that she mentioned it, his soft bed did sound inviting.

"Mr. Michaels. Miss Christian," he said, rising to accompany his wife.

Miss Christian yawned delicately, patted her finely sculpted pink lips with her thin, fragile fingertips and rose slowly to her feet—her small, elegantly clad feet.

"It is a bit early, but it seems later. I believe I will retire, as well."

Michaels looked up at the deserting party and settled himself more firmly, if possible, into the comfortable leather chair he had claimed. He held up his own book, a book of political essays from a bygone regime, to account for his decision to stay in the parlor. A better explanation might have been provided by the sounds of activity in the kitchen, which were still floating into this room, but only Michaels understood that.

It was after Miss Christian was in her room and Mrs. Bern had been instructed to make sure all the lights were extinguished once Mr. Michaels went to bed, that the young lady rang for the warm milk.

Dutifully, if not with a glad heart, Maggie heated the milk, poured it carefully from the saucepan into the glass container and carried it up the stairs and down the hall to the luxurious room that had been assigned to Miss Christian.

"Come" was the reply to Maggie's short, hard knock.

The little maid opened the door and entered. The room was darkened except for the lamp on the writing table. Miss Christian sat at that table in a white, flowing dressing gown. She should have been luxuriously sprawled on her bed, surrounded by pillows and comforters. Instead, she was writing busily in a rather bulky notebook.

"Bring that over here," she told the girl, barely glancing up.

As Maggie bent to place the glass, with the doily underneath it, on the desk at the lady's elbow, her eyes fell on Miss Christian's writing. Since Miss Christian made no attempt to cover the text, it is very likely she assumed the maid could not read. But Maggie Landers had been reading since she was a child at her mother's knee and Mrs. Landers had turned the pages while Maggie struggled to decipher the thrilling story about the terrible wolf and the damsel with the red cloak. In fact, Maggie had doubtless learned to read before Miss Elizabeth Christian did.

Stanley and Geraldine Barker was the heading on the paper. Underneath that was printed a careful column.

£12,000 per annum
36 rooms, Oxford
4 domestics

Then there was a space, and in a separate paragraph that she was just finishing as Maggie bent over the desk, the young woman had written, "Two children. Daughter, married, Scotland. Son, Claud. Studying abroad."

Miss Christian drew a line under the last two phrases and then become alerted to the fact that Maggie was looking over her shoulder and had been for a very long moment. Hastily she shut the notebook, more an automatic response than from any fear that the serving girl could read what she had written.

"That will be all."

Maggie, like a courtier from a royal chamber, backed obsequiously from the room.

She stood peering over the railing, waiting impatiently for Mr. Michaels. In only a few minutes, as if in answer to her urgent summons, she saw the light from the sitting room dim and go out as the lamps that lined the room were snuffed one by one. At last, the wavery glow of a candle preceding him, Mr. Michaels came out into the main hall and crossed to the stairs.

Maggie meant to call out to him as soon as he left the sitting room, but she took a moment to appreciate the glow of the candle on his face. It was a handsome face, certainly, but the girl was no longer most impressed by that, as she had been the day he first presented himself at the Denton town house. Now she saw his honesty, his dedication, his passion and compassion. And she also saw the frown of concentration and dared believe she knew why and about whom he was troubled. She whispered his name.

Although he had been listening for her from the sitting room and knew when she left Miss Christian's room overhead, still her form, which hovered almost transparent at the head of the stairs, startled him. As soon as he was close enough to be heard in a loud whisper he spoke.

"What is it?"

"In your room," she whispered back.

When he reached her side he took her hand and pulled her behind him into the dark chamber.

"What is it?" he repeated.

"The door," she whispered up at him, spraying him with a fine mist. He closed the door. She started to speak, but with his fingers against her lips he stopped her and took a moment to light two more candles and to set his candlestick down. Finally he turned to her.

"What is it?" he said in a voice that he meant to be fairly normal but which came out very low and mysterious in the dark room.

"She has a notebook full of very curious notes," Maggie said, or rather half whispered.

"Who has? Ethel?"

"No. Miss Christian."

"Maggie, you must forget about Miss Christian. Let us concentrate our efforts on the cook, find out where she goes of an afternoon when she is ostensibly in her room, discover, if we can, what she did with that box of silverware."

"Listen to me," she shushed him. "Just listen to me. I know you are reluctant to suspect the lovely Miss Christian of any wrongdoing, but surely you will find *this* questionable."

Michaels relented, unintentionally dividing his attention between what Maggie said and the thought that, speaking of lovely, there was surely nothing more lovely in the world than this silvery gold fine meshwork of hair in the gentle warmth of candlelight.

"As I said, she is keeping some curious notes. I happened to see what she was writing tonight, and on a sheet labeled Stanley and Geraldine Barker she has listed his annual income, the location and size of their home and their family, son and daughter. She seemed particularly interested in the son, who is studying abroad."

Michaels half turned, forced at last to admit that this *was* interesting. As he seemed to study the thick rug underfoot, Maggie helped supply the excuses.

"It could be argued that she is conscientious. Careful to remember new acquaintances," she said.

"New to this part of the country, she is making every effort to fit comfortably into society," Michaels offered.

"Perhaps she found Mr. Barker terribly fascinating. The notebook could be a diary and she wrote down every detail of a wonderful evening she never wants to forget."

"A thick notebook, you say?" Michaels asked. Maggie nodded. "It could be a list of all the homes she has visited."

"I believe it is," Maggie said seriously, and Michaels turned to face her squarely again. "I believe if you studied that notebook you would find a list of homes that would match a Bow Street police list of homes that have been burglarized."

"Can you get that notebook for me?" Michaels asked. Maggie shook her head.

"I don't think so," she said. "I believe I saw it once in one of her dresser drawers, but I have not seen it since then. She must keep it about her person now."

"Then maybe I can lay my hands on it," Michaels said, smiling wickedly. Maggie scowled predictably and shook her head again, this time even more vehemently.

"Absolutely not!" she cried, momentarily forgetting that they were being secretive. Then the candles highlighted the mocking light in his eyes. "It would be too dangerous," she told him coldly. "You could never be commended for a delicate touch, Officer Michaels."

Michaels raised his eyebrows to admit "touché" and continued to smile, at least until he remembered the seriousness of the question. Then he shook his head.

"Any one of the explanations you offered for the notebook could be true. I know you don't trust Miss Christian, but I still believe Ethel Cranney is the thief we are after."

Maggie sighed and raised her hands, ready to protest, then dropped them hopelessly.

"How much more do you need, Mr. Michaels?"

"Stolen goods."

"That bracelet!"

Michaels reached forward and brushed at her cheek gently.

"I found that bracelet in *your* room, Maggie."

"But I told you I found it in her room. Don't you believe me?"

"What I believe is immaterial. The magistrate would consider only the fact that the stolen property was in your possession, hidden by you, and he would draw the only conclusion he could. We have to have something more, Maggie. And we have to have it soon."

His tone had become very serious as they stood close together in the dark room. Now his voice dropped to a rough whisper. He put his fingers against her cheek.

"Oh, Maggie," he murmured. He drew her face to him with the slightest pressure and kissed her softly on her warm lips. "What would I do without you?" he whispered against her cheek. The strength had left her knees, so to support herself she put her hands on his strong shoulders. He took one of those hands and pressed it to his lips and face.

"My love," she sighed.

In one swift motion he gathered her into his arms. He held her carefully, as if she were a piece of fine crystal. Gently he smoothed the hair back from her brow, bending to kiss her eyelids, her temples, the lobes of her ears. He continued to whisper loving phrases against her hair and at last took her hand again and kissed each fingertip. In short, in a rather lengthy good-night, through which Maggie did not hurry him, he proved conclusively that he had, contrary to her claims, a wonderfully delicate touch.

Chapter Twenty

"Now see here, Michaels, I must insist that you do something about this. I have been more than patient in allowing you to carry on your investigation as you saw fit, cooperating in every way I knew, corroborating your story and demonstrating, I do think, the patience of Job with your reluctance to act and the presence of that little crook in my house. What you needed, you said, was more tangible proof. There can be nothing more tangible than the proof of this theft. You must stop the girl or I shall speak to your superiors about your performance, and to my bank about the efficacy of the Bow Street people."

Denton had worked himself into something of a flurry. Sweat stood out on his brow and he had the pleasing sensation in the back of his mind of having delivered himself a very fine speech.

"Mr. Denton, I understand your concern. But are you absolutely certain that vase has not merely been misplaced?"

"Oh, it has been misplaced, certainly. And we both know who it was who misplaced it."

The gentlemen were in Denton's private study. It was the morning following the tea party and Maggie's discovery of Miss Christian's interesting notebook and Mi-

238 *Thief in the Night*

chaels's delicate touch. It was early the next morning.
Earlier than Michaels had planned to rise, in fact. But the
policeman's plans were changed with Mr. Denton's knock
on his bedroom door and the whispered instructions that
gentleman gave to meet him in his study as soon as he was
dressed.

The banker obviously had news of some import and
Michaels had hastily washed his face and pulled trousers
on his bare legs. As a policeman, having been roused
from his bed on more than one occasion, he had discovered that the speed with which he could answer one of
these nocturnal summons was improved the less he wore
to bed. Through the years his speed kept improving until
now he slept buck naked. In less than five minutes he
joined Mr. Denton in his study.

The older gentleman had not launched directly into his
diatribe against the policeman and his performance. He
prefaced that speech with the report that he had noticed
today that his aunt's vase was missing. It was missing
from a knickknack shelf in a dim corner of this very
study. It had been a hideous thing, justly kept from the
public eye as far as Denton was concerned, but it dated
from one of the ancient Chinese dynasties and was, in
point of fact, a *very valuable antique*, which phrase
Denton delivered in a chilling tone of voice.

Michaels made the unfortunate inquiry as to which
Chinese dynasty the vase dated from, because for the
moment, he could think of nothing else to say. It was
then that Denton, correctly interpreting the question as
a stall to save the officer from immediate action against
the Landers woman, delivered himself of his fiery speech.

"You claim to be an experienced investigator, but evidently experience has not increased the speed of your
investigations. What else must I lose before you act,

man? What, exactly, are you doing to bring this thief to justice?"

"I have been watching Miss Landers with a policeman's trained eye, I assure you, and I have seen nothing suspicious in her actions. We are hasty to suspect the girl, but, just for example, how would a simple girl from the country know that particular vase had any value at all?"

"Because she is *not* a simple country urchin. Your words, Mr. Michaels—she is clever, a master of disguise."

Michaels, desperately trying to think of some way to pacify Mr. Denton or at least slow him in his headlong haste to have the officer dismissed and Maggie prosecuted, hit upon the unique idea of telling the man the truth.

"I do not believe Maggie is the thief."

"What do you mean?" Denton asked. He was not as stunned by Michaels's pronouncement as Michaels had meant for him to be. Mr. Denton was a fairly intelligent man who could also tell when it was raining outside and whether or not his wife had shaved her head. Now he only tried to make the lad see reason once again. "You suspected her from our first interview in my office. Before you ever met her you described her to me. You found the silver set in her room. Yet she has had free run of my house, as a result of which, an ugly, valuable vase is now missing as well as a set of ugly, valuable silver. The girl has a true financial eye, though admittedly deplorable aesthetic taste."

"Maggie Landers is not the only person in this household, is not the only one with free run of the house."

Denton opened his mouth, then closed it again. He took a calming breath and admitted to himself that Michaels was an experienced officer of the law. Perhaps, just perhaps, what he said had merit.

"Cranney?" he asked when he opened his mouth again.

"That is one possibility."

"She really isn't a very good cook, is she?" Denton said thoughtfully. Then he looked up as Michaels's reply registered completely. "*One* possibility? Who else could you suspect? My wife? Myself?"

"It is my understanding that Miss Christian was not personally known to you or your wife before her introduction on, I believe, the very day that I met her, as well."

"Miss Christian? She is a friend of the Randolphs."

"Introduced to you by them?"

"No.-No, they were leaving for France. A letter of introduction, if I remember correctly."

"Signed by one of the Randolphs?"

"I don't really know." Denton found himself floundering and struggled to find a foothold on good sense. "But see here, Miss Christian is a young woman of quality."

"The thief for whom I am looking is, as you reminded us both, a master of disguise. She has been described as everything from a titled lady to a charwoman."

"But surely you cannot believe..." Denton sputtered. Michaels held up his hand.

"I did not say that I suspect Miss Christian. I, myself, do not. But certain questions have been raised, and even though I am concentrating my investigation for the time being on Ethel Cranney, I wanted you to be aware that there *are* other avenues to pursue before I can make a valid arrest."

"What about the belongings that are disappearing from my house? Must I watch my possessions vanish one by one before my eyes while you are pursuing red herrings up and down every outlandish back street in the kingdom?"

"Certainly not, Mr. Denton. I still believe that the thief, whoever she may be, has not been able to dispose of the merchandise. It must be somewhere in the immediate area and I will be able to return it to you as soon as I apprehend the thief."

"This cannot go on much longer, though, Michaels."

"No, sir."

"Three days."

"Three days? Mr. Denton, police work cannot be scheduled to a specific timetable. I cannot say that within three days the thief will tip her hand."

"The thief has already 'tipped her hand.' I will give you three more days to amuse yourself with your other avenues, and then I want an arrest made and these robberies stopped. You've had nearly a month already. I have no desire to make a permanent houseguest of a Bow Street runner."

"Mr. Denton..."

"Three days."

Before Michaels could protest further, the banker had the study door open and was greeting Mrs. Denton with a surprised comment about how early they were all arising that morning.

Three days was a ridiculous time limit. In London, Bow Street runners would sometimes pursue a criminal for months, assuming elaborate disguises, sometimes adopting a completely foreign way of life in order to bring a criminal to justice. And Denton demanded his results in three days!

Michaels stopped to remind himself that Denton was right. It had been a month since his meeting with Danny in the Brown Bear. And the banker's impatience now could be attributed directly to Michaels himself. The policeman had been suspicious of the newly hired maid, which suspicion Denton had converted to conviction in his own mind. It is very difficult to alter the opinion of a man who believes he has found the light of truth.

Michaels sighed. Three days didn't allow him time to participate in any more of Mrs. Denton's outings and he was afraid his reputation as a convivial guest was about to suffer. With a grim smile, though, he admitted that Mr. Denton was not likely to invite him down to Dover again anyway.

Besides, perhaps he shouldn't be quite so concerned about his future social engagements. His immediate task was to save Maggie Landers's frail little neck from a hangman's noose.

When Maggie awoke that morning she sensed an air of urgency about the house. Mr. Denton and Michaels arose not much later than she did, and as the morning advanced, with Michaels's grim look and Mr. Denton's short replies, with the ladies calling for her and occupying her precious time, the gauze of disbelief that had shrouded this whole robbery accusation began to clear and leave behind it a serious sense of danger. Michaels had told her before, from the very moment he had confronted her with the bracelet, that her very life might be required of her if she was convicted of these thefts, and now the policeman's words would not leave off their ringing in her ears.

Automatically she hurried about everything she did. Time was short and there was much to be done.

She served the breakfast of hot porridge and boiled eggs, aware of Michaels's every breath but unable to delay, to take the time to appreciate his presence.

For his part, the frown of concern never left Michaels's brow. Not when he talked with Mr. Denton, of course. Indeed, talking with that gentleman unfailingly deepened the frown. But Mrs. Denton, offering her most innocuous comments on the weather or Miss Christian's choice of dress that morning, was met with a furious scowl, as well. And Miss Christian, who had always been one of the pleasanter aspects of this assignment—bearing in mind that Michaels was very probably in love with Maggie Landers, in love, not comatose—he now viewed askance, with a certain amount of suspicion that Maggie had forced upon him and also with a crease across his forehead.

Maggie was clearing the table as the house party rose to leave. Mr. Barker's suggestion of going after game of one kind or another was prompting Denton to check his land to see if there was any game on it of one kind or another. Mrs. Denton claimed Miss Christian and told her they really must look over some clothes packed away in an old trunk.

"We might find something amusing or even practical," Mrs. Denton said cheerfully.

Though seemingly otherwise occupied, that good lady had heard Miss Christian's comments to Mr. Barker the day before and her heart had unexpectedly been touched. And for her part, Miss Christian, though not striking one as the domestic sort, seemed perfectly willing to look through the trunk. Mrs. Bern was summoned, but she very practically suggested Maggie attend the ladies if there was going to be a great many errands required. The housekeeper quietly told Maggie she would clean the kitchen if the girl would do the running that day. Maggie readily agreed, since running was exactly what she wanted to be doing.

The trunk was stuffed full of dated clothing of high quality material. Miss Christian may not have been domestic, but she had an excellent eye for value.

"Oh, this brocade is divine. Look, not a thread lost through wear, I am convinced of it." The young woman held up the heavy dress for Mrs. Denton's inspection. It was a glossy dark gray, and looking at it as Miss Christian held it below her chin, Maggie could imagine the young lady in a more modern dress of that material, with perhaps a red flower in her hair or at the waist. She would look, as she was sure Mr. Michaels would agree, spectacular.

"I believe you are right, Elizabeth. This belonged to Mr. Denton's aunt, so there is a great deal of material there. Why, I have a marvelous idea. Rather than let that lie moldering in this trunk, why don't you take it with you? Perhaps you can find a dressmaker who could make you something out of the cloth?"

"Do you think? It is awfully old. Of course, as I said, it is remarkably well preserved."

Miss Christian hesitated; Mrs. Denton continued to press the dress on her. In time the young woman acquiesced and handed the gown to Maggie, to take back to Miss Christian's room.

"I am sure I can put it to some use," she said, looking after Maggie's departing figure doubtfully.

In this game of charity and acceptance, careful rules had to be observed to allow everyone to emerge victorious. The tendered article must not seem too valuable to the giver, nor too eagerly accepted by the taker. It must never be mentioned again. Miss Christian must smile

with a certain superiority and Mrs. Denton must assume
the expression of someone for whom a great service was
being performed.

They found a few other things that Miss Christian
agreed, after prolonged insistence, to "take off Mrs.
Denton's hands." Maggie hauled everything back and
forth, brought out the clothes, showed the material to
either lady, folded, unfolded, packed and repacked. She
was grateful for the opportunity to observe Miss Christian so closely and frustrated when that young woman
did absolutely nothing suspicious or underhanded.

At last the session ended and Maggie was excused. For
once when she entered the kitchen it was spotless. There
were no piles of food of which to dispose, no spilled
flour, no encrusted pots and pans. She stood quietly for
the first time that day and allowed herself to glory in the
cleanliness and the fact that she had not been required to
produce it. But even as she stood, Mrs. Bern and Ethel
entered from either door of the kitchen. And curiously
enough, neither came from the direction one might have
expected. Ethel entered from the dining room door and
it was Mrs. Bern who came through the doorway that led
down the short hall to the bedrooms.

Mrs. Bern, matching the feeling of the whole day, was
slightly out of breath as she reminded Maggie to hurry,
that it was time to prepare lunch, that the table had to be
set, that Ethel wanted some green beans from the garden.

"Where are you going?" Mrs. Bern asked as Maggie
started toward her room.

"I need to get a sunbonnet if I am going to pick
beans," the girl called back to her. Mrs. Bern frowned at
the delay—everybody seemed to be worried about de-
lays—but didn't try to stop her. Besides, she needed to

give Mrs. Denton some idea about when lunch would be served, and Ethel had already gone outside to see what else the garden had to offer.

Maggie rushed into her room, grabbed the bonnet and turned to go. But the handle of her brush caught the corner of her eye and she remembered that she hadn't given her hair a real brushing that morning. And, too, the consideration that she would soon be serving lunch to Mr. Michaels *did* present itself, so she grabbed up the brush and noticed that the bottom drawer of the dresser on which it sat was open. Maggie ran the stiff brush through her hair a time or two and then really did mean to hurry outside to get the beans, but the opened drawer and the sleeve of the nightgown that poked out nagged at her like a pin on the floor of a careful housekeeper. She knelt beside the drawer to straighten things but when she pulled out the length of thin flannel something hard clattered onto the floor. Curiously she picked it up and found it was a miniature painting. Maggie was hardly a connoisseur of the arts, but she recognized the diminutive painting as being valuable. She hadn't ever seen it before, but it was of the size where it might hang on the wall for years and still never be noticed. More probably it had been tucked into this drawer sometime past, perhaps even in some past decade, and only now had become entangled in the sleeve of her nightgown.

Curious, though, she thought as she stood and continued to study the painting. I thought that drawer was empty when I put my things in it.

"Maggie, no one was in the kitchen and I need to talk to..."

Mr. Denton had not asked the young policeman to join him in his inspection of the fields. Michaels could not blame him. Mr. Denton had made it abundantly clear that the younger gentleman was not here to revel in his hospitality but to catch a thief. Michaels appreciated that fact, so watching for his opportunity, he had come to have a few words with Maggie. He noticed that her door was ajar, so he pushed it open, but stopped abrupty when he saw Maggie standing there, when he saw that she was holding something. Something that looked old, and heavy, and possibly valuable.

"What is that?" he asked.

"A miniature painting," she said.

"What are you doing with it?" he asked, more carefully this time.

"I found it in my dresser drawer," she answered, slowly and carefully herself.

"Oh?" he said.

"Yes," she answered.

They stood watching each other silently while the seconds ticked away.

Chapter Twenty-One

A day had passed. The first of the precious three that Denton had given him.

Mrs. Denton wondered aloud if Mr. Lennin would like to join her husband and Stanley Barker when they went shooting, and what it was that Geraldine would arrange for the ladies, but as for that day, she seemed willing to leave her husband and young guests to their own devices. That did not preclude the possibility of some spur-of-the-moment evening fete she might come up with, but for now at least everyone was careful to let sleeping dogs lie.

Michaels made some vague comment about "things he had to catch up on" and excused himself after breakfast. With great show he went up the stairs to his room, only to sneak quietly out and down the narrow back stairs ten minutes later. He was determined to find out what Ethel Cranney did when she wasn't in the kitchen or in her room. Unfortunately, after breakfast she did go directly to her room and stayed there, making audible noise, until she came out to prepare the noon meal. Frustrated, Officer Michaels returned to his room and answered the summons to lunch forty-five minutes later.

Maggie had been kept busy all morning. She could feel the oppressive weight of personal danger gathering about her shoulders with every passing hour, and it was frustrating for her, as well, to be trapped by duties that kept her from helping herself.

Michaels hadn't said anything more to her when he surprised her in her room the day before. He even forgot what it was he had come in to tell her. He appeared to accept her story and believe that the painting she held had only just been discovered by the girl. He made no protests when she silently returned it to the drawer out of which it had fallen. But Maggie was acutely aware of the picture she had presented. It would take a very great amount of either stupidity or fawning love to make the policeman blind to what he saw, and Maggie was sure he was not stupid, and just as sure that any love he might have for her was not the blinding sort.

Nevertheless, or perhaps because Maggie continued to be his most likely suspect, Michaels seemed more determined than ever to fix the blame on the Denton cook.

The lunch she served was a bland hodgepodge of yesterday's this and warmed-up that. To Michaels's eye or, more precisely, to Michaels's palate, it was as sure a proof of the cook's guilt as Maggie's guileless manner had been to Mr. Denton.

Everyone ate sparingly and immediately after lunch they all went their separate ways again. It puzzled Mrs. Denton that her two young, attractive guests did not spend more of their leisure time together, and she determined to address that problem personally. Tomorrow.

This time Michaels said he thought he might go for a walk. Mr. Denton was the only one who took much notice of the announcement, and he only glanced up to frown at the younger man. In his opinion, taking after-

noon walks was not the most efficient method of catch
ing thieves. Michaels refused the challenge and merel
left by the main door. He walked past the windows, dow
the front lane, which could be seen from those window:
not turning until he got among the trees that would hid
his movements from anyone interested enough to b
watching.

He hurried around to the back of the house, trying t
find the kitchen entrance as he came from this unfami
iar angle and which he could see through the trees an
bushes that marked the end of the lawn. He thought b
had found it and was about to step out from his cove
when Ethel Cranney herself stepped out of the door h
was watching and hurried around still yet another co
ner of the house, just when Michaels thought he had bee
around every corner the house could possibly have.

The cook's bulky figure disappeared and Michae
raced across the lawn to the side of the house. Crouch
ing low, he looked around the obstructing corner just i
time to see the last fold of the gray skirt being swallowe
up in the black doorway of one of the outbuildings. F
waited a minute or more, watching the door to make su
the cook was not coming right out again, and then, r
turning to the row of bushes, he kept among them to a
proach the outbuilding. He had the feeling that at last I
was about to discover something of great import.

There was a window at the end of the large shed t
ward which Michaels was making his way. One lo
through that window would put the nails in Cranney
coffin. At last he came parallel with the building an
almost crawling, he sneaked under the window. T
building was large, and the afternoon chatter of birds a
insects seemed unusually loud, so he was not able to he
anything from inside the shed, even with his ear press

against the weatherworn boards. Ever so carefully he raised himself to the height of the window, and then dared the last five inches when his head would be visible from inside the room and he could see through himself.

At last his eyes were level with the window, and then, wide and searching, they were scanning the glass. But it was useless. For many years that glass had been accumulating dust and grime and machinery oil and fly-specks. The window was perfectly opaque. Michaels couldn't see a thing through the glass.

Mrs. Bern shook her head disapprovingly over the lunch Ethel had served. Mrs. Denton would have something to say about this. And she would say it all to Mrs. Bern, at great length, several times over, with few variations. The housekeeper had planned to check the flower garden this afternoon, cut back some of the overgrown autumn flowers and gather a fragrant armful of roses for the front hall. Now, of course, she must keep herself at the mistress's convenience, ready to take her place at the whipping post as soon as she was called.

None of that changed the fact that the flowers ought to be looked to or that roses in the receiving hall would still be very nice, so Mrs. Bern instructed Maggie to see to those labors. It was a pleasant, outdoor job, which she meant as a little reward to the serving girl, but Maggie's gloomy face and dragging step hardly looked rewarded.

The problem was that this would take the girl away from the house, keep her apart from its occupants and prevent her from monitoring the actions of one of its occupants.

But she was the maid in this house, at least until she was charged and convicted of grand theft, so she had no choice but to take the garden shears, put the basket over her arm and attend to the flowers.

The long, dry stalks of last autumn's mums had to be trimmed back to allow the summer growth, so Maggie first dropped her basket there, at the base of the chrysanthemums behind the lilac bushes, and then knelt down beside them with her shears. But before she leveled even one stalk she heard the sound of someone walking, hurrying it seemed, around the house from the front door. She knew immediately who it was and bent herself even lower behind the greenery.

Elizabeth Christian passed quickly in front of the flower garden, and pushing aside leaves and branches, Maggie watched the young woman swiftly cross the back lawn and enter the rickety old building where Mr. Denton kept the farm implements that hadn't been used for fifty years or more. Maggie hadn't ever been in there, but Mrs. Bern, familiar with every spot on the Denton property after so many years, explained its purpose, having fetched a small handsaw from the building herself one day.

Miss Christian was not looking for a handsaw. In fact, Maggie could imagine no legitimate reason in the world why Miss Christian should be skulking into that outbuilding. Admittedly, it was Maggie who was doing the actual skulking, but Miss Christian's actions were undeniably suspicious. Breathlessly, Maggie watched the black doorway at this end of the building, waiting for the young woman to return, hoping fervently that she wouldn't leave by the door at the front of the building, which Maggie couldn't see clearly from her vantage point next to the ground, behind the greening chrysanthemum plants, hidden by the lilac bushes.

She thought that surely she had huddled there for a
half hour or more, when finally the billowy, pale yellow
skirt filled the doorway again and Miss Christian came
back across the lawn, passing directly in front of Maggie. The young woman never glanced down, and Maggie
was as still as death until Miss Christian went around the
house and the girl heard the front door close.

Then, like a jack-in-the-box, she sprang to her feet,
only to drop immediately to her knees again. When she
stood she was able to see the front entrance to the shop
quite clearly, and also quite clearly she saw Ethel Cranney coming out of that door.

Michaels checked his pocket watch. Twenty minutes.
What was Cranney doing in there? For twenty minutes?
He could have put his fist through the glass when he
found he couldn't see in the window. Instead, he stood
stiffly against the boards, waiting for the cook to come
back out again. But it had been twenty minutes and it
occurred to him that a bold confrontation might provide
the evidence he needed, and possibly a confession.

The thought was action, as they say, and he stepped
boldly around the protecting edge of the building, eyes
ablaze, dark hair tousled, shirt pulled loose and trousers
smudged and disheveled. The very picture of an aveng-
ing angel.

What he saw surprised him so much that he almost
didn't duck behind the building to avoid being seen. It
was Miss Christian who had just come from the same
building, hurrying across the lawn in front of the flower
garden. Moments later, Ethel Cranney came out of the
door that faced the back of the house, and Michaels
melted around the building as gracefully as he was able
in his stunned condition.

The cook returned to the kitchen entrance, forcing
Michaels entirely around to the back of the outbuilding.
There he discovered what he would have given fifty
pounds and his firstborn child for twenty minutes
sooner—a clear window that revealed the entire room.
Tempted once again to put his fist through a glass, instead he shook his head and ran his fingers through his
hair, which did nothing to tame his appearance. All he
could do now was inspect the room and try to find out
what made it such a popular meeting place.

From her lookout, Maggie could just barely see the
cook's gray skirt stir the grass as she walked along. When
she couldn't see that anymore she decided Ethel had
reached the house, and then in confirmation of that as-
sumption Maggie heard the faint sound of the dutch
doors being opened and closed.

Once more she stood, this time not so flamboyantly
and gathering her skirts in both hands to raise them well
above her knees, she ran across the open lawn to the side
entrance of the outbuilding Miss Christian had used.
Coming from the bright outdoors, Maggie found the
room pitch-black, and she stood in the doorway for a
minute or more to allow her eyes to adjust. It was just as
well that she had stopped at the entrance, because when
she could see into the building at last, she saw a tipped
wheelbarrow directly in front of her that she surely would
have run into if she had entered blindly.

The shed was a nightmare of grease, broken machinery for which there was not now, had not been for fifty
years and perhaps never had been, a use. Hand plows,
horse plows, a broken spinning wheel and an assortment
of handcarts were shapes that became recognizable to
her. As she picked her way across the floor she also saw

craps and broken machinery that were not at all familiar to her, such as the big, cumbersome collection of boards and metal that might have been anything from a seed planter to an egg sorter at one time.

She was not completely sure what it was she was looking for. But Ethel Cranney and Miss Christian had just spent twenty minutes in this building. Evidently there was something positively compelling about the room. What was it?

Unconsciously, her steps were leading her toward the back of the building, toward the only source of light in the room: a relatively clean window.

"I am looking for a pin," the good wife told her husband one day.

"Is this where you lost it?" he asked her.

"Oh, no," she replied. *"I lost it over in the corner, but the light is better here."*

The same questionable logic brought Maggie to the circle of light coming through the window and a collection of odds and ends sitting on top of a wooden tool chest.

The sun was at the precise place in the sky so that its rays highlighted the odd conglomeration. Distractedly, Maggie looked down at the clutter and the box, her mind running questions about the meeting between the cook and the young guest, wondering if they mightn't have found a more convenient spot to hold a dietary consultation, wondering, vaguely, why the top of the tool chest didn't have any dust on it.

Sharply her attention focused.

Maggie was a tidy little soul who couldn't help but notice that this place was filthy. Some of these things, she was sure, had not been touched in all the years Mr. Denton had owned the property, and who knew how many years it had been before that since his long-dead uncle had used this machinery in his farming? And yet, in the room foul with greasy dirt, there was no dust on top of the toolbox.

Maggie picked the odds and ends carefully off the top of the box because they *were* dirty and lifted the lid. In the center was a small, very ugly oriental-looking vase. Next to it was a miniature painting. It was the same painting she had found in her room and carefully, under the policeman's watchful eye, replaced in the drawer. Someone had taken it out of that drawer and put it in the trunk. Not someone. Now she knew who had done it.

There was also the dull glitter of silverware, brushed with ivory handles, a bulging coin purse and a small box made of unsanded wood that Maggie had last seen in Mr. Michaels's hand as he accused her of being a thief.

Maggie, in her unspoiled country freshness, felt as if she had uncovered the fabulous booty of a pirate king.

Michaels, who had been watching the girl's action surreptitiously from the edge of the window, being very careful not to cast a shadow into the room, felt that way too.

Chapter Twenty-Two

She closed the lid and carefully piled the small household articles on top of it, hoping that she had replaced them so it would not be noticed that they had been disturbed.

"Both of them?" she whispered.

Michaels stood outside the building, his back resting weakly against the wood. He was looking up into the sky, asking himself the same question. More or less. His went something like, The cook and the girl...and Maggie? He endeavored valiantly to unthink the last name and concentrated instead on the other two women.

That would be a perfect partnership. It would explain a lot about the elusive thief. The descriptions and activities of the thief the Bow Street police had been pursuing would be practically impossible for one person to assume. This made much more sense.

"Obviously," Michaels murmured. "I have them."

But it wasn't a happy murmur. He had them, but he was not sure who he had, and the third name would not erase itself from the list.

He hurried back to his room and waited for the girl. He knew she would come; there was no doubt in his mind about that. With the calm faith of a child he sat in his chair, facing the door.

"Come in, Maggie," he said when the tap finally came.

Carefully she opened the door and peeped in.

"Jared?" she whispered.

"Here," he said.

She barely pushed the door open far enough for her to squeeze through. When she finally got past the panel and pushed it closed behind her, Michaels saw that she was holding her apron in one hand, gathered together like a sack. It was bulging and made faint clicking noises when she moved.

"I found it!" she whispered triumphantly.

"Found what?" He still had not risen from his chair. He might have been a judge hearing a case.

"Why, *everything!* Look!"

She went to his bed and emptied the contents of her apron onto the mattress. A tiny metal frame encasing a painting and fifty pieces of silverware or more fell onto the bed, along with an unsanded wooden box Michaels was surprised to see. She turned excitedly back to him.

"I have been watching Miss Christian, as you know," she said. "Actually, today I was cutting flowers, but I saw Miss Christian come out the door, and then I saw *Ethel* come out the kitchen door, and they both went into that old building behind the house. Well, I waited, and when they left I went inside to look around, and I found *this!*" She waved her hand at the bed and then turned back to him, her face shining with pleasure and relief. "So I guess that answers your question, doesn't it?"

"What question is that?"

"You wondered which one it was, and it looks like it is both of them," she said, her voice vibrant with excitement.

"It looks that way, doesn't it?" he said. Michaels was a trained investigator and his voice sounded excited, too. His eyes shone and his lips were upturned, so no one, certainly not a trusting, guileless girl who loved him with every fiber of her being, might have guessed he was not sincere in his pleasure.

But how could he be? The silverware was there, yes, and on top of that was the painting she had been studying in her room. And the bracelet. Everything he had accused her of taking was there. But there were no ivory brushes and no coin purse and no oriental vase. She had not emptied the box, or suggested that there was any more to be retrieved.

"What did you do with it?" Denton asked.

"I had her put it back where she found it," Michaels told him flatly. "I told her we did not want to rouse their suspicions."

"Excellent story."

"It was not just a story, Mr. Denton. We do not know that Ethel and Miss Christian are not involved. In fact, I am firmly convinced one, if not both of them, is."

"Yes, I suppose all three of them could be in it together," Denton admitted thoughtfully. "They *are* all three new to the house."

"Or it might be *only* Mrs. Cranney and Miss Christian," Michaels said. He hoped his voice didn't sound as desperate as he felt. Denton smiled indulgently.

"Yes, all right. It might be any of them. You say you did not actually see any of them add to the box, and

Maggie only brought back what she had been accused of stealing?"

"That is correct."

"And the girl says she was watching Miss Christian Certainly it has occurred to you that what the girl was more likely watching was the building? That she had vested interest in who goes in and comes out of there and what they do and what they may find?"

"That did occur to me, yes," Michaels admitted.

"What was it the girl told you? How did she claim she discovered the box?"

"She said there was no dust on it."

"In a dark building, cluttered and grimy, Miss Landers just happened to notice that there was no dust on the lid of the box. A lid, if I understand you correctly, that was nearly covered with gadgets of one sort or another How very clever and observant our Miss Landers is."

"I knew you would present these arguments, Mr Denton. That as sure as I am that Maggie is not the thief you are that convinced that she is. But you have suggested nothing that would explain the meeting between your cook and your young guest of quality in a farm building in back of your house."

"An explanation may not be necessary. Coincidence."

"Unlikely."

"Granted. And you are correct, most probably not dietary consultation. What we are faced with, Mr. Michaels, is a conundrum. We seem to have three eminently viable suspects, all with motive, means an opportunity, if I understand your police jargon correctly. How do you propose that we 'nab' the real culprit?"

The men were once again in Denton's study. It was a small, cramped room, with bookshelves and desk and two chairs. It didn't allow much room for pacing, but Michaels put what there was to full use.

"We know now where your stolen property is, Mr. Denton. From what I could see, the box surely holds everything you know is missing and a good deal you were not even aware was gone. The danger of you losing anything is past. I suggest, therefore, that we give our thief the opportunity to make one more irresistible take. Cash."

"Cash?"

"Bank notes. A sizable amount."

"Money? *My* money?" Denton spoke with a slightly disbelieving wonder. Michaels had struck a most tender chord.

"That is correct. But it mustn't be your money, not pocket money or even an amount with which the bank has entrusted you."

"It must not?"

"Surely you have noticed that our thief has been taking things that were not readily missed. An old set of silverware, unused for years. A vase, nearly hidden in the shadows of this room. A bracelet supposedly locked away in a safe." Denton looked up sharply and Michaels remembered he had not said anything to the banker about the bracelet. "For example. So she wouldn't take any money that would be readily missed."

"I would readily miss any money," Mr. Denton claimed flatly.

"Yes, I know you would. But for argument's sake, let us say that your aunt left you some money or, better still, left some money unbeknownst to you in this house somewhere."

"If I have not discovered it in twenty-five years, how is our thief to make the miraculous discovery in two days?"

"How indeed?" Michaels said, turning sharply and nearly running into Mr. Denton. "What if..."

He paused, but Denton did not interrupt his ruminations. Despite what he told the police officer, he had considerable respect for his skill.

"What if it is a box *you* found. In with your aunt's things, hidden in a closet or a cupboard. Something you hadn't seen before, or perhaps *had* seen and ignored. There could be stories about certain wealth your aunt was known to have possessed but which was never accounted for. But you..." He paused again and took another turn or two around the room while Denton patiently waited. "You find the box or chest or something, suspect of course that there is money in there... I mean, after the stories you've heard all your life... but you decide not to open the box until a witness from the bank is present."

"I do?"

"Again, unlikely. But not impossible, considering the care you take with money."

"Allowed."

"The box must be placed in the sitting room, awaiting the witness."

"The household aware of it."

"Everyone."

"Talk will no doubt be exclusively about what may be in the box, both in the parlor and in the kitchen."

"Absolutely."

"Is the box locked?"

"It must be."

"Then how will she...?"

"It will be a simple key lock, and the thief we are pur-
uing will surely know how to open such a simple lock.
Doubtless without leaving a trace that it has even been
ampered with."

"Doubtless."

"Then when she takes the money..."

"There must really be money in the box?"

"A great deal of money."

"But I thought that whoever opened the box would be
ur thief."

"Not necessarily."

"No?"

"After the wild speculations, anyone might be tempted
o preview its contents. Even Mrs. Denton."

Mr. Denton nodded his understanding, easily able to
magine his wife sneaking into the sitting room in the
ead of night and forcing the box open. After they re-
ired he might have to tell her...well, something, any-
ay. He hadn't wanted to worry her about any of this so
ar, so his trusting wife still blindly believed they had
ired a passable cook, a maid almost too good to be true,
vere entertaining a friend of friends visiting France this
ummer and a young protégé of his from the bank. Yes,
e might have to tell Caroline just a thing or two.

"So when she takes the money...?"

"Our thief will be the woman who takes the money
nd puts it in the box in the shed."

"Ah," Denton said, nodding sagely.

Chapter Twenty-Three

They stood around the table, silently staring at it. When they did speak it was in hushed undertones, as if in the presence of a holy relic. It did not look like a holy relic. It looked like an old metal box; like any one of the battered metal boxes lying about on the floor of the out building so recently visited by many of them. In fact, the is precisely from whence it had come.

It had taken nearly a week to make all the arrangements. The money had to be wired for and picked up, a without arousing suspicion. The box had to be found cleaned—but not too well—filled, locked and hidden a corner of the massive armoire that sat, largely undi turbed, in the Denton master bedroom from year to yea Mrs. Denton put her heavy riding things in one of th drawers, and Mr. Denton hung his worn, lounge-abou clothing on the rod occasionally. There were old cast-o clothes that had belonged to his aunt and uncle pushe back against the wall of the cabinet, which made it a ideal hiding place for the supposed forgotten cash bo and provided a perfect explanation for its sudden di covery.

"I thought I might find some of Uncle Carlton's hunting things," Denton murmured. "Shooting with Barker, you know." His wife nodded dumbly.

Although it was only the Dentons and their guests in the sitting room, as Michaels had predicted, the box was also the sole topic of conversation in the kitchen.

"Mrs. Denton said she always knew the old woman had more than they ever got," Maggie whispered to Ethel. Ethel nodded.

"A *lot* more is how I heard it," the cook said.

"So what do you think is in the box? Jewels? Gold?"

"Too quiet for jewels," Ethel said, pausing to consider. "Not heavy enough for gold. Bank notes would be my guess."

"Really?" Maggie gasped.

"Really what?" Mrs. Bern asked, coming through the kitchen door.

"Ethel thinks the box is full of bank notes," Maggie confided softly.

"Stuff and nonsense," Mrs. Bern said. She had just left this conversation in the sitting room. She might have been forgiven if she sounded weary of the subject. But like the rest of the household, the other two servants couldn't seem to get enough of it. It had been their breath of life since Maggie raced back to the kitchen with the news that morning. She had been cleaning up after breakfast when Mr. Denton lugged the box downstairs and plunked it onto the dining table, right in the middle of the dirty dishes.

"You will never *guess!*" she cried, hurtling into the kitchen, dropping a teacup, which shattered on the floor ignored. "Mr. Denton only just found a tin box in his closet he thinks has been there since his aunt lived here." She lowered her voice to the conspiratorial whisper where it had remained for the rest of the day. "He *believes* there is treasure in it. Old Mrs. Bellweather's forgotten treasure, he says."

Michaels, for his part, was beginning to feel like a scurvy villain for keeping Maggie in the dark this way. When the truth finally came out and she was vindicated as he knew she would be, it would appear to her that she had been suspected just as seriously as Ethel Cranney or Elizabeth Christian. And of course that was not true. Not at all. That is, Denton continued to suspect the girl, yes, but not Michaels. Certainly not.

Nevertheless, his silence made him feel guilty during the preparation period, and his excuses for the additional time they had been allowed were weak at best.

Even with the extra week, they made no further discoveries, either of them. They witnessed no more strange meetings, nothing else was taken from the house, and no one but Mr. Michaels, searching for a metal box with a simple key lock, went out to the shed.

During that week, Mrs. Denton turned her full attention to "getting the young people together." Her effort failed dismally. Try as she might, the young people refused to be paired.

She would suggest they see if the apples were coming on yet. It would have been a cool, romantic ramble under the shady fruit trees. But Miss Christian was nervous about the bees, so Mr. Michaels checked the apple trees alone and reported that the crop would probably be sparse this year. Mrs. Denton was not surprised.

Since their evening of cards, neither had seemed anxious to have the other as a playing partner, and Miss Christian did not sing nor did Mr. Michaels play the piano. Their literary tastes were extremely dissimilar, and

Miss Christian had evidently lost interest in Michaels's colorful stories of crime.

None of those considerations needed to have mattered. The fascination and attraction of their mutual good looks alone should have been enough to pair the two of them. And Mr. Michaels, to credit his male gender sufficiently, *was* spellbound by Miss Christian's somber beauty for a time. He might have been held spellbound indefinitely had Miss Christian, extremely adept as she was at the art of fascination, flattered his ego a bit more. But the young woman seemed to have wearied of Mr. Michaels's stories *and* Mr. Michaels.

When first they had met, she gave the distinct impression that she found Mr. Michaels intriguing. She sought out his company, she spoke to him in private undertones when they were together, her eyes seldom left his face, whether she was sitting next to him or he was across the room.

Now she did not choose to sit next to him if the choice was hers; she would just as often, or more often, turn to talk to Mr. Denton instead of the younger man; she would gaze off into the distance when he spoke to her, and even once, delicately to be sure, she yawned.

Mr. Michaels, of course, was aware of the change, but Mrs. Denton was determined that these two become romantically involved. So she had them take the phaeton out together and run a few errands. They ran the errands, not exchanging more than a dozen words while they were gone.

One evening she thought it might be jolly if they read a scene from a play, each taking a different part. She insisted on the tragically romantic suicide scene from *Romeo and Juliet*—which was not her husband's idea of jolly—and gave, predictably, the lead parts to Miss

Christian and Mr. Michaels. Her husband was Friar
Laurence, Mrs. Bern was called upon to be the nurse, and
Mrs. Denton supplied the additional voices.

Her two young guests were terrible actors. They read
their parts woodenly, they refused to do any physical
business, and by the time the long scene had dragged to
its final, dreary, "For never was a story of more woe/
Than this of Juliet and Romeo," Mrs. Denton was forced
to agree with her husband that perhaps this had not been
her jolliest choice of entertainments.

She and Miss Christian had called upon Geraldine
Barker one afternoon.

"Caroline, my dear, you look a little fatigued. Are you
feeling quite well?" Mrs. Barker commented.

Mrs. Denton was not surprised that she looked wrung
out; she felt wrung out.

"But, Miss Christian, you are as fresh as a daisy. This
sea air certainly agrees with you."

Mrs. Denton was also not surprised that Miss Christian looked untired.

Tea was served and the ladies sat around the tea table
quietly munching cress sandwiches and tea cakes. The
men were not included in this little party so nothing more
substantial was offered.

"Stanley just brought the news back with him from
town," Mrs. Barker offered. "It appears Sir Averly is no
letting his cottage this year. I regret that. Usually Sir Av
erly's guests are a convivial group. But we shall have to
make merry ourselves this year, I suppose."

If Mrs. Barker regretted the failure of the Averly cot
tage to be filled, Mrs. Denton was devastated. She cam
away from the tea nearly a beaten woman. What she had
imagined would be a wonderfully lively, gay and roman
tic summer with two beautiful, energetic young people

was wearing her to a frazzle. It might not have if the young people had been only a touch energetic themselves, but Mrs. Denton was finding it exhausting to supply the energy for *everyone* in her house. Usually she only had to entertain Franklin, who, after forty years, had become relatively easy to please.

And then this morning, her husband had staggered down the stairs with a bulky metal box, saying something about the unaccounted-for wealth his aunt had surely possessed. Hadn't he always told her there must be something more? Actually, when first he said it this morning she couldn't remember that he had ever suggested any such thing, but by the time he had repeated it to Mr. Michaels and Miss Christian, Mrs. Denton was speaking of it herself as an old family legend.

"And this could be it after all these years," she told Mrs. Bern.

Mrs. Bern, after spending two-thirds of her life with these people, both in London and here at the Dover place, was the only one who seemed skeptical about the box and its contents. When Mrs. Denton breathed her awed confirmation to the housekeeper about this being the box they had been looking for all these years, Mrs. Bern looked at her askance. After all these years, considering Mrs. Denton's careless self-control, surely she would have mentioned something about a missing portion of Mrs. Bellweather's estate to her housekeeper, from whom she kept no other secret, including her husband's confidential advancements at the bank or her own scandalous flirtation with Charles Atgood, a flirtation that might very well have developed into something really scandalous if Mr. Atgood had had his way.

Nevertheless, it was hard for even the levelheaded housekeeper not to be charged with the electricity in the air. It filled the house as if the old cottage had just been struck by lightning. Here in the kitchen and back there in the sitting room.

"Oh, Franklin, surely you are not going to wait until tomorrow to open that thing? How could you?" Mrs. Denton wailed.

"Caroline, if that box contains what I think that box contains—" he looked meaningfully around at all of his audience, not wanting a syllable of this explanation to be lost on anyone "—then I shall want everything carried out with unimpeachable propriety. There was no stipulation made for undisclosed money in my aunt's will, but our longtime ownership of this house, the general instructions in the will, my position as Aunt Hildegard's closest living relative, all should unquestionably ensure my claim."

"And the fact that possession is considered the major portion of the law," Michaels offered.

"Exactly. So our lawful possession must be attested to in the presence of a legal and certified witness," Denton continued loftily. He played his part with such conviction that there could be no doubt in the house that he believed his aunt's money was in that box and he wanted it. Franklin Denton was positively inspired in his performance and came near to believing the story himself.

"It has been sitting in back of that armoire for twenty-five years," Miss Christian breathed. Until this instance Miss Christian had seemed absolutely unflappable, but even she seemed impressed by the wealth that box might contain.

"Who would have thought it?" Mrs. Denton said. "I thought there was nothing but old clothes in there."

There was a general shaking of the bent heads that surrounded the old metal box.

Back in the kitchen Maggie and Ethel kept up their own version of the same conversation as they peeled vegetables.

"I hear it has been sitting in the back of that closet for thirty years or more," Maggie said. "No one ever bothered to move the clothes."

"Who would have thought it?" Ethel rinsed her carrot in the pan of water on the table and reached for another.

"Who indeed?" Mrs. Bern said scornfully. The cook and the maid looked up, shocked by the housekeeper's irreverent tone.

"Don't you believe it's Mrs. Bellweather's long-lost money?" Maggie asked, her blue eyes wide and wondering.

"I do not know about any long-lost money. What I do know is that I have been cleaning this house every summer for twenty-five years now and I guess I know what in every cupboard and closet and drawer and hidey-hole on the place. Don't you think I might have run across something like this in all those years?"

"Maybe not." Now Ethel reached for a potato. Maggie, usually uncommonly deft of hand, was distracted this afternoon and Ethel was outpeeling her, three vegetables to one. "I heard it's a big old chest up in the master's bedroom. It seems to me that a proper housekeeper doesn't go through every drawer and cupboard in the master's private room."

Mrs. Bern was caught unawares by an undeniable argument from the cook. She did not appear to be pleased by that.

"You see?" Maggie chirped. "You see? It could have been there for twenty-five years without anybody knowing it, and tomorrow we all get to see it. Mr. Denton said

we must all be witnesses to the opening of the box, take
a proper look at what's inside and sign our names right
on a barrister's ledger that a judge in court will see.'
Maggie sounded as thrilled by that prospect as she would
have been had the imagined wealth been coming to her.
And indeed, she couldn't imagine how she could be any
more excited.

The day's duties dragged at Maggie. She kept invent-
ing excuses to hurry into the sitting room. She would in-
quire if anyone wanted some cool water or hot tea or
cake, or if someone had called. She watered the house
plants—the poor darlings were hearty souls and would
most likely survive the double watering—and dusted
everything, very slowly and painstakingly. She burned to
talk to Jared about it, to find out how much *he* thought
was in there, how much the box could hold and how large
the denominations of the notes would be. But Michael
was never alone in the room. In fact, he left the room
once to take a short walk, get a breath of fresh air, but his
absence was short-lived and Maggie would have been
forced to leave the house herself to join him and she just
couldn't seem to pull herself away.

Of course, they didn't just stand around the table all
day. They sat and read and talked some and occasionally moved to another chair, which would give them a
different perspective on the box. Oh yes, and Denton left
too, sometime after lunch, telling them he was arranging
for the bank official to be there the next day. He returned in an amazingly short time from such a mission,
but nobody thought to comment on how quickly he had
made the arrangements.

The box was put in the place of honor at the head of
the table and the dinner of roast beef and vegetables was
consumed in weighty silence.

Finally, Michaels excused himself and went up to his room. Maggie, showing less discretion than she ever had before, was directly behind him.

"This is the most exciting thing I've ever been part of," she said, closing the door behind her, which she had caught before he shut it. "Isn't it the most exciting thing you've ever been part of?"

"You have led a protected little life there in Huntington, my dear," he said wearily. He and Mrs. Bern would have been ideal companions tonight after a full day of his box business. Michaels was beginning to regret that he had ever devised the scheme, especially when he saw that light in Maggie's eye. It might have been childlike excitement, but was there a harder glint there? A hunger?

Oh, Maggie my darling, don't let it be you, he found himself praying, and then was ashamed of himself and his doubt and was more unhappy than ever.

"What is it?" she asked, instantly all dear, sweet concern for him. He had sunk into the seat by his writing desk and she hurried to kneel by his side.

Somehow, so quickly, their relationship had changed, had deepened into these tender beginnings of love. Michaels was frankly amazed at his depth of feeling for this girl. He could no longer believe the deceit and intrigue that had prompted his outburst of seemingly uncontrollable passion that day in her room. The importance of his job, this assignment, the well-being of the Dentons or, for that matter, anybody else on earth had somehow paled to insignificance since he had come to know Maggie. He could not understand it.

Maggie had no nagging questions. She merely accepted the fact that Jared Michaels was the most important person in her world, and that his happiness outweighed any and every other consideration.

Forgotten in an instant was her unbridled enthusiasm, her fascination with the box that sat on the dining room table. As she knelt by his side she put the back of her hand carefully against his cheek.

"Are you well?" she asked. He nodded against her hand. Seriously she peered under his beetled brow. "Are you unhappy? With me?"

"I only want..."

"Yes?"

"I want us ... to be us," he murmured.

She didn't understand exactly what he meant, but she knew that somewhere in there he had told her he loved her. She sighed happily and rested her cheek comfortably against his knee. Perhaps a box full of money was not the most exciting thing in her life, after all.

The minutes ticked away as Maggie rested her cheek on Michaels's knee. Eight o'clock struck and Michaels stroked the silk of her hair. Maggie sweetly slept and Michaels's hand cupped her head in a warm caress. Nine o'clock struck.

"Maggie?" he whispered, so softly it might have been supposed that he did not really want to waken her, that he wished he could keep her safely here at his side through this long night. "Maggie?" She stirred and smiled against his knee. He felt her lips move, even through the material of his trouser leg, and his throat tightened into a knot. "Maggie, it is nine o'clock. Mrs Bern may need you."

"Oh," she said sorrowfully. "Must I leave so soon?"

Michaels wanted to clasp her to him, to assure her that indeed she did not have to leave him—ever. Instead he took his hand off her head.

"They will wonder where you have gotten to after so long. Dear Mrs. Bern may know."

Mrs. Bern's added vigilance had not been entirely fruitless. She had seen Maggie come out of Mr. Michaels's room one night after their brief discussion of the case," which they still held every night, and their more prolonged good-night. Not surprisingly, Maggie's cheeks were flushed when she emerged from the room and her eyes reflected a dreamy, faraway look that could neither be manufactured nor misunderstood. Mrs. Bern, neither blind nor with the intellect of a legume, couldn't help but suspect that Maggie and Mr. Michaels, against her most solemn cautioning, had become, in the delicate phrasing of the day, "involved." Mrs. Bern may have had an exaggerated idea of what went on behind Mr. Michaels's closed door, even with the enhanced good-nights, but her deduction that Maggie Landers was falling, or more likely had already landed squarely, in love was right in the money.

"Mrs. Bern," Maggie groaned. She sat up and stretched, first her arms, then, rising to her knees, her back, and finally, supporting herself on one of his knees, she stood, groaned some more and stretched the entire length of her body.

She took his hands and pulled him to stand before her.

"Tell me that you feel better," she demanded.

"Tell me *you* feel better," he returned, smiling.

She reached up, so far up, and put a small, soft palm on either of his cheeks.

"I always feel better when I have been with you," she said earnestly.

He did take her in his arms then and held her as if he
would never let her go; held her until she laughed into his
ear and reminded him that Mrs. Bern would be looking
for her; held her until he was sure he would always know
the imprint of that body against his own.

At last he released her and she hurried to his door, now
honestly concerned about the length of time she had been
from the kitchen and steeling herself for the disapproving looks Mrs. Bern would be directing her way all night.
Before she opened the door she turned and blew him one
last kiss.

"Oh, my sweet, sweet darling, please God don't let it
be you," he murmured after the door clicked shut behind her.

Chapter Twenty-Four

Officer Jared Michaels and Mr. Denton had agreed to meet at the shed at midnight. They considered it a pretty safe bet that their thief, experienced and cautious, would not attempt to open the box any earlier than that. She would, in fact, doubtless wait until two or three o'clock in the morning, but the two gentlemen were taking every precaution to make sure that they apprehended her.

"Michaels? Is that you?" Denton groped in the dark toward the vague bulk.

"I am here," the policeman affirmed. "Was anyone stirring when you left?"

"Only my wife."

"What did you tell her?"

"That I was worried about the money and was going to sleep downstairs."

Michaels nodded in the dark, so his agreement was completely lost on Denton.

"Anything out here?" Denton asked.

"Nothing yet."

"Well, I have come prepared," Denton said proudly, and Michaels was appalled to see a metallic shimmer in the other man's hand.

"What have you got there?" he asked, but he knew. The man was obviously determined to protect his property at all costs. He also no doubt imagined he would be a great help to the representative of the law with that thing.

"Just a little persuasion," Denton whispered cheerfuly.

"Mr. Denton," Michaels said, keeping a tight rein on his patience, which was not easy; Officer Michaels was already stretched to the breaking point. "We are going to capture one female thief this morning. I believe that between the two of us we have sufficient muscle without complicating matters."

"Yes, well..." Denton sounded only a trifle subdued. "It never hurts." He patted the heavy firearm and slipped it beneath his belt.

Michaels watched the dim outline of the man's actions and smiled grimly. If Mr. Denton was not very careful with that thing it could, contrary to his prediction, hurt him very badly.

The men took up their watch posts without any further conversation. They positioned themselves just inside either door of the outbuilding. From there they could see any approach to the building, coming from any part of the house. Michaels took the side door, which would allow him to see anyone coming from the kitchen entrance. He told himself and Denton that this was because he was expecting Ethel Cranney to be coming to the shed that night. Ethel was a large woman and Michaels' more athletic physique would ensure that she would be subdued. But the pictures of the metallic glint of Denton's firearm and Maggie's soft, white, throbbing breast rose before his eyes unbidden. He would not allow Denton anywhere near this door.

"Michaels!" Denton hissed at him through the dark.

"What?"

"Remember that you said anyone might be tempted to open that box tonight?"

"Yes?"

"So what if someone other than the thief gets there first? The money in there would be a temptation to anyone."

"I do not believe our lady will allow anyone else to beat her to it."

"But what if . . ." Denton began plaintively.

"Don't worry, Mr. Denton. Your money is safe."

Actually, the same idea had already occurred to Michaels, and the comforting assurance he had given himself was that in that case, Mr. Denton would be out a sizable sum of money.

The minutes slipped away, their ripples almost imperceptible in the dark pool of the night. The hum of sleepy insects and the occasional call of a night bird fell into the silence but did not fill it. The first hour of the summer day was cool and Michaels and Denton both wrapped their coats about their shoulders and watched the house through lids that, despite their best efforts, began to weigh heavily.

Inside the house all seemed quiet, but the night hid more than any of them would have imagined.

Ethel Cranney had retreated to her room as usual directly after the evening meal was prepared. But she was not there now. She had not been there for some time. She and Elizabeth—Miss Christian, she sometimes reminded herself and grinned—had devised a schedule where they could meet and talk in the younger woman's room.

Usually. Unless that moony-eyed young man or the busy little maid insisted on getting underfoot. Then, of course, alternative meeting places had to be employed. Tonight there had been no difficulty, which was fortunate, because the conference had taken a good deal longer than usual. Their run in this house was almost over and new plans had to be made.

"Twelve thousand a year. That's healthy. Healthy enough I think." The "cook" sounded pleased, and Miss Christian smiled her lazy cat smile.

"I think," she agreed.

"But this boy—Claud?" Elizabeth nodded. "What will be his portion?"

"All of it. He is an only son. Doted upon by both parents. The apple of their eyes."

"For whom they couldn't hope a more elegant wife."

Miss Christian nodded her head modestly, smiling a smile that was not so modest. Ethel patted her hand.

"I don't mind telling you," the woman said, "that Michaels fellow had me worried. He's a handsome devil. How did I know you wouldn't fall in love with him and spoil all our plans, Lizzie?"

"Papa was handsome and how much good did that do you?" Elizabeth asked, then shook her head. "No, not after all our work. Mr. Michaels is as poor as a church mouse. Good looks will not buy furs nor jewelry, or even put food on the table. I simply couldn't allow it." She spoke matter-of-factly, as if that was all there was to it, but there was an echo of regret in her voice. Ethel patted her hand again. She certainly understood her daughter's temptation and only wished she had been as strong when Daniel Cranney had come along selling his load of wares.

"Well, now," Mrs. Cranney said briskly, quickly covering the regret. "We're almost finished here. Maybe we houldn't have tried it this way. Cooking isn't my trongest suit, Lizzie. Denton hasn't ever been pleased."

Miss Christian smiled again and waved her hand.

"To the Barkers you shall be Mrs. Eleanor Christian, st surviving relative of Miss Elizabeth Christian, living France. Even if the Barkers glimpsed the Denton cook hen they were here, they will not recognize her in the uiet, dark, dignified French lady I will introduce as my unt. The Barkers can hardly refuse to include my dear, ail auntie in their party, and how very loving and con-ientious I will be. It will melt their hearts. Why, I will se to sainthood in their eyes within a fortnight."

"We *could* start this one with a healthy bank ac-unt," Ethel said, suddenly dropping her voice to a bare hisper. "We've never had any money before."

The girl looked at her sharply.

"We could," she said, matching the other's vocal level.

"Do we dare risk it?" Ethel asked. The girl shrugged.

"So far no one knows what's in that box. If it is empty hen they open it tomorrow, who is to say it was not al-ays empty?"

Maggie lay tossing fitfully in her bed. This wasn't fair. astor Meacham had taught them from the pulpit since e was a little girl that we are never faced with a temp-tion too strong to resist.

"The Spirit of God shines in you all," he used to say, s face raised so it caught the shaft of sunlight shining rough the little stained glass window, making the pas-r appear to be simply bursting with the Spirit. "And by e light you are stronger than Satan! You are better than tan! You can conquer Satan!"

Maggie, an impressionable child, was stirred to her ry soul by the preacher's passion and knew as well as

she knew that the corn would burst through the soil
week after it was planted that she *was* stronger than Sa
tan, that she *could* conquer him.

She admitted to herself now, on this hard cot, under
blanket that had become damp with sweat, that there ha
been times she had forgotten that lesson, times when sh
had allowed herself to yield to temptation, to take th
easier or more pleasurable route, but she had never be
lieved the temptation was too strong to resist before.

Everything would be solved if she opened that tin box
if she emptied that tin box. Her worries would be ove
her obligations met. Then when she kissed Jared an
heard him murmur against her hair that he never wante
to lose her, she could tell him that he wouldn't. Ever.

No one would know. As far as anybody knew, the bo
was empty. If it was empty when they opened it in th
morning, who was to say that it had not always bee
empty?

She threw the wet and sticky blanket back and sat u
in bed. Her hair flew about her face and her eyes glowe
with a wild, feverish light.

Michaels couldn't see his pocket watch, but he thoug
it must be nearly three o'clock. He was aware that he ha
been dozing, but so lightly that the merest disturban
would bring him instantly alert.

It was Denton's "Hist!" that roused him. He kne
what it meant. They had not practiced signals or r
hearsed precisely what they would do, but Denton sa
someone coming and slipped back into the black sha
ows away from the door.

Michaels was a startlingly agile man who could mo
his large frame with the swiftness and silence of a jung
cat. While Denton's sibilant hiss still vibrated in the a

he left his post and melted into the shadows at the back of the shed, near the box of stolen goods. He had already decided to take up that position when the thief entered, even before Denton brought his gun, but now it was doubly advantageous in that it would practically ensure his capture of the thief, and it would move him out of the line of any of Denton's wild shots.

He waited, willing himself to breathe silently through his nose, aware that his heart was pounding, aware that perspiration stood out on his forehead, was running down his sides, had plastered his shirt to his back.

He strained his eyes to the lighter blackness of the door, aware that any form that appeared there would be only a black silhouette. Would he know it? Would he recognize it? Had he held it against himself last night until he thought she had melted into him?

Someone stood in the doorway.

Don't shoot her! he thought wildly, afraid for a split second that he had shouted it out loud.

The form paused at the doorway and then hurried into the shed, obviously familiar with the obstacles in the way. The glimpse of the dim shape had been too brief and Michaels was still in an agony of uncertainty. It might have been any of them: Miss Christian, his own Maggie, even the bulkier Ethel Cranney.

The figure was now not fifteen feet from him, at the box. She moved the things from the top, not sweeping them carelessly to the floor but rising and falling in and out of the black shadow, putting everything carefully and quietly on the floor. She lifted the lid to the treasure chest and then put her arm inside her cloak. When she withdrew it she had a bundle of something in her hand.

Michaels knew what it was. She knew what it was. But just for one more look, just to confirm the wonderful fortune that had fallen to her, she leaned forward, toward the very dim starlight that was coming through the window.

"Mrs. Bern!" Michaels gasped. This time he did speak out loud and the woman whirled toward him.

"Mrs. Bern?" Denton called unbelievingly. She whirled in the other direction, trying to find either or both of her assailants in the dark.

Neither of the men assailed her. They merely came to stand on either side of her, looking in disbelief first at the venerable, gray head and then down at the handful of bank notes that had fluttered into the box, on top of the silverware, on top of the unsanded wooden box, on top of a metal-framed miniature painting and one singularly ugly oriental vase.

Chapter Twenty-Five

Ethel Cranney and Elizabeth Christian, neé Cranney, mother and daughter, had sneaked down to the sitting room and the metal box that sat on the table, but Michaels had been correct: the thief they were after had not allowed herself to be beaten to the prize.

Maggie had not come into the parlor. She did not leave her bed until the great hubbub brought them all into the sitting room as dawn was about to break, or was threatening to break eventually, or at least when night no longer seemed as if it would last forever.

"Mrs. Bern!" Mrs. Denton exclaimed. She was surprised to see her housekeeper coming in from outside, walking between her husband and Mr. Michaels. Mrs. Denton had no idea how surprised she was about to be.

"Sit down, my dear," Mr. Denton said, and then turning to Mrs. Bern, a look of wonder on his face, he said, "and won't you sit down, as well, Mrs. Bern?"

Mrs. Bern did. She said nothing. Her lips were set in the straight line that Maggie had come to recognize as iron determination.

"What is the meaning of all this?" Miss Christian asked.

"Officer Michaels, perhaps you had better explain," Denton said, and, well, there was some head jerking then.

"*Officer* Michaels?" Mrs. Denton shrieked. Mrs. Denton, it will be remembered, was the only one of the household who had gotten any sleep during the night and her uptake was therefore generally much quicker than anyone else's.

"Hush, Caroline. You will want to hear this."

"I apologize, Mrs. Denton, for coming into your home, invading your hospitality, under false pretenses. My name *is* Jared Michaels. Officer Jared Michaels of the Bow Street police." Mrs. Denton's jaw dropped, but she didn't interrupt. Mrs. Bern, for her part, seemed extremely displeased by the disclosure. "A month ago I spoke to your husband and explained to him that the Bow Street runners have been in pursuit of a certain female thief for some time. We had received a tip that your home was about to be victimized, and your husband and I devised this ploy for my inclusion in your house party. I was hoped that if I came, posing as an acquaintance of your husband's from the Fidelity National Banking Concern, I could carry on an intensive investigation unbeknownst to any of the principal parties and apprehend the thief. Which—" he paused and cast a troubled glance at Mrs. Bern "—I have. I believe."

"'Believe' nothing, old man," Denton crowed. "There she was, putting the notes—*my* bank notes—with everything else she has stolen from us. Caught in the act, red-handed, bold as brass!"

His wife looked dismayed at her erstwhile housekeeper.

"Mrs. Bern? Is this true?"

"I am afraid it is, Mrs. Denton," Michaels said. "The metal box with the money in it was actually a trap we set to catch the thief." Ethel and Miss Christian exchanged a shocked glance, and Maggie looked up accusingly at the policeman. "Mrs. Bern, I might add, was not the thief we expected to catch." Now he looked at Ethel, Maggie looked at Miss Christian, and Mr. Denton leered down at Maggie. Mr. Denton, the thief caught, his possessions returned to him, was as giddy as a schoolboy.

"Me?" Ethel sputtered.

"Me?" Miss Christian asked in a shocked, arched one.

"You, young lady," Denton said to Maggie.

"Well, I never!" Miss Christian exclaimed. "I really do not know how I could stay in this house a day longer, finding that I have ignominiously been under a cloud of suspicion."

"And I'm not cooking another meal for you folks!" Ethel exclaimed. Her outraged announcement met with no argument at all.

"Jared?" Maggie asked softly. The hurt wonder in her voice was like a knife in Michaels's side.

"Mrs. Bern?" Mrs. Denton repeated dazedly.

Mrs. Bern's lips had softened their tight line and now she turned a sympathetic eye on her forlorn mistress.

"I *am* sorry, Mrs. Denton. I thought . . . I hoped they were things you would not miss."

"Would not miss!" Denton cried. He was ignored.

"You *took* things of ours?" Mrs. Denton asked, struggling to understand this betrayal after almost forty years.

"Things you did not need or want. Things that quite often you did not even know you had."

"But why? Your wages are generous. You have been like one of the family."

Mrs. Bern looked down at her hands and carefully smoothed the skirt across her lap. Finally she spoke, but very softly. Denton and Ethel Cranney, farthest from the housekeeper, had to lean forward to hear her.

"Yet I am not one of the family, am I? Someday, and judging from the ache in my bones on cold mornings it may not be a distant day, I will be unable to serve you. I realized that, oh, not long ago, and began looking at myself and my life. After a lifetime of living and working here, Mrs. Denton, Mr. Denton, I have nothing. If I were no longer able to work to earn my living, I would be destitute."

"You talk as if we would throw you out onto the trash heap like a broken water pitcher," Denton objected indignantly. Mrs. Bern looked at him soulfully, her motherly eyes shining damply. "Well, that is simply ridiculous," he finished.

"It is," Mrs. Denton seconded her husband, then took the housekeeper's hand in hers. "You *are* part of the family, Leticia. You have been sister, aunt, cousin and mother to me through the years. It has been your influence, your training, your direction that have made our house a home. And when your arms and legs will no longer do the work, we will hire more help, and under your guiding hand our house will continue to be home."

Misty eyes were shared all around, especially by the Dentons and their housekeeper. After Mrs. Denton's pregnant speech, she put her arm around Mrs. Bern's shoulders and hugged her affectionately. Beginning to feel that he had been cast unfairly through this whole li

e drama as the antagonist, Michaels cleared his throat
ncomfortably.

"Mrs. Denton," he interrupted softly. "I am afraid
Mrs. Bern must be taken in front of the magistrate now.
is very likely that she will not return to this house."

"What!" the lady cried. "Franklin, what does he
mean?"

Denton, too, cleared his throat uncomfortably.

"She is a thief, my dear. Caught in the very act. You
ught to see the volume of goods we have recovered."

"You recovered everything?"

Mr. Denton hesitated. He recognized the glow he be-
an to see in his wife's eye. If Mrs. Bern's tight lips were
signal to Maggie of iron determination, the light in Mrs.
enton's eye would have been compared to diamonds.

"I believe so," he finally said.

"Then Mrs. Bern has actually stolen nothing at all."

"Why of course she has stolen something! She has
olen a great many things. From us, Caroline."

"You just told me you recovered all of your property,
at Mrs. Bern no longer has any of it."

"Caroline..."

"Am I right or am I mistaken, Franklin? Has Mrs.
ern anything in her possession that you claim as
ours?"

"Not now," he said petulantly.

"Mrs. Bern, have you sold any articles taken from this
use for your own gain?"

"Well, no, ma'am. I didn't have a chance..."

"Officer Michaels, surely the moving about of certain
our possessions from one of our private properties to
other of our private properties does not constitute
eft?"

"I am not sure I understand you," Michaels said.

But her husband did.

"Now see here, Caroline," he began. "If you think I am going to overlook this and keep a known thief under the roof of my house..."

"Oh, Franklin, use the mind with which you were endowed for just the tiniest moment. Imagine this place *without* Mrs. Bern."

Franklin Denton did that for the first time since the heady moment when he and Michaels had triumphantly accosted the woman in the shed. And as he contemplated the scene his wife suggested, it would not be an exaggeration to say that he paled visibly.

"Perhaps..."

"Perhaps nothing. Mr. Michaels, we appreciate your trouble, and my husband will see that you receive a generous stipend for services rendered. But I am afraid that you have *not* caught a thief." Mrs. Bern gasped and the tears that had filled her eyes now fell onto her cheeks. Mrs. Denton looked around at all of the surprised faces in the room. "I simply cannot do a thing without Mrs. Bern," she explained helplessly.

"What is it?" Maggie asked him.

They had left the scene in the sitting room and the unexpected denouement of Michaels's month-long assignment. Morning had dawned while they sat in the parlor listening to the confessions and Mrs. Denton's firm decision.

Ethel Cranney and Miss Christian had left shortly after that, putting on a great show of being in a huff, both of them. Actually, this would fit in with their timetable ideally. Elizabeth had learned from Stanley Barker that he and his wife were going to visit their son in Paris later this month. Mrs. Barker had issued a vague invitation

hich she would make definite as soon as Miss Chris-
an arrived on the Barker doorstep. Miss Christian, as it
ould turn out, had just heard from her ailing aunt and
as going across the Channel to her aid and comfort.
nere was no question that Mr. and Mrs. Barker would
sist that the single young woman accompany them.

Mrs. Cranney's French accent was only marginally
tter than her cooking, but she would claim to be from
e south of France and to the English ear it would be
fficient, if she spoke as little as possible and Elizabeth
anney got Claud Barker to propose quickly enough.

The Cranney women had lived for a number of years,
nce that frosty December morning when Mr. Cranney
d walked through the front door of their tiny cold-
ater flat never to return, on the bounty of households
ey invaded variously as rich young heiress and travel-
g companion, forgotten great-aunt and maid, strug-
ng but worthy student—sometimes art, sometimes
erature, but never music—and tutor. Friend of friends,
sent or deceased, was one of the easier ploys, but it al-
ved for only one of them, so they alternated the serv-
g position. Ethel had come to the Dentons expecting to
engaged as a maid and was surprised to find herself a
ok. The Dentons, as has been pointed out on a num-
r of occasions, were surprised by the cook, as well.

Elizabeth was now of the marrying age, and before her
me was passed, they had been keeping their eyes and
s open for the perfect mate. Claud Barker sounded
nt-minded and indulged but young enough to be man-
ed, especially by a beautiful wife and her sickly aunt.
d more than anything, he was rich and would be even
her when his father, admittedly a hale and hearty old
tleman, passed away. That consideration alone made

Claud Barker the man of Mrs. and Miss Cranney
dreams.

So they rushed to their rooms to pack, called for
conveyance they would share and were out of the De
ton home before anyone had time to wish them farew
properly. They had plans to make, traveling to do, wan
robes to overhaul, and, as usual, they were operating
a shoestring budget.

Maggie had also returned to her room to dress. She h
looked around at the walls, brightened by her sample
expanded by her imagination, and smiled at herself. S
suspected, judging by the look in Jared's eye, that s
would not be coming back to this room many more tim

Now, though, as they stopped to watch a farmer gui
his lazy cows to the milk barn, a frown creased N
chaels's brow and his eyes, his beautiful dark eyes, had
troubled intensity. He shook his head when Maggie ask
her question and turned around to rest his back and
bows against the logs of the fence.

"That wasn't right," he said. Maggie opened her ey
her beautiful, sky blue eyes, wide in surprise.

"To let Mrs. Bern go? Jared, my love, you mustn't
so very strict about the letter of the law. She really had
taken anything *away*. Mr. Denton got everything ba
and you told me yourself, when you were so shamefu
accusing me, that getting his things back was always l
Denton's main concern. And Mrs. Bern *said* she v
sorry...." Maggie was pleading with him, trying to ma
him see the real justice of it, but he shook his head.

"Not that. Yes, certainly, if the Dentons do not w
to charge Mrs. Bern and there has been no actual cri
committed, I can have no objection to it. But I me
Mrs. Bern herself. *That* was not right." Maggie look
her confusion and Michaels smiled and kissed her on

of her nose. "I mean," he said, trying one more time,
hat Mrs. Bern was not the thief I was chasing. I was
mmissioned to stop a notorious thief who has struck a
umber of wealthy London homes, in various imagina-
e disguises, over the past several months or even years.
rs. Bern has been in this house for forty years. She has
ver been anyone else, anywhere else, disguised as any-
ing else but the Dentons' housekeeper." He shook his
ad again and Maggie ran her warm fingertips up and
wn his arm.

"Maybe the Dentons weren't the next victims after
," she suggested helpfully.

"But Danny is usually completely reliable. What a wild
incidence that on the one occasion when his informa-
n was incorrect, I should come to a house where ac-
al robbery *is* in progress, that I should stop the thief,
urn the valuable property and—" he stopped and took
 girl into his arms "—find the woman I love. Mar-
et Landers, I have told you that I want us to be to-
her forever, that I never want to lose you, that I will
 whithersoever thou goest, but it occurs to me that I
 y not have asked you to marry me."

"No, you haven't," she said, smiling up, so far up, into
 face. "But I thought you might get around to it
 ntually." He bent and kissed her berry red lips, sa-
 ring their sweet flavor. When they finally parted she
 ispered against his cheek, "My answer, provided you
 interested, is yes."

Epilogue

Maggie Landers and Officer Jared Michaels were married in a lovely church ceremony at which Pastor Farrington, who had replaced Pastor Meacham two years earlier, officiated, and at which her five brothers were a perfect study in uncomfortable embarrassment, dressed up as they were in their Sunday best with their collars starched *twice,* and Maggie going around kissing everybody, including each of them, on the lips.

Mr. Denton had, not with an entirely cheerful heart, given Michaels the stipend his wife had promised, and Mrs. Denton saw to it personally that it was even more generous than the policeman had hoped or her husband feared. With the money, the Michaelses spent a lovely honeymoon at a quaint country inn near the white cliffs of Dover. Maggie finally got to see the ocean, to go bathing in the sea and to go on a country drive with her handsome husband.

At last they returned to London, and with the rest of the money they set up housekeeping in a small, clean flat that Michaels promised her they would trade for a little cottage someday soon.

Maggie and Jared were as happy as they imagined they would be, even considering a policeman's far-from-

nerous wages and the dangers to which he would be li-
ble as long as he was a policeman. But he loved his
ork, and then he loved to come home to Maggie and
rget his work.

With Officer Michaels returned to his Bow Street la-
ors, his pretty little bride threw herself cheerfully into a
udy of proper housewifery. She cooked—considerably
tter than Ethel Cranney—and cleaned and darned her
usband's socks. On Tuesdays, because bread was two
aves for a penny on Tuesdays, she went shopping.

And one Tuesday she went to the Greenleaf Employ-
s Agency.

The door creaked slightly when she opened it and the
tumnal gloom of the room, which made it seem more
e a musty old attic than a place of business, was mo-
entarily relieved by the outside light and air. But then
e door swung shut behind her and the agency was re-
rned to its brooding shadow.

The room was as stark as she remembered it, un-
anged in the months since she had seen it last, even to
e number of unnecessary chairs lined against the wall
ross from the stove.

The door to the other room was open and Maggie also
cognized the sounds of mammoth effort she heard is-
ing from that room. In another moment the doorway
s completely filled by a pallid shape. The light was too
n for Maggie to distinguish his features, but she rec-
nized the man. It was the owner of the Greenleaf Em-
yers Agency. Not Mr. Greenleaf. There had long since
ased to be a Greenleaf associated with this agency. No,
e gentleman's name was Briggs. Grant Briggs.

Mr. Briggs, his eyes already accustomed to the gloom,
whole body sensitive to any change in his environ-
nt, like some great white slug uncovered in the garden

sod, immediately recognized, for his part, the slight fig
ure near the counter.

"Ah, Miss Landers," he said. "Come back at last.
must admit I was beginning to have the gravest misgiv
ings about you and the fulfillment of your half of ou
bargain. As you know, there are serious consequences fo
failure to meet your obligations. But all is forgiven nov
Or will be soon, I am sure." The puffs of flesh around h
eyes tightened. "Join me, won't you?"

Maggie wanted this interview, this episode of her lif
to be over as quickly as possible. But, guiltily, she als
acknowledged that she did not want to be caught, *fl*
grante delicto, in consultation with this man by a
stranger who might come into the shop while she w
here. Reluctantly she came around the corner.

"Very well," she said coolly, drawing her elbow in s
as not to stroke the man's belly as she edged past hi
through the doorway.

This room, too, was as she remembered it. If not mo
so. The divan seemed looser and sloppier in its stuffin
the table covered with more indelible stains, the shelv
protruding more into the room. The air was rank with t
odor of an open salami on one of the planks of the t
ble.

"Would you care for a bite to eat?" Briggs asked h
settling himself onto his protesting chair and indicati
the other chair to the young woman.

"No."

"Right to business, is it?" he huffed. "Very well. Y
know, Maggie, so far our business dealings have not be
entirely satisfactory."

"I paid you your stipulated fee months ago."

"That is not what I am referring to, as you are ve
well aware." He pulled the salami onto the table and

f a circlet of the highly seasoned meat. He stabbed it
rough the center and motioned with it again to the chair
ross from him. Maggie shook her head.

"I'll stand," she said.

"As you wish, my girl. As I was saying, you have not
en as industrious as others I have placed in house-
lds of even meaner circumstances. And then you dis-
peared altogether. Dropped completely out of sight.
hat was I to think? I was distraught, my girl, that's
lat I was. All in all, you have been a bitter disappoint-
nt to me." He wagged his head mournfully and took
bite of the salami. Still chewing, he looked up at her
d smiled, revealing shreds of meat caught between his
:th. "But perhaps you will justify my hopes in you,
ter all."

"I do not believe so," Maggie said.

"Oh, my girl, but you had better. Indeed, you had
tter. I can't allow this sort of blatant disregard of an
reement. Can you imagine the consequences through-
t my entire network?"

"You cannot threaten me, Mr. Briggs."

The big man opened his little eyes to their widest lim-

"Threaten you? Is that what you believe this is? Is that
you believe this is?"

Without warning he slammed the point of the knife
o the top of the table. Maggie jumped violently. There
s silence while they both watched the tremors in the
ife handle diminish and then cease.

"Let us by all means be very careful, my girl. You
ew the terms of your employment when you took the
sition. So what have you got for me? I trust that all
nt well."

Maggie could not seem to draw her eyes away from th
knife handle.

"I have nothing for you, Mr. Briggs." With a struggl
she transferred her gaze to his moonlike face. "And ev
erything went splendidly, thank you."

She could see the blood bubble up from his loosene
shirt collar and fill his face.

"Now see here, girl, we had an agreement. And m
girls know how to keep an agreement. I place you in
prosperous home, and you see to it that we all share som
of that prosperity. If you wanted to be an independer
concern, you should have made that decision before yc
came to me looking for work. And you might have trie
to find work, too, a grand position like the one I place
you in, you country bumpkin, rude and backward, wi
no experience and no references. Now pay your dut
Maggie, my girl, the duty fairly contracted—seventy-fi
percent of your take. You get a fourth of it for your ow
plus a place to stay until another place opens up."

"I don't have anything to give you," she repeate
fighting back a strong urge to step away from the tab
to put some distance of safety between herself and t
man. But she stood her ground, determined not to
bullied by this man any longer. "I didn't take anythin
I will not steal anything for you, Mr. Briggs."

She started to turn her back on him, but in a white bl
his fist darted out and his doughy fingers grabbed b
wrist.

"Just a moment, Miss Landers," he snarled. "You w
give me money or you will give me flesh, but you will gi
me one or the other."

She shook his hand away from her arm with a streng
that surprised them both and threw him off balance.

"It is Mrs. Michaels now, and I will give you neither money nor flesh, Briggs. But I will tell you what I will do for you. I will not interfere with this ring of petty thieves of which you are the mastermind. I wouldn't dream of it, considering the wealth the enterprise has brought you." She let her eyes rove scornfully over the watermarked walls and the shabby furniture, finally letting them rest on Brigg's slovenly form. "And if you leave me strictly alone, I will not say anything about you or this place to my husband, Officer Jared Michaels of the Bow Street Police."

Briggs jerked back as if she had pulled a poisonous snake from inside her shawl and threatened him with it.

"But he and the other runners are clever men, Mr. Briggs. I cannot guarantee that even with my silence you will remain in business long."

She did turn then, and with head held high, she strode from the inner living room to the outer office and finally into the fresh air of the street beyond the door, which kicked shut behind her. Briggs watched her exit in stunned silence. He suspected he was in serious trouble, that his little empire was about to crumble.

But Maggie was true to her word. Officer Jared Michaels never learned from her that Grant Briggs was the ringleader of a gang of thieves. But she was also correct about the Bow Street runners. They *were* a group of very clever men.

The Greenleaf Employers Agency was closed less than a year later.

* * * * *

my VALENTINE 1992

Celebrate the most romantic day of the year with
MY VALENTINE 1992—a sexy new collection of four
romantic stories written by our famous Temptation
authors:

GINA WILKINS
KRISTINE ROLOFSON
JOANN ROSS
VICKI LEWIS THOMPSON

My Valentine 1992—an exquisite escape into a romantic
and sensuous world.

 Harlequin Books ®

VAL-9

HARLEQUIN
PROUDLY PRESENTS
A DAZZLING NEW CONCEPT IN ROMANCE FICTION

One small town—twelve terrific love stories

Welcome to Tyler, Wisconsin—a town full of people
you'll enjoy getting to know, memorable friends and
unforgettable lovers, and a long-buried secret that
lurks beneath its serene surface....

JOIN US FOR A YEAR IN THE LIFE OF TYLER

Each book set in Tyler is a self-contained love story;
together, the twelve novels stitch the fabric of a
community.

LOSE YOUR HEART TO TYLER!

The excitement begins in March 1992, with
WHIRLWIND, by Nancy Martin. When lively, brash
Liza Baron arrives home unexpectedly, she moves
into the old family lodge, where the silent and
mysterious Cliff Forrester has been living in seclusion
for years....

WATCH FOR ALL TWELVE BOOKS
OF THE TYLER SERIES
Available wherever Harlequin books are sold

Take 4 bestselling love stories FREE

Plus get a FREE surprise gift!

Special Limited-time Offer

Mail to Harlequin Reader Service®

In the U.S.	In Canada
3010 Walden Avenue	P.O. Box 609
P.O. Box 1867	Fort Erie, Ontario
Buffalo, N.Y. 14269-1867	L2A 5X3

YES! Please send me 4 free Harlequin Historical™ novels and my free surprise gift. Then send me 4 brand-new novels every month, which I will receive months before they appear in bookstores. Bill me at the low price of $3.19* each—a savings of 80¢ apiece off cover prices. There are no shipping, handling or other hidden costs. I understand that accepting the books and gift places me under no obligation ever to buy any books. I can always return a shipment and cancel at any time. Even if I never buy another book from Harlequin, the 4 free books and the surprise gift are mine to keep forever.

*Offer slightly different in Canada—$3.19 per book plus 49¢ per shipment for delivery. Canadian residents add applicable federal and provincial sales tax. Sales tax applicable in N.Y.

247 BPA ADL6   347 BPA ADML

Name _____ (PLEASE PRINT)

Address _____ Apt. No. _____

City _____ State/Prov. _____ Zip/Postal Code _____

This offer is limited to one order per household and not valid to present Harlequin Historical™ subscribers. Terms and prices are subject to change.

HIS-91   © 1990 Harlequin Enterprises Limited

H A R L E Q U I N®

A Calendar of Romance

a part of American Romance's year-long celebration of love
d the holidays of 1992. Celebrate those special times each
onth with your favorite authors.

xt month, live out a St. Patrick's Day fantasy in

MARCH

S	M	T	W	T	F	S
1	2	3	4	5	6	7
8	9	10	11	12	13	14
15	16	17				21
22	23					
29						

**#429 FLANNERY'S
RAINBOW
by Julie Kistler**

d all the books in *A Calendar of Romance*, coming to you one
month, all year, only in American Romance.

---

u missed #421 HAPPY NEW YEAR, DARLING and #425 VALENTINE HEARTS AND
VERS and would like to order them, send your name, address and zip or postal code
with a check or money order for $3.29 plus 75¢ postage and handling ($1.00 in Canada)
ach book ordered, payable to Harlequin Reader Service to:

In the U.S.

3010 Walden Avenue
P.O. Box 1325
Buffalo, NY 14269-1325

In Canada

P.O. Box 609
Fort Erie, Ontario
L2A 5X3

e specify book title(s) with your order.
dian residents add applicable federal and provincial taxes.

COR3

presents
MARCH MADNESS!

Come March, we're lining up four wonderful stories by four da:
zling newcomers—and we guarantee you won't be disappointe
From the stark beauty of Medieval Wales to marauding *bandidos* i
Chihuahua, Mexico, return to the days of enchantment and hig
adventure with characters who will touch your heart.

LOOK FOR
STEAL THE STARS (HH #115) by *Miranda Jarrett*
THE BANDIT'S BRIDE (HH #116) by *Ana Seymour*
ARABESQUE (HH #117) by *Kit Gardner*
A WARRIOR'S HEART (HH #118) by *Margaret Moore*

So rev up for spring with a bit of March Madness . . . only from
Harlequin Historicals!